L

Lucy took a sip of her own tea. "That's good. Just a touch of cinnamon. I've been writing all morning." She gave Sky a pat on the head. "I assume Brent told you about the mirror."

"He didn't. What happened?"

She paused. "Well, it's no secret. I'm sure he wouldn't mind you knowing. He found an antique mirror in one of the trunks and hung it in that room with Violet's possessions. He stepped back to make sure it was level and saw a face looking at him."

I felt the familiar press of cold wrapping around my body. It occurred at times like this when I came face to face with the inexplicable. I knew what Lucy was going to say next. Still I said, "Whose face was it?"

"A pretty girl with long chestnut hair. She was wearing sapphire earrings and a lacy white top."

"That's how I described Violet time and time again."

"The face was only there for a second. He blinked, looked again, and saw his own reflection. He swears he didn't imagine it."

I was certain he hadn't and wondered why he hadn't told me about it.

"You'd think he'd take that mirror down and pack it away in the trunk," I said.

"That's what I would have done. Not Brent, though. To him, that house is a challenge, and I think he wants to see Violet, even though he won't admit it.

"He may get his wish," I said. "That house is haunted."

"I'll go further. The house is evil."

Other Works From The Pen Of

Dorothy Bodoin

Treasure at Trail's End (Gothic romance)—The House at Trail's End seemed to beckon to Mara Marsden, promising the happy future she longed for. But could she discover its secret without forfeiting her life?

Ghost across the Water (romantic suspense)—Water falling from an invisible force and a ghostly man who appears across Spearmint Lake draw Joanna Larne into a haunting twenty-year-old mystery.

Darkness at Foxglove Corners—Foxglove Corners offers tornado survivor Jennet Greenway country peace and romance, but the secret of the yellow Victorian house across the lane holds a threat to her new life. (#1)

Winter's Tale—On her first winter in Foxglove Corners Jennet Greenway battles dognappers, investigates the murder of the town's beloved veterinarian, and tries to outwit a dangerous enemy. (#3)

A Shortcut through the Shadows—Jennet Greenway's search for the missing owner of her rescue collie, Winter, sets her on a collision course with an unknown killer. (#4)

Cry for the Fox—In Foxglove Corners, the fox runs from the hunters, the animal activists target the Hunt Club, and a killer stalks human prey on the fox trail. (#2)

The Witches of Foxglove Corners—With a haunting in the library, a demented prankster who invades her home, and a murder in Foxglove Corners, Halloween turns deadly for Jennet Greenway. (#5)

The Snow Dogs of Lost Lake—A ghostly white collie and a lost locket lead Jennet Greenway to a body in the woods and a dangerous new mystery. (#6)

The Collie Connection—As Jennet Greenway's wedding to Crane Ferguson approaches, her happiness is shattered when a Good Samaritan deed leaves her without her beloved black collie, Halley, and ultimately in grave danger. (#7)

A Time of Storms—When a stranger threatens her collie and she hears a cry for help in a vacant house, Jennet Ferguson suspects that her first summer as a wife may be tumultuous. (#8)

The Dog from the Sky—Jennet's life takes a dangerous turn when she rescues an abused collie. Soon afterward, a girl vanishes without a trace. Ironically she had also rescued an abused collie. Is there a connection between the two incidents? (#9)

Spirit of the Season—Mystery mixes with holiday cheer as a phantom ice skater returns to the lake where she died, and a collie is accused of plotting her owner's fatal accident. (#10)

Another Part of the Forest—Danger rides the air when a kidnapper whisks his victims away in a hot air balloon, and a false friend puts a curse on a collie breeder's first litter. (#11)

Where Have All the Dogs Gone?—An animal activist frees the shelter dogs in and around Foxglove Corners to save them from being destroyed. Running wild in the countryside, they face an equally distressing fate and post a risk to those who come in contact with them. (#12)

The Secret Room of Eidt House—A rabid dog that should have died months ago from the dread disease runs free in the woods of Foxglove Corners, and the library's long-kept secret unleashes a series of other strange events. (#13)

Follow a Shadow—A shadowy intruder haunts Jennet's woods by night, and a woman who can't accept the death of her collie asks Jennet to help her find Rainbow Bridge where she believes her dog waits for her. (#14)

The Snow Queen's Collie—A white collie puppy appears on the porch of the Ferguson farmhouse during a Christmas Eve snowstorm. In another part of Foxglove Corners a collie breeder's show prospect disappears. Meanwhile, the painting Jennet's sister gave her for Christmas begins to exhibit strange qualities. (#15)

The Door in the Fog—A wounded dog disappears in the fog. A blue door on the side of a barn vanishes. Strange wildflowers and a sound of weeping haunt a meadow. The woods keep their secret, and a curse refuses to die. (#16)

Dreams and Bones—At Brent Fowler's newly purchased Spirit Lamp Inn, a renovation turns up human bones buried in the inn's backyard, rekindling interest in the case of a young woman who disappeared from the inn several decades ago. As Jennet tries to solve this mystery, she doesn't realize it may be her last. (#17)

A Ghost of Gunfire—Months after gunfire erupted in her classroom at Marston High School, leaving one student dead and one seriously wounded, Jennet begins to hear a sound of gunshots inaudible to anyone else. Meanwhile, she resolves to find the demented person who is tying dogs to trees and leaving them to die. (#18)

The Silver Sleigh—Rosalyn Everett was missing and presumed dead. Her collies had been rescued, and her house was abandoned. But a blue merle collie haunts her woods and a figure in bridal white traverses the property. (#19)

The Stone Collie—Jennet's discovery of a collie puppy chained in the yard of a vacant house sets her on a search for a man whose activities may threaten Foxglove Corners' security. Meanwhile, horror story novelist Lucy Hazen is mystified when scenes from her work-in-progress are duplicated in real life. (#20)

The Mists of Huron Court—The house was beautiful, a vintage pink Victorian in a picturesque but lonely country setting, and the girl playing ball with her dog in the yard was friendly, suggesting that she and Jennet walk their dogs together some time. Jennet thinks she has made a new friend until she returns to the house and finds a tumbling down ruin where the Victorian once stood and no sign that the girl and dog have ever been there. ((#21)

Wings

Down a Dark Path

Dorothy Bodoin

A Wings ePress, Inc.

Cozy Mystery

Wings ePress, Inc.

Edited by: Jeanne Smith
Copy Edited by: Joan C. Powell
Executive Editor: Jeanne Smith
Cover Artist: Trisha FitzGerald

All rights reserved

Wings ePress Books
www.books-by-wings-epress.com

Copyright © 2017 by Dorothy Bodoin
ISBN 978-1-61309-714-4

Published In the United States Of America

February, 2017

Wings ePress Inc.
3000 N. Rock Road
Newton, KS 67114

Dedication

To Max and Gavi

One

The howl shattered the pre-dawn silence, seeming to send its primeval lament deep into my soul.

"What in the name of everything that's holy was that?"

I froze, the fork suspended over the bowl of beaten eggs. The collies abandoned breakfast to converge at the kitchen door in various stages of agitation or excitement, depending on their personalities. All except for Sky, the timid blue merle. She tried desperately to melt into my side.

My husband, Deputy Sheriff Crane Ferguson, took a swig of his coffee. "Coyote," he said.

"It sounds like it's right outside the door. It couldn't be."

"Sure it could," he said. "They're all around us."

"I didn't think they came so close to the house."

I glanced out the kitchen window. The sky was about to break into the luminous graying light of early morning. A thin layer of snow covered the landscape. The trees, tall and gaunt, swayed in a strong wind. It was an inhospitable vista and a deserted one.

There were no woodland interlopers in the yard, nor on Jonquil Lane, and none near the yellow Victorian house across the lane. The cry must have come from the woods, which was still too near the house for comfort.

It had seemed so close, practically on our doorstep.

Of course I had heard coyotes yipping in the woods at dawn, at dusk, and during the night. They sounded like dogs. I knew the difference, though, as did the collies who lived with us.

I lowered the first piece of egg-soaked bread into the frying pan. "Raven's out there alone."

Raven, the rare bi-black collie, lived outside (her choice) in a dog house custom built by Crane in imitation of our green Victorian farmhouse.

"I wouldn't worry about Raven," he said. "She can hold her own against any critter."

"Well, I don't like it."

"It's all part of country living, Jennet." Crane's voice still held a hint of a southern accent even though he'd lived up north for years.

"We humans *have* taken over their habitat," I said. "Still…"

Coyotes reminded me of dogs. A small smooth collie or German shepherd. They were, of course, members of the same family. *Canis latrans*. Country cousins of our dogs. But they were still wild animals. You wouldn't want to pet one. You wouldn't try to teach it to shake hands.

I set the first pieces of French toast on Crane's plate and brought the syrup pitcher from the counter. In less than a half hour, we would be parted. Crane would leave to patrol the roads and byroads of Foxglove Corners, and I'd begin the hour-long commute to Oakpoint, Michigan, where I taught English at Marston High School.

But today was Friday. I lived for weekends.

Satisfied that my breakfast table was complete, I sat in one of the oak chairs and stole a glance at Crane. The overhead light shone on his silver-streaked blond hair and the badge he wore with pride.

I missed him so much during the weekdays that anyone would think I was newly married. This wasn't an attribute aspired to by an independent twenty-first century wife, but it was the way I was wired.

"Coyotes aren't known for attacking humans," Crane said, helping himself to a slice of bacon. "Dogs maybe, but small ones or puppies, and cats. Not big collies."

"Suppose I meet a coyote when I'm walking the dogs?" I asked.

"You might try a technique known as hazing, as long as the coyote doesn't look like it's sick or protecting pups."

"What's that?"

"Make a lot of noise. Be as loud as you can. Wave your arms. Clap your hands. Grab a fistful of pebbles and throw it at the coyote. Not to hurt it, just to scare it. It probably won't hurt you."

"Probably isn't good enough."

"Take the gun then."

I didn't want to do that. I had a gun for protection, had lobbied hard for the right to own it, against Crane's initial objection, but I didn't want to shoot an animal. Ever.

"I guess I'm overreacting," I said.

"You can't be too careful, honey."

Crane always had his gun when he was out and about.

Because Candy, our most aggressive collie, had proved too rambunctious for me to handle, I usually took the other dogs for their walks and left Candy's exercise to Crane. Sometimes Raven, another feisty canine, liked to accompany us, walking off leash. I'd have to rely on her for protection. If it came to that.

I didn't think it would. After that first howl, the deep country silence had returned. The coyotes would stay in their woods, and I would stay safely in the rest of Foxglove Corners. It was known as co-existing.

~ * ~

Our house and the yellow Victorian across the lane, where my aunt by marriage, Camille, lived with her husband, Crane's Uncle Gilbert, were the last inhabited dwellings on Jonquil Lane. Beyond our property and a stretch of woods lay one of the most unsightly areas of Foxglove Corners. Here a builder had begun the construction of a group of French chateaux-style mansions. Subsequently he went bankrupt and fled Foxglove Corners for parts unknown, letting his project come to a standstill.

Over the seasons, entire walls of half-finished structures had fallen, along with broken panes of glass, roof shingles, and miscellaneous building debris. A few of the mansions, mere shells, remained more or less intact while nature slowly reclaimed her own. Instead of new families, wildlife moved in, along with an occasional vagrant and evil-doer.

Everybody complained about the crumbling houses, everyone agreed they were a menace, but no one took action until one summer, Sue Appleton, the president of the Lakeville Collie Rescue League, and I had joined forces to collect signatures for a 'Raze the Construction' petition. Other matters had intervened, and, in the end, we didn't have enough names to present to the proper authorities.

So the abandoned construction remained untouched, a gloomy, overgrown, forbidding place for people, a source of never-ending fascination for dogs.

On Saturday morning, I leashed Halley and two of my rescues, Star and Misty, and set out for the first walk of the day. Raven, lying in front of her house, watched us but didn't move.

I often took the collies to visit the horses at Sue's farm on Squill Lane, a route which took me past the crumbling mansions. Invariably the dogs found something to interest them in that ungodly wilderness, a scent or sound that eluded me, and I made it a point to hold on tight to their leashes.

Misty was in an exuberant, saucy mood this morning, tugging on her leash, her lustrous white fur blown back in the gusting November wind.

"Misty, heel," I said and gave the lead a tug of my own.

The young white collie had a stubborn streak and the strength to back it up. For the moment, though, I was in control.

As we approached the abandoned construction, Star gave a little whimper. I noticed she was limping, favoring her right leg.

Bringing us to a stop, I bent to examine her paw. I ran my hand over the rough, cold pad and neatly trimmed nails, looking for a foreign object lodged between her toes.

Nothing. That wasn't good. Star was the oldest of our canine brood. Maybe I should take her home, out of the wind. We hadn't gone that far. Yes, that would be best.

I turned around, but before I could take a single step forward, Misty wrenched the leash out of my hand and with an excited yelp bolted into the shadowy expanse of disintegrating houses and their surround of woods. Her leash trailed behind her.

You little devil!

"Misty, come!" I shouted, and the wind carried my voice away.

Apparently she didn't choose to hear, and I could no longer see her.

What now?

I didn't have a choice. A dog running free in Foxglove Corners was vulnerable to all sorts of dangers from predators to motorists driving too fast on lonely country roads.

Darn. I shouldn't have let this happen, should have had a tighter grip on Misty's lead and been quicker to react.

But it happened. With a guilty glance at Star, I led her and Halley, the docile ones, into the heart of the lost development.

I hadn't gone a dozen yards before I realized the folly of my decision. Star struggled to keep up with us, casting me an imploring look, accompanied by a pitiful whine.

But I had to find Misty. At the same time, Star couldn't continue to walk. If only Raven were with us.

Trying to find a way out, I looked around. A fallen many-branched limb lay across our path. I looped the leashes securely around a sturdy branch.

"Stay, girls," I said, and repeated. "Stay."

Confident that they would be all right, I stepped over the log and plowed across light snow cover through a forest of scrub and seedlings. I had never ventured so far into the development, and my unease began to mount. I couldn't see the lane from my vantage point, and while I wasn't afraid of getting lost in this wood, I wanted to find Misty quickly and get back to Jonquil Lane.

Another wall had toppled over, a victim of the winds, leaving its stark interior open to the elements, but the neighboring mansion, about an acre away, looked whole, if not new.

The snow-topped house brought an old fairy story to mind: the witch's cottage that beckoned to Hansel and Gretel.

What nonsense!

The imitation French chateau was a far cry from a little cottage built of candy. But by what magic had this structure withstood seasons of neglect and wild winds?

I shouted into the silence. "Misty! Where are you?"

In answer came a low, threatening growl.

Coyote?

One growl, and the abandoned development fell silent. Like the howl I'd heard yesterday.

That didn't mean the growler had left the area.

I couldn't tell the creature's location. It seemed to originate in the woods to my right. Or behind the house. Or… I didn't know, but its message was clear. "Get out of my territory."

I should have brought the gun.

Then I remembered Crane saying that coyotes weren't known to attack humans. Misty was a full-grown collie.

But I'd left my two older dogs tethered to a branch. Helpless.

Leave it to you, Jennet, to turn a morning walk into a disaster.

Not knowing whether to go forward or retrace my steps, I stood for a moment.

Go back. Trust Misty to come home.

Before I could do that, a crashing sound broke the quiet of the woods.

Two

Oh, no! No time to search the ground for a big stick. No time…

Misty bounded out of the brush, tail wagging, eyes sparkling with secret delight. Burrs clung to her coat, and her paws were muddy. I'd just groomed her this morning.

"You bad dog!" I said. "Where did you go?"

She gave a joyous yelp.

You'll never know.

Thankful that she hadn't tangled with the creature that had growled, I grabbed her lead, which was cold and wet from its journey through the snow, and dragged her back to the branch where I'd left Halley and Star.

She didn't want to go with me, kept tugging on her leash to show her displeasure. Spoiled brat. Well, I'd spoiled her, along with all my dogs.

"Heel," I said sharply.

The woods were silent. Too silent. Silence wasn't always good. The sooner we were back on Jonquil Lane, the better.

I needn't have worried about my girls. Halley was lying down, chewing a stick, while Star was busy licking her paw. She had probably dislodged the foreign object herself as she appeared to move more easily. They were eager to resume walking.

I was no longer in the mood for a walk, especially with an unknown animal lurking in the woods. I didn't think any of us were, except Misty who kept looking over her shoulder.

"Forget it," I said.

The older dogs wouldn't mind an abbreviated walk, not with the cold wind blowing, and I could visit with Sue Appleton another day. All that mattered was that we'd gotten out of the house for a while— and lived to walk another day.

I couldn't help thinking about the mansion that had retained its shape. How close to being finished was the interior? Perhaps if the rest of the houses were demolished, that one house could be spared. Technically, I imagined, it still belonged to the absent builder.

I would love to see the inside, but I had no intention of returning to that godforsaken development anytime soon. The unseen creature had warned me away.

~ * ~

Later that afternoon I put a roast in the oven, added potatoes and carrots, and with dinner covered, treated myself to a few hours of leisure reading. I had found an old Gothic paperback, *Nella Waits*, at the Green House of Antiques last week, and it was riveting.

At five o'clock, a vintage yellow Plymouth Belvedere with white fins parked behind my new Ford Focus, and Brent Fowler emerged, bearing gifts as always. A large bouquet, wrapped in dark red foil that matched his hair, and a bottle of wine.

The dogs flew into their 'welcome friend' mode. They knew the sound of Brent's car and undoubtedly his scent outside the walls of our house.

He was dressed like the hunter he was, green plaid shirt showing behind a brown suede jacket and boots. Brent was the Huntsman of the Foxglove Corners Hunt. He owned stables, numerous horses and dogs, and courted whatever lucky girl caught his eye.

He could do all this because he had plenty of money and an endless supply of time.

I opened the door and smiled as I took the flowers from him.

"I was in the neighborhood and thought I'd stop by and see what's for dinner," he said.

"You're in luck. Pot roast and lemon meringue pie."

"Guess I'll stay then."

I found a vase for the flowers, a sumptuous flower shop bouquet, and filled it with water while Brent set the wine on the coffee table. Always one to make himself at home, he collapsed into the rocker. Sky settled down at his feet, and Misty leaped into his lap. The other collies, their greeting complete, retreated to their favorite spots in the house.

"What have you been up to?" I asked.

"Funny you should ask that. I've been visiting your old stamping grounds."

That could only mean the pink Victorian on Huron Court, the house Brent had purchased intending to open it to the public as an inn after extensive renovation. The pink Victorian, the scene of my last terrifying misadventure.

"Weren't you going to wait until spring?" I asked.

"Yeah, but I couldn't. I got to thinking about the house sitting there empty, and figured, what the heck? I have the time. Someone has to keep an eye on the place anyway."

"Has anything unusual happened?" I asked.

He knew what I meant by unusual. On Huron Court, time was unstable. Without warning, it had been known to move backward to the past, and, for all I knew, forward to the future as well.

"Can't say that it has," Brent said. "I don't spend much time there."

In spite of my resolve not to think about the Victorian or Huron Court or Violet, who once lived in the house, my thoughts drifted back to the time when I thought I'd lost my happy life forever. Only a few short weeks ago, I had been trapped in the past. I had irrefutable proof of my time slip, tucked into a handkerchief box.

"I've been making plans and lining up painters and contractors," Brent said. "In the meantime, I'm moving Violet's possessions into the room we think was hers and setting aside bags to donate to Vietnam Veterans. I'll have to buy a bed, though. I wonder what they did with her bed?"

"Moved it? Sold it? Who knows?"

A burst of raucous barking interrupted my speculation as the dogs dashed to the kitchen door. Misty leaped down from Brent's lap to join the pack, a dazzling white comet flying through the air.

Crane came stamping in, tail-wagging collies on either side, and locked his gun in its special cabinet.

"Evening, Fowler," he said.

"Sheriff."

"Bringing my wife flowers again?"

"They're for the house," he said. "For the dinner table."

"And the wine?

"For the roast."

Crane dropped a kiss on my cheek. It would have been more thorough had we been alone. But Brent wouldn't stay all night.

"How did you know we were having roast for dinner?"

"Good guess," he said.

"I might have heard a coyote today," I told Crane. "This time it growled at me."

"Near the house?"

"No, in the abandoned development. I didn't see it, though."

I told him about Star's temporary lameness and how Misty had broken away from me.

He frowned at Misty but knew not to reprimand her so long after the incident. "Maybe I'd better take over Misty's walking," he said. "She's grown into another Candy."

"She's gotten all her naughtiness from Candy, her mentor," I said. "But this was a one-time-only event. The dogs are always interested in those falling-down houses. Today she caught me unaware."

"Are you guys having coyote trouble?" Brent asked.

One heartrending howl. One menacing growl. No sightings.

"Not yet, but I think they're moving in," I said.

Crane joined me on the sofa. "I told Jennet what to do if she meets up with one."

"What's that?"

"The fine art of hazing."

"I'd better check on my roast," I said.

I rose and so did Candy. She followed me into the kitchen and paced underfoot as I assembled a quick salad. Dinner was ready. All I had to do was add another place setting. We often had company, and quite often it was Brent. Sometimes I thought he was lonely, although he could have a date every night of the week if he so desired.

But he was lonely for home cooking and good company. He couldn't buy that.

I moved the flowers to the center of the table and lit the heirloom candlesticks that had belonged to Rebecca Ferguson, Crane's Civil War-era ancestress, trying not to trip over Candy. She was my shadow this evening, pot roast being her all-time favorite meat.

In the living room, Crane and Brent were still talking about coyotes. I simply couldn't get away from those pestiferous intruders.

We're the intruders, I reminded myself.

At any rate, it was better to discuss coyotes than the house on Huron Court. I didn't want to think about it. Now, thanks to Brent, it was going to stay in my mind for a while.

Three

All of a sudden, coyotes were in our lives and in the news. Sunday's edition of the *Banner* devoted most of the third page to the grim story of Pippa, a little powder puff mix who had been attacked by a coyote in her yard. Pippa's owner had let her out before bedtime but didn't go with her.

The owner, who wasn't named, scared the coyote off by hurling rocks from her garden at it— Crane's hazing technique— but the damage had been done. Pippa was in the Foxglove Corners Animal Hospital in serious condition. Her owner was incredulous. "My dog was in her own backyard. She should have been safe."

Accompanying the article was a sketch of the coyote and facts such as average height, weight, and habits. Nothing I didn't know.

Poor Pippa. She was on her property. The coyote was in his one-time territory. Wild animals didn't understand development.

Thinking of Pippa, I lost my appetite for my doughnut, but the coffee tasted good. I turned the page, hoping to find happier news, and Candy grabbed the entire plate from the table. It hit the floor, and the doughnut disappeared into Candy's mouth.

She was shameless.

Imagining her in a life or death combat with a coyote, I let the transgression pass with a half- hearted reprimand.

I didn't feel like taking the dogs for a walk today. I definitely didn't want to take the gun. Still, they needed to go out. Dogs like following a routine, and this was our walk time.

Collies aren't powder puff dogs, I told myself. Even so, I'd been lax about letting them out in the yard alone. From now on, I'd stay with them.

What a nuisance!

Probably nothing would happen, but it was better to be safe than sorry.

Although I was loath to defer to Crane's edicts, not wanting him to think he could dominate me, I'd better take the more easily managed Halley, Sky, and Gemmy. For a while anyway.

I finished my coffee and called the lucky three to heel. Misty, cuddling her precious toy goat, didn't seem to mind being excluded.

Or the little fur brat was sulking.

As I buttoned my jacket, I glanced at the gun cabinet. Crane's gun was gone, as always while he was on duty. My own rested in its appointed place like a forsaken antique.

So, should I go? Halley was watching me and waiting.

All right, but I'd walk in the other direction, away from the abandoned development. I always enjoyed seeing the majestic houses built along the lane, although the black and white vista of November lacked the enchantment of daffodils and jonquils and summer wildflowers shimmering in sunlight.

I'd still have to pass the stretch of woods across the lane and adjacent to the yellow Victorian but wouldn't encounter any ghostly deserted structures. Could the howl I'd heard yesterday have originated in that wilderness?

Oh, for heaven's sake. Go, but don't take the gun. Don't overthink this.

Plenty of rocks lined the lane. Coyotes were most active at dawn and dusk, and it was almost noon. But like deer they could be unpredictable...

Do you want to stay in the house forever, worrying about something that might never happen?

I attached three leads to collars, filled my pocket with treats from the Lassie tin, and led the dogs out to the lane. This was my home. Darned if I was going to let a hypothetical coyote spoil my cherished walk time with my girls.

~ * ~

Later that day, Crane folded me in his arms for a long, thorough kiss. A wave of cold air and pine and wood smoke washed over me.

"No company tonight?" he said.

"Just us."

"Good. I drove by Fowler's place today."

"His house or the barn?" I asked.

"The pink Victorian."

I hadn't expected that. "You were on Huron Court?"

"Briefly. I saw his car parked in front of the house and stopped."

I tried to ignore the chill that traveled over me. "That was dangerous."

"Not for me. He just had the living room painted a light purple color."

"He was going to wait until spring," I said. "He planned to knock down a wall and make other extensive changes. You'd think painting would be last on his list."

"What Brent says isn't the same as what he does."

He moved to the cabinet in the living room and locked his gun inside. "What did you do today, honey?"

"Took the dogs for a walk without any drama, did a little school work, and roasted a chicken. Typical Sunday. How about you?"

"Arrested a drunk driver. Met a new deputy. Typical day."

On the surface, our life sounded dull, but it was the life I wanted.

I often marveled at my good luck. When a tornado damaged my house in Oakpoint, I found the house of my dreams in Foxglove Corners and the man of my dreams practically in my own front yard.

God bless the tornado, I thought.

Had anyone ever said that?

Life with Crane hadn't always been easy, but it was glorious.

Trailed by Candy, Crane went upstairs to shower, and I put the finishing touches on dinner. A salad, rolls, we had half a lemon meringue pie left... The table was set, the candles lit, the dogs fed.

While I waited for Crane, I picked up the newspaper. I might as well finish reading it before the news became history.

Wars, murders in Detroit, killings in foreign lands, a group of young musicians hoping to raise money for a trip to Germany. And buried in the middle of the first section, the picture of a gorgeous tricolor collie beneath the heading, "Reward Offered for Lost Dog."

Her name was Trista— Trista Summer Thunder— and she'd been separated from her breeder en route to her new home when her truck was involved in an accident on Spruce Road. Trista, a show prospect, a daughter of champions, had wandered away from the chaos following the crash. This had happened yesterday morning, and she'd hadn't been seen since.

That meant she could be anywhere in Foxglove Corners. Anywhere at all, for that matter.

Her new owner was offering an amazing reward of twelve hundred dollars for her safe return.

That sum should inspire people to search for her in every nook and cranny of the Corners. It was curious, though. Why would she choose that amount? I could almost hear the cynics say, "Just take the money and buy another dog."

I wondered if Sue Appleton knew about Trista. A dog on her own in the countryside was at high risk, and we were in the business of rescuing collies. I'd call her, but later. I could hear Crane on the stairway. It was our dinner hour, time to set aside distressing conversation.

~ * ~

Mondays always rolled around too soon. A few hours passed, then the night, the morning, and I was driving to Marston High School. My friend and fellow English teacher, Leonora, sipped a carry out vanilla latte in the passenger's seat.

Snow fell on the freeway, not much yet but enough to make the pavement slippery. I drove carefully, liking the way my new Ford Focus held the road, liking the fact that Leonora and I had carpooled to Oakpoint since her move to Foxglove Corners. Having a companion paved the way to face a school day which would more likely than not be hectic.

I had four pleasant classes, a difficult one, and an overbearing principal. After a rocky start, I was able to cope with the most recalcitrant of students in my so-called class from hell. Usually.

A half hour into our drive, we'd exhausted our news: Leonora's Sunday date with Deputy Sheriff Jake Brown, the man she hoped to marry; my sudden awareness of coyotes in the neighborhood; the plight of Trista, the lost tricolor, and Brent's decision to paint the living room of the pink Victorian before renovations began.

"If he waited till spring, I thought he might lose interest in it," I said.

Leonora paused to take a sip of her latte. "Brent never impressed me as a patient man."

"I wish he'd sell the place and concentrate on his fox hunting or his other inn. I wish..."

A truck whizzed past me, exceeding the speed limit, but I refused to drive faster. You never knew when an icy patch lay in waiting for the distracted motorist.

"I wish we could forget all about that house," I said. "That won't be possible as long as Brent owns it."

Leonora glanced at me. "You don't mean that, Jen. You're as curious as ever."

She was talking about the mystery that went with the house as if it were one more amenity, the possible murder of the girl, Violet Randall, who had lived there until her disappearance.

"You're right. I'm curious. But I can learn everything I want to know without ever setting foot in Violet's house again."

"That's true," Leonora said.

Whenever I thought about that house, I seemed to grow instantly cold, even as I talked about it to Leonora on this snowy morning with the heater on its highest setting.

"It's just that I'm afraid," I said.

Four

I could always count on my fourth period American Literature class to be rowdy and unruly. They wouldn't like the day's story or assignment, no matter what it was. They'd be starving, for the next hour was lunch, and there would be a thousand matters that needed to be discussed— immediately and loudly.

Oh, and they'd be too cold in the room, or too warm. They needed a drink of water from the fountain or a trip to the bathroom. If I were momentarily distracted, a few rebellious souls, always the same ones, would slip into the wrong seat after attendance.

I could count on an hour of pure aggravation.

We had reached American author Ambrose Bierce in our survey. *An Occurrence at Owl Creek Bridge* contained beautifully written passages and at the end, a twist they'd never anticipate.

"Is this another boring story?" asked Slade Johnston, my chief nemesis.

"Aren't they all?" That was Jasmine, Slade's girlfriend.

"Not this one," I said. "It's set during the Civil War. As the story opens, a Confederate supporter is about to be hanged as a spy."

Pauline Carson raised her hand. "Shouldn't that be hung, Mrs. Ferguson?"

"No," I said. "Hanged is correct."

"Hanged doesn't sound right."

I pointed to the dictionary in front of the room, open on its stand. "Look it up."

"Naah," she said. "That's all right."

"Maybe I'll show you the movie," I said, "but we have to read the story first. I'll start."

My goal was to have them realize the written story was a thousand times better than a film.

I waited for the noise to subside and began:

A man stood upon a railroad bridge in northern Alabama, looking down into the swift water twenty feet below. The man's hands were behind his back, the wrists bound with a cord. A rope closely encircled his neck...

Encouraged by the unusual silence in my classroom, I read on. An occasional glance told me no one had fallen asleep. Bierce's fiction was as clear and riveting today as it had been decades ago. No wonder this story had endured and found its way into high school textbooks.

Even I, who knew the tale well, felt my heartbeat quicken as I followed Peyton Farquhar's daring escape from the Federal soldiers. Finally free, he set out on foot for his plantation home.

At last he found a road which led him to what he believed to be the right direction.

Abruptly I stopped reading as memories of my own intruded on the story's crystal-sharp images. In my mind I travelled a different road, Huron Court, in a seemingly endless attempt to reach Sagramore Lake which lay just ahead.

It *had* to lie just ahead. The lake wouldn't have moved. It was the road, that accursed road. While imperceptibly, inexplicably, the season advanced, somehow the road turned me around and sent me in the wrong direction. Back to the house.

Back to the past.

He had not known that he lived in so wild a region.

I stumbled over the words. My mouth felt dry, and my heart was pounding.

This was a good place to stop, to leave my audience hanging.

"Please finish the story for homework," I said. "There isn't much, but it's— er..." I searched for the best word, settled on *dynamic.*

Ignoring the groans and objections of thirty-three disappointed listeners, I glanced at the clock. Ten minutes until lunch. Never had fourth hour gone by so quickly.

~ * ~

The bell rang, and I retrieved my packed lunch from the closet. Minutes later, Leonora joined me, carrying her lunch on a tray. The cafeteria had a student favorite today, meatballs and spaghetti.

She set a can of ginger ale on the large table we used in Journalism to lay out the school newspaper.

"It was so quiet in your room last hour, Jen. What was going on?"

"We were reading *An Occurrence at Owl Creek Bridge*," I said. "I finally found a story they like."

"What's wrong then?"

Leonora and I had known each other for a long time. She could read my moods and knew about practically everything I did.

I told her. "I never know what's going to set off the memories. Today it was a story. Peyton Farquhar realized he was on a wild, unfamiliar road, and I remembered."

"Well," she said, spearing a meatball with a plastic fork. "You had a nightmare experience. If it had happened to me, I probably couldn't function at all."

"I still dream about it. Sometimes. All I want is to stay in my own world and live my own life."

"Then don't go near Huron Court. Ever again."

"I don't intend to," I said.

~ * ~

I hoped I wasn't going to be haunted by flashbacks of my long, terrifying walk on Huron Court. I'd left that time behind me, or so I thought. But some memories have staying power. They re-emerge when least expected and in unexpected places. Like in my classroom when I needed to be focused on my teaching. Or in dreams.

Heaven knew I had enough everyday problems clamoring to be solved. Each new day in American Lit brought a new challenge. I could never let my guard down.

The next day I showed a film version of *An Occurrence at Owl Creek Bridge*. The class was always more manageable on rare movie days. By then everyone knew the ending. Peyton Farquhar was dead. During his harrowing escape from his executioners, he was seconds from death.

I was elated that as a whole my students didn't find the movie as good as the story. More important, I was able to watch it without a single frightening memory. Having a pleasant day with the class from hell made an enormous difference in my outlook and energy level.

That evening was going to be busy. After dinner, I had to attend a meeting of the Lakeville Collie Rescue League. As usual, when I was pressed for time, I drove to Clovers, my favorite restaurant, for carry-out dinners and delectable homemade desserts. Leonora decided to order in as well.

Clovers was off-the-beaten-path on a rural section of Crispian Road. The owner, Mary Jeanne, specialized in old-fashioned comfort food. An added bonus was the frequent presence of one of her waitresses, Annica, my young friend and sometime partner in detecting. Annica worked part time as a waitress to finance her college education.

She looked elegant this afternoon, in one of those dresses that take the wearer from day to night, with sparkly chandelier earrings and a matching barrette in her red-gold hair.

"Are you girls here for dinner?" she asked, as she led us to a booth by the window with a view of the bleak November woods.

"We came for take-out," I said, scanning the chalkboard menu.

"We have stuffed cabbages today," she said.

Ah, look no further. They were a favorite of ours, and I'd never mastered the knack of making them.

"I'll have two."

"Do you have enough for a third dinner?" Leonora asked.

"We sure do. Mary Jeanne just turned out a fresh batch."

Annica jotted down our order and handed it to Marcy, her fellow waitress.

"My shift's over," she said. "I'll join you for a few minutes. How was the Marston madhouse today?"

"Pretty tame," I said.

Leonora added, "The cold weather helps. Kids aren't so anxious to skip school when it's snowing."

"Are you going out later?" I asked.

"I have a date," Annica said. "With Brent."

I could have guessed.

Annica had a long standing crush on Brent, who dated her frequently. Hence the dramatic attire and glitter. On an average day, Annica was the essence of brightness. This day she radiated brilliance.

"Aside from my date to look forward to, it's been a bad day," she said. "I got a ticket this morning for driving eight miles over the speed limit. Hey, Jennet, did you know there's a new deputy in town?"

"Crane said something about it."

"She's gorgeous. Just like a movie star with that long glossy hair. She's mean, though. No sense of humor."

"Crane didn't mention that it was a woman," I said.

Or that she was gorgeous.

"Just thought I'd warn you," Annica said. "Slow down. I wouldn't have minded if Crane had pulled me over, but that chick... I didn't like her."

Without setting eyes on the new deputy, I decided I wouldn't either.

Five

After dinner I drove the short distance to Sue Appleton's horse farm on Squill Lane for the League meeting. Crane took Candy, Misty, and Star for a walk in the opposite direction, and Raven stayed behind to watch the house.

It was already dark, and on the way I had to pass the abandoned construction. I stole a glance at the crumbling walls in the embrace of encroaching woods. A luminous moon rode high above the treetops. Thank heavens for moonlight. Except for my headlights there was no other source of illumination. As long as I stayed in the car, I should be safe.

Don't be over confident, I told myself. *Danger assumes many forms.*

By night, the lane looked different, alive with grotesque shadows and vaguely menacing. For a moment, I thought I saw a light shining from the heart of the ruins. It flickered and died. Imagination probably. Or a vagrant sheltering in one of the shell houses. He'd need a light.

That was the most likely explanation.

But there could be another one.

That's right. Scare yourself. You still have to drive home.

I stepped on the accelerator, knowing the police didn't patrol Jonquil Lane. Once I'd left the construction behind, I breathed more easily.

Sue's sprawling ranch house sparkled with Christmas lights strung around the door and windows. A half dozen parked cars suggested that the meeting would be sparsely attended.

They usually were. Most of the members had jobs and families to take care of, not to mention their collies. But this was the last meeting of the year. In December, Sue would host her annual Christmas party, and we'd celebrate another successful year of rescuing collies.

The door was open. Icy and Bluebell, Sue's blue merle rescues, formed the greeting committee. I gave them each a pat on the head and followed the chatter and muted Christmas music to Sue's family room.

It was a comfortable meeting place with pictures of Sue's horses and collies on the walls and bunches of dried flowers in floor baskets. Flames rose in a wood-burning stove, and a delicious aroma of popcorn filled the air. Sitting with the familiar league members, I saw someone new, a tall woman with a swirl of ash brown hair anchored to the top of her head by a jeweled barrette.

"Here's Jennet," Sue said, setting a bowl of popcorn on a table next to an assortment of soft drinks. "Jennet, I'd like you to meet Irene, our new member. Irene, this is the famous Jennet Greenway Ferguson."

I felt my face grow warm. "Hardly famous," I said.

"Don't be so modest. You've been in the paper. More than once."

"I've seen your picture," Irene said. "It's a pleasure to meet you in person."

I found an unoccupied chair by the wood stove and settled into it, hoping the conversation would shift from my various activities.

Icy raced to the window barking as if the fiends of hell were descending on the house. His face, outraged and angry, glared back at him back at him reflected in the darkness outside.

"Deer in the yard," Sue said. "Icy loves to chase them."

That observation led to a side discussion of the deer of Foxglove Corners and how close they came to houses, how much damage they could do to gardens, but how beautiful and graceful they were.

"Let's get started," Sue said. "First, everybody, be on the lookout for this dog."

She held up two eight by ten pictures of the missing tricolor collie, Trista Summer Thunder. In one she sat in front of a red flowering bush, looking proud and regal. The other was a stunning profile.

"Isn't she a beauty?" Sue murmured.

Beauty was an understatement. Trista conjured images of stormy skies. Her coat was black with sable markings. On her right side, a shawl of black broke the wide snowy ruff, and on her head she wore a white star mark. Her expression radiated intelligence and collie charm.

"She's exquisite," Emma Brock said.

"Trista is a daughter of a blue merle, Champion Graybrook Winter Rain," Sue said. "You may have seen the story in the *Banner*. She went missing when the truck she was riding in collided with a speeder. She might be in our area. Her owner is offering a reward of twelve hundred dollars. Apparently she can afford it, and she wants her back."

"If one of us were to find her, that sum would pay for a lot of vet care," Emma said.

Sue sent the pictures circulating through the room. "Of course we wouldn't accept the reward. After all, we're the Rescue League."

"We could consider it a donation," Irene said.

Irene was right, though. That sum would be a welcome windfall, making life easier for some poor foundling.

Sue rummaged among the papers on her desk and held up another picture, a smaller one of a sable collie gazing longingly out of a crate.

"This is Lolly from Oscoda. I'm going to pick her up next weekend. She's almost a year old, sweet and gentle with young children and pets. Does anyone have room to foster her?"

Silence. The fire in the wood stove crackled. Someone opened a can of root beer. No one spoke.

"Anyone?" she asked.

I had just added a seventh collie to my brood, an elderly dog named Star whose owner didn't have time for her.

"Well, I'll let you think about it," Sue said. "Lolly's owners are moving to California after the first of the year. They can't take her with them."

More likely, they didn't want to take her. People surrendered their dogs for a variety of reasons, few of them legitimate, in my opinion.

Sue sighed and set Lolly's picture back on the desk. "There are two sign-up sheets for our potluck holiday party going around, one for food, one for gifts. Let's see. Our treasurer couldn't be here tonight, but we're in good financial shape. What we need are more foster homes."

Her audience shifted uncomfortably in their seats. We were a small group but a dedicated one. Still, a person can only care for so many large dogs. Sue had six collies at present, all rescues.

Irene said, "I could take Lolly as a foster. Maybe. I'll let you know in a few days, but I'd like to see her first."

"Wonderful. Let's all keep an eye out for Trista. We're heading into winter. It won't be so easy for a dog to survive on her own out there in the elements."

"Such a beautiful collie," Emma said. "Let's hope somebody didn't help himself to her already."

~ * ~

I heard the coyotes as I turned on Jonquil Lane. Could any other creature make so mournful a sound?

They were too close to our house for comfort. Sue had told us a chilling true story about a pack of coyotes that had lured a farm dog into the woods where they'd attacked him.

They were too intelligent, those four-legged predators. How else could they survive? I didn't like to think about those to-the-death struggles taking place in my neighborhood. For the same reason, I didn't allow myself to think of slaughterhouses when I made a meatloaf. It might make me a hypocrite, but it was the truth.

The howling continued. Would a stray dog think the coyotes were calling to him?

A dog had to be twice as clever as a coyote. Mine were, I thought. Halley's breeder had bred collies for intelligence and good health. My other dogs were rescues, but they'd proven themselves many times over.

No sneaky coyote would lure one of them into the woods.

I passed the abandoned construction. No mysterious light flickered. The howling had faded. I sped past our property line and Raven's house and parked in our driveway behind Crane's Jeep.

Home and safe.

I turned off the lights, dropped my keys in my purse, and opened the door.

A creature stood in the pool of light that poured from the front windows, a piece of the night come alive. My mind registered darkness. A canine shape. Stillness.

A moment later, it disappeared. A creature of the night returned to the night. I wondered if I'd imagined it.

The creature hadn't made a sound but had stood like a stone statue. Watching and waiting. Too large to be a coyote.

Or so I'd thought in the moment I'd become aware of it. Now I wasn't so sure I'd seen anything at all.

It couldn't have been a living creature. If it had been, if it had invaded Raven's territory, she would have sailed through the night air, bent on driving it away.

And dogs in the house would be barking. Misty's face appeared in the window, then Candy's. They hadn't started barking their welcome yet. I didn't hear a sound from Raven's house.

I had an unfortunate susceptibility to dark tales. A combination of Trista's tale and coyotes howling had set my wild imagination in motion again.

You're the only life form in the immediate vicinity, I told myself.

Nonetheless I hurried into the house. In case I was wrong.

Six

Brent handed me his phone. "What do you think, Jennet? Does it look authentic?"

I scrolled through numerous pictures of a room in the pink Victorian, the one I thought might have been Violet's room. I recognized her Cupid lamp and collie figurines. The narrow white iron bed was new, as was a bookcase with a distressed white pine finish. Brent had found a small French provincial desk and a bench with a lavender velvet top.

The blue and white quilt we'd found in the attic covered the bed, and the bookcase held the childhood classics and series books we'd found packed in boxes. A picture over the wall painted in blues, yellows, and white depicted a fairy or angel hovering over the bed of a sleeping child. That image was more appropriate for a young girl, but I thought perhaps Violet had had it as a baby.

It was a pretty bedroom with a view of woods, the kind any young girl would love to have. In her diary Violet had referred to it as an ivory tower, or words to that effect, where she could be apart from her family and still be near them.

I felt the familiar icy chill wrapping itself around me. Maybe Brent's bringing Violet's room back to life— his version of Violet's life— wasn't a good idea.

"I never ventured beyond the first floor," I said. "When I was with Violet, I mean."

"Sometimes I feel that if Violet were to come back, she'd be right at home in this room," Brent said. "Her things would be there. Well, a few of them."

He had donated Violet's clothes to the Vietnam Veterans. It would be too creepy to keep them in the closet. Creepy? There was a word I didn't often use. Somehow it seemed to fit the situation.

I wanted to ask Brent if he thought this re-creation were wise. I almost did. Instead I said, "Are you planning to let a guest sleep in this room when you open the inn?

"No," he said. "It'll be a kind of one-room museum."

That was fortunate. I wouldn't sleep there myself.

Crane had already scrolled through the pictures while I cleared the table. I hadn't heard his reaction, but he sat quietly drinking coffee, a slight frown on his face. I already knew his views on Violet's house and Brent's plan to turn it into an inn. He thought—in his own words— that Brent was playing with fire. He'd ordered me to stay away from it. Ordinarily I would have chafed at this dictatorial pronouncement. However, in this case it coincided with my own feelings.

"I had the walls papered," Brent said. "They were a washed-out shade of light blue. Annica found a print with violet flowers."

Annica? I wasn't surprised. She lost no opportunity to be a part of Brent's life. He'd probably mentioned decorating, she'd suggested violets for Violet, and proceeded to find the perfect wallpaper pattern.

"Weren't you going to wait until the renovations were complete to decorate?" I asked.

"I've decided against knocking down walls," Brent said. "I'll just do what's necessary to make the place safe."

"What about the tea room?"

"It'll be the dining room. Or should I say the parlor? I'll buy six or eight round tables and chairs and one of those china cabinets."

I refilled our coffee cups and brought a platter of cookies down from the mantel where it had stayed safe out of the reach of collie paws and jaws. Candy and Misty followed me, hoping a cookie or even a crumb would fall to the floor.

At one time, Brent had talked about extensive renovations. The dated kitchen with its shades of bright lemon and robin's egg blue counters, in particular, had been slated for gutting. He intended to buy all new appliances to accommodate the customers he hoped to attract. I reminded him of this.

"I'll replace a few of them," he said. "But it's a funny thing. The more time I spend in that house, the more I like it as it is. I don't think it wants to be changed. Not drastically, anyway. I had it thoroughly cleaned from top to bottom. Now I'm ready to furnish it. Annica's looking for china and lamps."

Crane masked a cough and concentrated on drinking his fresh, hot coffee. I stared at Brent, wondering when the outspoken earthbound fox hunter had changed. For heaven's sake. The house didn't *want* to be changed? As if the house's feelings were to be taken into consideration? He sounded like Lucy Hazen.

Go ahead, I thought. *Say it.*

"Aren't you getting carried away, Brent? Just a little?"

"What do you mean?" he asked.

"Well, you're talking about the house as if it's alive."

He appeared to be confused. "How so?"

"Saying it doesn't want to change."

"Oh, that. It's just a figure of speech. You use them all the time."

Technically Brent was endowing inanimate objects with human qualities, which was indeed a figure of speech. When that object was a house with a dark history, though, it could be worrisome. It *was* worrisome.

"The inspector assured me the house is structurally sound," Brent said. "Why tear it apart? I'm going to have new stairs installed outside and the windows replaced. It needs a new roof, too, but there's no point in unnecessary construction. I've decided to call it the Gingerbread House," he added.

I'd suggested Ginger's House, thinking of Violet's sable and white collie, Ginger. But I liked Brent's choice better. I gave him his phone back.

"These pictures make me feel like I'm right there with you," I said.

With a growing photo album, I could follow Brent's progress and never set foot in the pink Victorian.

"I'd like to have the house ready for Christmas," Brent said.

"So soon?"

"I can't think of a better time to open a new inn. Christmas lights and wreaths and a big tree in the living room. Presents for all the guests."

When Brent's opening date had been months away, the project seemed unreal. I didn't have to think about it. Now, however, the situation had changed.

Almost imperceptibly. Like Brent's attitude toward the house.

~ * ~

Brent left and Crane and I were alone. This was the first opportunity we'd had to talk without interruption all day. I refilled our coffee cups again, and he tended to the fire. Candy watched him anxiously, knowing the time for her walk was drawing near.

"That house has become an obsession for Fowler," he said.

"I know. He went from renovating practically everything to not wanting to change anything. Do you think…" I paused to give

Misty a pat and take a drink of my coffee before it cooled. "Do you think he's falling under the house's spell?"

"Assuming that were possible, it'd take a person susceptible to— uh— supernatural influences."

"Like me, you mean?"

He sidestepped my question. "Not like Fowler. He has an opportunity to turn a house with potential into a unique inn. You know he's never been patient."

"That's true. The kind of renovation he was talking about could take a year or two."

"Besides," Crane said, "no one ever claimed that house was haunted. It was the road, Huron Court."

"You're right."

But I remembered Misty scratching at the floor of the living room under which Annica thought a body had been buried. Still, the road was the culprit, not the house, that once elegant pink Victorian that had been neglected and uninhabited for decades.

"There's something else," Crane said. "We're all interested in knowing more about what happened to Violet Randall. Weren't you going to go to the library and look through old newspaper articles?"

"I've been too busy at school," I said. "Not to mention at home."

Demanding classes, schoolwork, meals, taking care of six collies and one husband— my schedule was full. As winter made itself known with cold temperatures and snow, still flurries, I found myself longing for the lazy days of summer when my time was my own.

"I'll find time to go to the library, though," I said. "I'm curious, too."

~ * ~

I knew Violet Randall was dead. We had visited her grave in the Old Resurrection Cemetery—Crane and I, along with Brent,

Annica, and Lucy. I'd made a second trip to her grave to fill the stone lamb's basket with fresh flowers.

But how did she die?

According to newspaper accounts of the time, Violet had disappeared while walking her dog on Huron Court. Missing, eventually presumed dead. Therefore, she could be a ghost, if accounts of Violet and Ginger sightings were authentic.

In her diary she had written about grim foreknowledge of her own demise. Something bad was going to happen to her. Apparently it had. She'd stopped keeping her diary and her name had vanished from the papers.

After a school day that had been remarkably free of angst, I dropped Leonora off at her house and drove to the Corners. The Foxglove Corners Public Library closed at six o'clock in the fall and five in the winter. That didn't give me much time for research, but at least I was making a start.

The old white Victorian had belonged to Elizabeth Eidt's family before she donated it to the town along with hundreds of her own books. Thus was born our library, a one of a kind institution and for many a home away from home.

In mid-November it looked tired in its surround of bare trees and leaves raked into flower beds. All of the furniture and Halloween decorations had been removed from the porch, packed away for another season, everything settled down for a long sleep like Miss Eidt's perennials.

Blackberry, Miss Eidt's cat, sat in a corner, her jewel-green eyes fixed on me as I climbed the stairs and opened the door. A pity she wasn't a dog. I missed the welcome bark of a canine and the wag of a friendly tail. You could never tell what a cat was thinking.

Miss Eidt looked as tired as her library, but was smartly attired, as always, in a soft lavender dress accentuated with ropes of pearls.

"Jennet," she said. "How nice. I was hoping you'd stop by. I've been saving this for you."

She brought a paperback out from behind her desk. *Legacy* by Florence Hurd. The old Gothic novel with its glossy, uncreased cover looked as if it had just been printed. Impossible. Its price was a dollar and ninety-five cents.

I touched it reverently.

"Where did you find it?"

"At an estate sale," she said. "It belonged to an eccentric woman who knew how to treat her books."

"I'll check it out."

"Just take it. I bought it for you. By the way, speaking of eccentric, there's someone here you know."

She leaned over the desk and said in a whisper. "It's Edwina Endicott. Do you want to take the book and run?"

Seven

I don't run away from anything. Although in this instance, I was tempted.

"Of course not," I said. "I might take refuge in your office, though. I need to check out something in the vertical file."

"Are you still looking for information on that cold case murder?" Miss Eidt asked.

"That and whatever else I can find on Violet Randall. Specifically on how she died."

Miss Eidt looked over my shoulder. "Uh oh, too late."

Edwina Endicott was bearing down on us, her gray coat brightened by a long red scarf. That was her only color.

I couldn't very well disappear into the office then. She dropped a book on Miss Eidt's desk and greeted me as if I were a long lost friend. We'd only met last month.

Edwina described herself as an amateur ghost hunter, although it seemed as if all she did was carry a camera on her person when walking on Huron Court. She claimed to have seen a ghostly girl walking with her dog on that lane and resolved to take their picture if she saw them again.

Without knowing why, I'd taken an instant dislike to her.

Well, maybe I knew why. She knew my name and private facts about my personal life, that I was married to Crane, for instance. It was as if she'd made a study of me.

"Look what I found in the Supernatural Section," Edwina said. "It's brand new."

Ghosts and Other Oddities Among Us, Volume Two.

Darn. Volume One had contained information about Violet, about people who said they'd seen her walking with her collie on Huron Court. There it was on the shelf with a space next to it. If only I'd seen the new book first.

Silently Miss Eidt stamped the card. "I don't recall seeing this one. Debbie must have catalogued and shelved it."

"When Volume Two comes back, would you hold it for me?" I asked. "And give me a call?"

"Of course. You wanted to use the vertical file?"

I glanced at the clock. How could twenty-five minutes have gone by already when I had just arrived? It was almost five-thirty, and I had dinner to make.

"I think I'll come back on Saturday when I have more time," I said.

"Good. Then we can have a real visit. I'll have Debbie pick up the doughnuts."

"Thanks for *Legacy*. I'll start it tonight."

Carrying her own book as if it were a treasure, Edwina accompanied me to the door. "I heard you mention Violet Randall," she said.

That was an example of what I disliked about Edwina. She'd eavesdropped on a private conversation.

"Yes," I said.

"Well, why do you want to know more about her?" She paused, holding the door open for us. "Did you see her, too?"

"I don't live anywhere near Huron Court," I said. "Supposedly she doesn't leave her territory."

"I thought you lived on Jonquil Lane."

"That isn't in the same neighborhood."

"It's close, though."

"You could say that."

"I've almost given up hope that I'll see the girl again," Edwina said. "But I never go out without my camera. Just in case."

Remembering a question I'd meant to ask her on a previous encounter, I said. "Did you ever see a beautiful Victorian house on Huron Court? It's pink, and it has twin turrets."

"You must be thinking about another road. The only house I've seen on that stretch of roadway is coming apart at the seams. It should be condemned."

"I just wondered."

She followed me down the steps. My white Ford Focus, one of the few cars in the parking lot, beckoned to me, promising freedom from an annoying conversation. I quickened my steps.

"There's my car."

"What a beauty! I love a white car."

At the moment it was dirty, courtesy of the country roads.

"I'm still hoping to see the ghost and her dog again," she called after me.

But that was unlikely. Violet was, I felt certain, an autumn ghost, and the season was practically over.

"Good luck," I said, and escaped into my car.

~ * ~

Where would an autumn ghost go when she wasn't haunting her territory? What did she do the rest of the year? Lie beneath the frozen ground and snow, waiting for the earth to awaken, waiting for summer and fall again? I thought of the phantom ice skater who appeared only in the wintertime on the lake through which she'd fallen to her death. The library's ghost never left the secret room of Eidt House.

Where was Violet? Did she ever leave Huron Court? Did she ever haunt the house that Brent planned to turn into an inn?

And why ponder the unanswerable.

I had more pressing concerns. What to make for dinner, for example. Ordinarily on a night like this, I would stop at Clovers for take-out. It seemed later than it was, though, and I wanted to be home before dark.

Steak was always a good choice. It was quick and Crane loved it.

Steak it was, then, with a salad and vegetables. Dessert? I hoped I had something in the freezer.

I drove on as the sky darkened. At this time of year, the daylight hours flew by, leaving an abbreviated evening— while school hours seemed twice as long.

I stepped on the accelerator, increased my speed to fifty, mindful of Annica's ticket from Foxglove Corners' new deputy sheriff. I didn't see any squad car in the vicinity, although this route contained many possible hiding places.

Live dangerously.

Although Crane would be livid if I got a ticket for speeding, all I wanted was to get home.

Two more miles, then I turned on Jonquil Lane. I saw the light in the bay window and Crane's Jeep, but no dogs were barking a welcome.

Odd. Usually no one could approach the house without the bark patrol sounding the alarm.

I swung into the driveway, and...

Oh, my God.

The coyote stood in a circle of light in front of my car. His eyes were fixed on the Focus. Or on me.

How could I ever have thought coyotes looked like smooth collies? This was a creature of the wild, lean and scrawny, with a ravenous eye.

From the house I heard barking. Not enough for six collies. And where was Raven? More to the point, where was Crane?

I grabbed my cell phone and dialed his number.

No answer.

"Get out of here!" I yelled loud enough to be heard through the windows.

I stepped on the accelerator. Drove forward. Slammed on the break. I couldn't just run a living creature down.

As if it knew my weakness, the coyote didn't move.

I had to do something.

The yellow Victorian across the lane was dark, and I didn't see Camille's car.

Remember. Hazing.

There were stones in the walkway. We'd dug them out of the ground for landscaping. Several were within easy reach of the car. If I dared open the door.

Wait! Noise! I had a noise source. I leaned on the horn, listened to the deep quiet of the country night break apart. On and on and on.

The coyote didn't move.

What now? What a bizarre ending to a long and tiring day.

If only I'd stopped at Clovers for take-out. I could toss a chicken drumstick or slice of beef out the window. A whole dinner if it came to that...

The minutes passed. I'd been in the car for ten minutes when I heard dogs barking in the distance. Moments before Raven burst into view, the coyote melted away, with Raven at his heels.

Smart creature.

And there was Crane with Candy, Misty, and Gemmy, the three collies who would have given the coyote a run for its money.

I pulled the car closer to Crane's Jeep, yanked the keys out of the ignition, and turned off the lights. I was shaking. Incident over. Delayed reaction.

What if Crane and the dogs hadn't appeared? I could have been trapped in the car like Stephen King's character in Cujo. Well, not exactly like her. The rest of my family would have come along sooner or later.

I opened the door, surprised that I was still shaking. I couldn't seem to stop.

"What happened?" demanded Crane, coming up to the car. "I heard the horn."

"A coyote," I said. "He wasn't going to let me get out of the car. If you hadn't turned up when you did, with the dogs…"

"I got home early and saw you weren't home yet, so I took the dogs for a short walk."

"Thank God it wasn't a long one."

The three collies were straining on their leashes, wanting to follow Raven. That wasn't going to happen.

Crane unlocked the door and ushered us all inside.

"They're getting too close to home," I said.

My voice was shaking, too. I needed a cup of tea.

Crane freed the dogs from their leads and laid his jacket on the kitchen table.

"I'll make it for you, honey. Would you like to go out to dinner?"

"I— no. Now that I'm home, I want to stay here."

He opened the freezer door. "Steaks okay?"

"That's what I planned. They can go in the broiler while they're still frozen."

Crane filled the tea kettle with water and put it on the burner. He poured water for the dogs who were more interested in their dinners. For himself, he opened a can of ginger ale.

"They're getting too close to home," I said. "That coyote was bold. Fearless. He didn't run away until I'd been blowing the horn for a while. Not even when I pretended I was going to run him down. That didn't scare him. Raven did."

Crane glanced toward the cabinet where he kept his gun. I knew what he was thinking. "We'll have to do something about that."

"What?"

"I saw an ad in the *Banner* for a coyote exterminator."

Exterminator? As in destroyer?

"I don't think I want them killed," I said.

"You don't want them threatening you either. What they do is trap the coyotes and euthanize them. It's kill or be killed, Jennet."

That was the law the coyotes adhered to. Eat or be eaten. Still…

That coyote didn't really resemble a dog.

"Let me think about it," I said.

If I'd had my gun in the car, I could have opened the window and fired into the air. Surely that would have been more intimidating than a horn. If the coyote was as smart as I thought it was, it would equate a gun shot with death. A car horn? It had probably heard horns before.

As I set about assembling a salad for dinner, I remembered the first coyote I'd seen. If indeed I'd seen a living creature and not a figment of my imagination. That one had been much larger.

Which meant there was more than one coyote in the area. Well, there was bound to be. They were pack animals.

The next time I left the house, I planned to arm myself.

Eight

On Saturday I surveyed as much of our property as I could see from the windows. All clear. Breathing more easily, I opened the door and led the dogs outside.

Even though the coyote who'd defied me yesterday had pranced through my dreams, my resolve to take a gun along on my walks with the dogs had faded. Along any route I chose there were plenty of easily-dislodged rocks for throwing. I *did* take a bottle filled with pennies, though. Shaking it would generate noise and do no harm. The bottle was slender enough to fit in the pocket of my jacket.

Thus emboldened, I set out with Halley, Sky, and Gemmy for Sagramore Lake Road.

The day was typical November, cold with a brisk wind and clouds that hinted of snow to come. I loved to see Sagramore Lake in winter weather, water like an endless splash of silver and a deserted beach.

We didn't have the beach to ourselves this morning. Jennifer and Molly, my young lemonade stand friends, were walking Jennifer's collie, Ginger. They wore bright jackets— one turquoise, one yellow— and Ginger had a red coat, hardly necessary for warmth as she had a thick, rich sable and white coat. But the girls were not too old for dress-up games with the tolerant collie.

Poor Ginger. She looked a trifle embarrassed as my trio greeted her with unbridled canine enthusiasm. Soon leashes were tangled together, and we were all smiling, collies included.

The girls were wearing make-up these days. A touch of rosy red, a hint of blush. Or perhaps, given their youthful glow and coloring, the blush was natural.

Jennifer handed Ginger's leash to Molly and adjusted her long knitted scarf that had come untied.

"Did you hear about the collie who went missing the other day, Jennet?" she asked.

"You mean Trista? Yes, the Rescue League is looking for her."

"So are we," Molly said. "Isn't Trista the prettiest name ever?"

"We want to find her, but we'd like to have that reward money, too," Jennifer added. "We're going to split it. I'm saving my half for college."

"Where are you looking?" I asked.

"In the woods," Jennifer said. "That's where I'd go if I were a runaway dog."

"We have a lot of woods in Foxglove Corners," I pointed out.

"We're searching a section at a time. Starting with Huron Court."

Every time I heard those words, I felt a twinge of coldness. Sometimes the twinge was a wave. Sometimes it was an entire block of ice forming around me. Even with today's frigid temperature, I was aware of icy nails running up and down my body, in spite of my warm cardigan and winter jacket.

"Be careful on Huron Court," I said. "That's a dangerous road. Do your parents know what you're doing?"

Jennifer reclaimed Ginger's leash. "Sure. We told them. They're looking for Trista, too."

"What's so dangerous about Huron Court?" Molly wanted to know. "When your Misty ran away, that's where she went."

I couldn't tell them what I'd experienced on that godforsaken lane. I wouldn't tell them if I could. So I prevaricated.

"When you come to that fork in the road, if you turn right, you'll find one of the most isolated areas in Foxglove Corners. There's nothing but woods, a lake and an old Victorian house. No one lives in it. Oh, and a cemetery if you walk far enough. If you must search Huron Court, turn left. And wherever you go, be on the lookout for coyotes," I added. "They're all around us."

"They don't hurt people," Jennifer said.

"Usually not, but don't count on it."

"We're going to go all over until we find Trista," Molly said. "She's a little smaller than the average female collie. Someone's liable to mistake her for a fox."

Jennifer scoffed. "She's not that small, and she's black, not reddish."

"How do you know that?" I asked.

"It was in the paper yesterday."

I'd just skimmed the *Banner,* one of my habits when I felt overwhelmed with housework and dinner preparations, and missed that follow-up story. Fortunately, Crane saved old papers.

"The article said no one has seen Trista. Maybe someone picked her up and isn't talking about it," Jennifer said.

"That could be."

But I hoped not. Also, Molly's words had set off a silent alarm. With coyotes roaming the woods and lanes of Foxglove Corners, I hoped some ignorant individual with a gun wouldn't mistake Trista for one and shoot her.

"All I can do is wish you luck, girls," I said. "But remember what I said. If you have to walk on Huron Court, turn left, not right. And watch out for coyotes."

As I said that, I wondered if it had been wise. So often young people did the opposite of what they were told.

"There's a lot of deer that way," I added. "Last month, when I was driving down Huron Court, I ran into one."

The girls were suitably impressed.

"Were you hurt?" asked Molly.

"Badly," I said, "and I found out later that the deer didn't survive."

"Well, we won't be driving," Jennifer said.

"Still, promise me you'll be careful."

"We will," Jennifer said. "We gotta go. Nice seeing you guys."

They walked on, heading toward Jonquil Lane, while I strolled to the end of the beach. Misty kept wanting to go in the water, but I held tight to her leash. This appeared to be a nice, safe walk. I didn't think coyotes would venture near a large lake. Why would they with so many ponds to choose from, not only in the woods but also as part of the homeowners' landscaping?

Coyotes were never far from my thoughts. The idea of encountering another bold, hungry creature dampened my great enthusiasm for strolling through the countryside with my dogs.

Remember the rocks, I thought.

Rocks in abundance and about five dollars' worth of copper pennies in a bottle.

The thought comforted me.

~ * ~

At home, I tended to the collies, ate a hastily thrown together sandwich, and drove to the Corners to devote an hour to research Violet Randall's murder.

Miss Eidt turned the library over to Debbie and ushered me into her office. She had the tea makings ready and a large bakery box open. Ah, yes, the doughnuts. What was research without tea and the Hometown Bakery's finest?

"Is she here this morning?" I asked.

"Not so far, but Saturday is her library day."

Edwina Endicott wouldn't be welcome in Miss Eidt's office. With luck, I'd be gone before she made her appearance.

File folders in a neat stack lay on the table waiting for me. *Supernatural Occurrences*, *Local Crime*, and *Legends of Foxglove Corners*. I noticed that the supernatural folder was crammed. In comparison, the local crime file was skinny. Well, that was about right.

I opened the local crime folder first.

"I went ahead and looked around," Miss Eidt said. "Violet Randall. Right?"

I nodded.

She busied herself making tea, pouring boiling water over leaves in a pretty teapot and stirring them vigorously.

"I found an obituary," she said, replacing the teapot's lid and fumbling through unfiled papers on a small desk. "Violet Randall died in 1986. Here, I made a copy for you."

I scanned the few lines. Violet was survived by her mother, Allyson, and her father, Gregory, and an aunt, Viola Randall.

She had such a small family. So few family members left behind to mourn.

"It doesn't say how she died," I said.

"It wouldn't in an obituary. Would it?"

"No, but sometimes there's a clue in a request for donations to a certain charity. There's nothing like that here, and that's what I need to find out. We're assuming it was a violent death. She'd disappeared while walking with her dog on Huron Court. That was in May," I added.

"My goodness." Miss Eidt covered her heart with her hand. "You walk all the time, Jennet. You're always taking one dog or the other for a walk."

"I usually have three at a time," I said, "so I don't worry."

Except about coyotes. But I couldn't tell Miss Eidt that and give her something else to fret about.

"Just be careful," she said. "I don't want to read about your disappearance someday."

"That makes two of us."

"I'll just take Debbie her tea and let you concentrate," she said.

I sighed. I had looked through these same folders before and found nothing relevant. What made me think I'd find something this morning?

But I hadn't seen the legend folder. Violet certainly wasn't a legend. Just a young girl whose unfortunate demise was lost in the mists of time.

Literally.

Nine

I almost didn't open the 'Legend' folder.

Violet Randall was a girl whose spirit haunted Huron Court in the fall of the year— if the accounts of the witnesses in *Ghosts and Other Oddities Among Us* were to be believed.

A girl whom I had met.

And Edwina Endicott. Edwina claimed to have seen a girl walking her dog on Huron Court. Convinced they were a pair of ghosts, she was determined to take their picture the next time they appeared.

Still, leave no stone unturned. That's the way a good investigator works.

I opened the folder and to my surprise, in this unlikeliest of places, found a half dozen articles about the Violet Randall case held together with a paperclip. They had been misfiled.

I glanced at the first heading: *Search for Missing Girl Ends Tragically.*

That much I knew.

I removed the paper clip and started reading. Violet's body had been discovered in June of 1986 by two hikers who had noticed a dog's leash caught on a low-growing branch. They looked for the dog, thinking it might be lost, and found a grave.

Well, it wasn't a grave. It was simply a resting place for a body, well hidden by the leaves of the huge tree that had fallen on it.

That discovery occurred a whole month after Violet's disappearance, more than enough time for a body to decompose in the hot summer weather.

I shuddered at the images conjured by that word, decompose. Poor, poor Violet.

It wasn't the tree that had killed her. Another article contained the autopsy report. She had been strangled and left in the woods. Her body had been identified by her clothing, shreds of blue and yellow material and by a pair of sapphire earrings.

When I'd last seen Violet, she had been wearing those earrings. I could almost see the blue stones sparkling through the strands of her long chestnut hair.

Wouldn't a thief have taken those earrings?

"That's what she was wearing," her mother said between sobs. "Her blue pedal pushers and a yellow jacket. What happened to the dog?"

A good question. What had happened to separate Ginger from her leash?

In all likelihood, the dog was dead, too.

I set the first article aside and read the others. From the beginning the police were baffled. They had no clues, no suspects, and asked anyone who had seen a stranger on Huron Court to contact them.

Who was there in that part of Foxglove Corners to see a stranger? Then, as now, Huron Court would have been a seldom traveled lane with dark woods to hide the killer and no one to hear Violet's cries or Ginger barking. The woods on either side of Huron Court had been searched, but apparently no one had seen a body under a tree or Ginger's leash. The fate of the dog was part of the mystery.

Unbidden, a line from an old folk ballad leaped into my mind: *In the greenwood he was slain...*

Change 'he' to 'she.' Violet had been cut down in the springtime with her whole life ahead of her. I recalled from reading her diary that she had been cursed with the foreknowledge of her own death, and that knowledge had cast a dark shadow on her last days.

The final article revealed that by July, the police still had no leads. Violet's death had already become a cold case. Whoever had filed the clippings— it had to be Miss Eidt— must have forgotten she had them.

Miss Eidt opened the door and stepped inside. "Jennet, what's wrong? You're crying."

I didn't realize it, but my face was wet.

"You found what you were looking for," she said, "and it wasn't good."

She handed me a box of tissues, and I gave her the news stories. She read them silently, while I dabbed at my eyes, then as silently she refilled the teakettle.

At last she said, "This calls for more tea. I'm so sorry, Jennet. I don't remember clipping these stories. I gathered so many over the years. If I had, I could have saved you some time."

"I have them now," I said. "Could I borrow them?"

"Oh, certainly. Or I could print copies for you. It looks like somebody got away with murder."

"It happened a long time ago," I said.

"She was killed in the woods of Huron Court," Miss Eidt said. "This makes me all the more worried about you. For heaven's sake, stay away from that road."

"I will. I do."

For other reasons, the ones I wouldn't reveal to Miss Eidt.

It looked as if I would also have to stay away from the mystery surrounding Violet's murder. If no one had come forward with information in 1986, how could I hope to find her killer today? Everyone connected to the case, including her assailant, might be dead. But maybe not.

When did you decide to try to find Violet's killer?

I didn't. I couldn't help being curious.

Murder will out. Most of the time. Sometimes it needed a helping hand.

Violet was so real to me. I remember she had loved her pretty collie and music. She planned to give piano lessons when she finished her studies. I still remembered the last song I'd heard her playing. Stephen Foster's *The Voice of Bygone Days*.

The melody played in my mind. Poignant and unforgettable. It would always be Violet's song.

"There is so much evil in the world," Miss Eidt murmured. "Why won't it stop?"

"That's life. A mixture of good and evil. All we can hope for is that in the end the good outweighs the evil."

"Well it's too late for Violet," she said. "I'll have Debbie make copies of these stories."

I glanced at the box of doughnuts. There were still an even dozen, half of them topped with chocolate icing, half with powdered sugar. Ordinarily they'd be irresistible. Today they were as appetizing as sand. But I was looking forward to a hot soothing cup of tea. Quietly I restacked the file folders and set them aside.

~ * ~

I'd found what I'd been searching for, the manner and the year of Violet's death. Why wasn't that enough? It should be, but...

Until I'd read the sparse accounts of Violet's death, I hadn't contemplated delving further into the mystery. Now, something had changed. I wanted to know more.

Surely you're not serious, I told myself.

I was just thinking about it. I'd found part of Violet's story but not the whole of it.

She lay in her grave in Old Resurrection Cemetery. Most likely Ginger was buried in the woods. So many years had passed since the day of Violet's fateful walk. If there weren't any clues to her assailant's identity then, surely there wouldn't be any now.

And if her killer had been found, surely it'd have been in the paper.

I concentrated on driving. The road had turned slick in places. While I was in the library, the sky had darkened. Snowflakes began to fall, landing on the windshield where they broke apart. I turned on the wipers.

Nature goes on, bringing snow and rain, sunshine and storm clouds, winter and spring. Nature doesn't care that two small lives were extinguished before their time.

Someone had to care.

I remembered the first time I had seen them— Violet laughing as she tossed a ball for Ginger, the collie leaping joyously after it.

That scene had been a time-out-of-time, I'd later learned. I had unwittingly slid into a crack in time and been whisked me away to the past.

Please, please God, never let it happen again.

The siren insinuated itself into my wanderings, a rude sound shattering my train of thought. Glancing in the mirror, I saw a vehicle bearing down on me, lights flashing through the snow. Oh, no. Not now. I wanted to get home.

The speedometer needle was frozen at sixty-five. What was the speed limit on this road anyway? Not sixty-five, I'd guess.

I pulled onto the shoulder and waited as the officer approached. It was a woman, her curves only enhanced by the uniform. She had black hair cut in layers that framed her face and blue-green eyes like iced granite.

In spite of her stony demeanor, she was a beauty.

Could this be the female deputy sheriff who had ticketed Annica on Crispian Road? The one Crane had mentioned in passing? With my luck, yes. I'd never gotten a ticket, not in my life. It seemed as if I was overdue for one.

Those granite eyes seemed to pierce me through.

"What seems to be the problem?" I asked, trying to look puzzled and no doubt failing.

"You're speeding in hazardous driving conditions," she said. "I clocked you at seventy. May I see your license and registration please?"

Seventy? Impossible. Sixty-five. Okay. Five miles difference? I could tell her that, but it wouldn't help. I might as well be quiet.

I pulled the documents out of my handbag. "What is the speed limit on this road?" I asked.

"Forty-five," she said. "On a dry, clear day."

I couldn't resist the response. "On this country road? There's hardly any traffic."

"Speed limits are established for a reason, and you may have noticed it's snowing. You might have run down a kid or a stray dog. Then where would you be?"

In trouble, I thought, *but don't say anything.*

With a smile that lacked even a modicum of warmth, she handed me the citation. "Have a nice day, and drive safely."

"Are you any relation to Deputy Sheriff Crane Ferguson?" she added.

"He's my husband."

"Then you should know better than to speed on a slippery road."

I'd known I wasn't going to like her.

Ten

Slipping the citation into my shoulder bag, I drove on at the correct speed limit, which I noticed no one had bothered to post, and didn't see a single running, distracted child or a stray dog. In fact I didn't see anything, living or dead, in the road. Only snow.

I marveled at the waste of manpower— make that womanpower— in Foxglove Corners. Why station an officer on a lonely country road that rarely saw a passing vehicle?

To catch a reckless motorist, of course.

That officer could have been Crane, which would have made the stop a disaster of gigantic proportions.

I decided there was no reason for him to know about the ticket. He would only worry needlessly, and I didn't intend to exceed the speed limit in the future. In this instance, silence was golden.

Besides, Crane hadn't seen fit to enlighten me about Foxglove Corners' new deputy. Oh, he'd told me he had met a new deputy but didn't mention that she was a woman, didn't mention her name, and hadn't seen fit to comment on the fact that she was a beauty.

Maybe he didn't consider her appearance relevant.

Ha!

Well, what's past is past. The snow was falling harder, leaving a fresh white cover on the roads and reducing visibility. Twenty minutes later, I pulled into our driveway with a sigh of relief, scanned the area for coyotes, and hurried inside. The dogs were barking and Raven, who had rushed out of the snow, almost knocked me over in her eagerness to beat me into the house.

Which was unusual behavior for her. Usually she liked to lie outside her doghouse and let the snow all but bury her. A few times in past winters, I'd had to check to make sure she was still alive.

Raven shook her coat free of snow

"It's snowing," I told the dogs, mitigating their disappointment with treats from the Lassie tin. "We'll go for a walk when it stops."

I needed a treat myself, still another cup of tea. I would have welcomed a couple of Miss Eidt's chocolate-iced doughnuts.

While the tea steeped, I settled in the living room rocker to watch the snow. It was so much more pleasant viewing it from inside and not having to worry about slippery roads or overzealous deputies.

Snow, coyotes, the lost collie, Trista. They ran through my mind, blending seamlessly together. I hoped Trista had found something to eat and a source of drinking water or, better still, shelter from the elements and predators. My thoughts drifted from snow falling on dead grass, to snow falling in the woods, to a snow-blanketed grave in Old Resurrection Cemetery, and I reviewed what I'd learned about Violet at the library.

Three decades had passed since the murder, but often a cold case is solved years after everyone concerned had given up hope of finding the killer.

Someone, previously considered unconnected to the crime, would break his silence. A new clue would surface. All it took was one lucky break and a person still interested in the case. I was that interested person, and perhaps I would be lucky.

Years of winter snow buried evidence, along with secrets, but every spring brought a thaw. Perhaps Violet still walked Huron

Court because she was unable to rest while her murderer remained unpunished. Assuming he or she were still alive.

I took a sip of tea, a rejuvenating sip, and reached for the material I'd brought from the library: copies of the news stories and Violet's obituary. Rereading them, I saw a place to start. I had three names, those of Violet's parents and her aunt, Viola Randall. They might still be alive and living in the area or nearby— and willing to talk to me. Time could erase old memories, but those of a great personal tragedy would still be clear.

Who knew? Maybe one stray fact, thought insignificant at the time, would emerge from a casual conversation.

Next project: find the survivors, I thought, and went back to watching the snow fall.

~ * ~

The next hour was the essence of tranquility. Work to do but no need to do it in the immediate future. Dinner in the oven. Dogs sleeping away a snowy afternoon.

Alas, tranquility never lasts in Foxglove Corners. In mid-afternoon, Brent burst into the house, bringing a bag from Pluto's Gourmet Bakery and much of the snow from the porch.

"I thought your fur kids might be getting bored," he said, as he stamped snow on the door mat. "Is it all right if I pass out treats now?"

It had to be all right. They had converged on him like a pack of starving beasts, even Star who had become a bona fide member of the pack in a short time.

"Be my guest," I said.

Because I was occupying the rocker, Brent flopped onto the sofa. Misty leaped up to take her place at his side, a biscuit shaped like a small T-bone steak in her mouth.

"I wanted to talk to you before the sheriff gets home," he said with a quick glance at the window.

"Oh?"

"Yeah. He doesn't want you to dwell in the past."

"I don't."

"Sure you do. So this is between you and me. It's our secret. I'm furnishing the living room of the Gingerbread House. Can you tell me what it looked like— from what you remember?"

I took a deep breath. I didn't like this.

"It was pleasant and comfortable. Very homey."

"I need details, Jennet."

"The sofa and chairs were burgundy. That's a deep red color. The drapes were light— cream colored. Crane said you had the walls painted purple. Purple and burgundy would inspire nightmares for me. There was a bookcase and Violet's piano."

"I had a piano delivered last week."

No, this wasn't good.

"You don't play, do you?"

"I never took lessons, but how hard can it be? I thought it'd be a nice touch to have one for the guests. For entertainment."

"Aren't you going to have televisions?"

"I'm thinking along the lines of an old-fashioned atmosphere for the Gingerbread House. No high tech. People who book rooms will be able to escape the pressures of everyday life."

"Okay, but you don't have to create a replica of Violet's living room," I pointed out. "Look in decorating magazines. Decide on a color scheme that goes with purple and settle for Victorian ambiance. Wasn't Annica going to help you?"

"She is, but she never saw the house the way it was in Violet's time. You did."

"Only the living room. I don't understand why everything has to be the same, or I should say, similar."

"It doesn't *have* to be," he said. "I'd like it to be authentic."

So authentic that if Violet were to rise from her grave in Old Resurrection Cemetery and float through the pink Victorian she would think she had come home?

Brent had taken the first steps down a dark path, and I wanted desperately to pull him back, to save him from the ramifications of this alarming new obsession.

"How's everything with the Hunt?" I asked.

He took a moment to catch up to my abrupt change of subject.

"Good. Just like always. We never let a little cold and snow slow us down."

"Are you going hunting in North Carolina this year? Or is it South Carolina? I can never remember."

"Probably. After Christmas. By then I expect the Gingerbread House to be up and running."

"And how is Alethea Venn?

Alethea was Brent's red-haired fox hunting pal. She was beautiful, a snob with a biting wit and a jealous streak. Although she was some years older than Brent, she considered him her personal property.

"You don't like Alethea," he reminded me.

"But you do. You're her friend."

"She's okay. I'll tell her you were asking about her."

Now I'd done it.

"About the living room," Brent said, "did you get a good look at the pictures on the wall? Were they prints? Oils? Landscapes? What?"

"I was only there for a short time, and I wasn't in a frame of mind to admire the art. Why don't you find a few prints of children and collies? That'll appeal to most people, and it'll give you a real turn-of-the-century flavor. You'll find some treasures at the Green House of Antiques in Lakeville."

"Good idea. I like that picture above the mantel." He pointed to one of my favorite paintings, the three white ghost collies who haunted Lost Lake. "I don't suppose you'd sell that to me?"

"I'm afraid not."

The dogs dashed out of the living room, barking their special welcome to their master. Crane had come home early.

"Remember, mum's the word," Brent said. "If he asks, we were talking about fox hunting."

That was true. Still, I intended to share our conversation with Crane. Brent was our good friend, and lately he didn't seem like the Brent of old. I was worried about him.

Eleven

After Brent went home, Crane and I settled down for a quiet evening in front of the fire with our drowsy, well-fed collies.

Crane said, "You may be right about Fowler, but what can we do? He's not looking for advice from us."

I leaned back against the cushions, glad that the day's work was done. I'd even made a sandwich for tomorrow's lunch with leftover ham from our dinner. "He's rushing to open his new inn before Christmas. That in itself is worrisome. Why the deadline?"

"What are you really afraid of?" Crane asked.

"That the pink Victorian has cast a spell on him."

"If you're talking about magic, honey, that's impossible."

He poked at the fire, which he'd replenished, and joined me on the sofa. Candy rose, stretched, and lay down again at his feet. Misty leaped up to lie between us. The other collies had stayed in the kitchen, no doubt hoping I'd dropped a piece of ham on the floor.

"Not magic, but whatever governs time on Huron Court. That crack in time, or whatever it is, works inside, too."

"You didn't think the house was affected," he said. "Just the road."

"At one time, yes, but I didn't think it through. I was forgetting Violet's own testimony."

In a diary entry, she had recorded her first time slip. She'd been sitting in her living room when without warning a force transported her to a future in which the house was abandoned and the room stripped of furnishings. She lost four hours before she was back in her own time.

Then, another day when we— Brent, Annica, Leonora, and I— were searching through boxes brought down from the attic, we heard a scream and barking. Violet had returned from a walk with Ginger, seen Brent's yellow Plymouth Belvedere parked in front of the house, and found the living room empty of furniture.

It was the scream that had whisked Violet and Ginger back to their own time, leaving us to wonder who had broken into the house and how she had disappeared so quickly. We wouldn't have known this if it hadn't been for Violet's diary. And how strange it had been reading about something we'd experienced in the present that Violet had experienced it in the past. I still couldn't comprehend how that could be.

"Strange things happen inside, too," I added.

"That's why you're going to stay away from that house," he said.

I didn't argue with him.

At dinner I had asked Brent if he'd seen or heard anything unusual at the house on Huron Court.

"Nothing," he'd said, but I detected a slight hesitation.

"Are you sure?"

"Maybe I heard voices once. It sounded like people whispering. I couldn't tell where it was coming from or make out what they were saying. I might have imagined it."

This was something new. Brent wasn't the imaginative kind.

He didn't appear to want to talk about it and avoided further talk of his future inn.

I reminded Crane of the conversation. "What about that whispering Brent heard?"

Crane shrugged. "It might have been the wind. The wind is always blowing in Foxglove Corners."

But was it likely that Brent had mistaken sounds inside the house for the wind blowing, though? I didn't think so.

"It's the house," I said. "Brent is hearing voices from the past. The house is evil."

"It's just an old house, Jennet, made of wood," Crane said. "I'll accept there's something odd about Huron Court. I have no choice but to do that. But I draw the line at giving a house human traits."

I recalled a remark Brent had made on another day when he was talking about the change in his renovation plans. He felt that the house didn't want to be changed, didn't want its walls broken down or rooms built on.

"Brent is trying to bring Violet's house to life, the way it was, whether he realizes it or not," I said.

"He realizes it, all right. But with him, it's all business. He wants to create an inn with a story behind it and a ghost."

I hoped it was that simple.

Candy nudged Crane's knee with her long nose, and he reached down to stroke her head. "Fowler hasn't asked you to come by and see what he's done, has he?"

"No. He shows me pictures on his phone."

"That's safe enough," Crane said, apparently satisfied. "Candy, Star, Misty... What would you girls say to a walk before bed?"

They were ready, tails wagging, eyes bright.

"Watch out for coyotes," I said.

Candy sprang to her feet and darted to the kitchen where we kept the leashes.

"Don't worry about me," Crane said. "I'm a match for any coyote."

I smiled as they got ready to leave. They were a formidable group, my deputy sheriff husband and three large collies. Four if Raven joined them. But what was that saying? *Pride goeth before a fall.*

"Take my penny jar," I said.

He laughed. "I'll reach for a big rock. Or a stick."

The coyotes were an ongoing problem, however, like Brent and that accursed house. As Crane had once said, Brent was playing with fire. I didn't think he realized it.

~ * ~

I heard the coyote pack howling in the night. They were close to the house. Not too close, I hoped. For the first time I was glad that one of our collies chose to live outside. Raven, too, was a match for any coyote, and she was intelligent. No coyote would lure her into the woods, and her barking would alert us to the presence of any unwanted intruders, whether they walked on four legs or two.

They were so loud. How could I go back to sleep with all the racket?

You'll get used to it, I told myself. *Before long you won't hear it. It'll be like the wind. Just another sound in the night.*

If the coyotes had moved into our neighborhood and weren't just passing through. We hadn't pursued Crane's suggestion to hire an exterminator. I would prefer that the pack decide to relocate for the winter— about a hundred miles south, which was unrealistic. I suspected the coyotes appreciated the amenities of Foxglove Corners as much as we did.

But how wonderful if some day they would leave. It would be a relief to walk without being afraid of what waited beyond the next curve in the road.

That reminded me of the pink Victorian, now the Gingerbread House, and Brent's obsession. His enterprise, he would call it.

And how was I going to trace Violet's survivors?

By then, I was wide awake. The coyotes were howling and ten minutes of trying to go back to sleep had turned into an hour. Somewhere in the night, the wind began to blow.

~ * ~

I woke from a confusing nightmare involving Huron Court and coyotes. I was walking alone, and how strange it was not only to be without my collies but to be strolling down the forbidden road as if it didn't hold unimaginable terror for me.

The coyotes were howling in the woods. Suddenly dark canine shapes emerged out of a mist. They didn't move, didn't threaten me. But their eyes were unnaturally bright. I couldn't look at them.

That must be how they immobilized their victims.

Desperately I searched the ground for the ever-present rocks of Foxglove Corners

There weren't any.

A stick then. A long fallen branch.

They were all still attached to trees.

There, thank heavens, the dream ended.

I woke up, surprised to be in my own bed next to Crane, who was a match for any coyote.

So don't be afraid.

But I was trembling and the front of my nightgown was drenched with perspiration. Dreams shouldn't be so real.

I made my way in the dark to the dresser and pulled out a fresh gown. The moon was bright, pouring light into the room. I paused at the window to look out— and down.

Not twelve feet from the house stood a coyote. It was much larger than the ones that had confronted me in my dream. At first I thought it was a dog.

It looked like a dog.

A memory flashed in my mind. It resembled the large coyote that had prevented me from leaving my car on the day of the League meeting. The creature that had melted into the night, making me wonder if I'd seen it.

I turned to wake Crane and felt a brush of velvet at my leg. Halley, our bedroom guardian, stood at my side. She placed her paws on the windowsill, and, when I looked again, the creature was gone.

Like the last time I'd seen it.

And, most telling, Raven hadn't barked.

Twelve

"When were you going to tell me about your ticket?" Crane asked the next day. "Or were you?"

As he was in the living room, locking his gun in its cabinet, I couldn't see his face, but he was using his stern deputy sheriff's voice. That wasn't good. So much for him not finding out about the citation.

I was in the kitchen gathering ingredients for a salad. He had given the collies an enthusiastic greeting. My own had left something to be desired. Now I knew why.

Darn and double darn. Did he know everything that went on in Foxglove Corners? That woman must have told him. She wanted to make trouble. Some women are like that.

I knew I wasn't going to like her.

Crane was waiting for an answer. I decided to stall.

"When you told me about the new deputy sheriff in town," I said.

"Veronica? I *did* tell you."

"When was this?"

"The other day. When I met her."

Her? He'd never mentioned the deputy's sex. Figuring I'd made my point, I said, "I didn't deserve that ticket. I wasn't speeding. Five miles or so above the speed limit isn't a hanging offense."

"Driving was hazardous that day. I saw two accidents. One put the driver in the hospital. You have to adjust your speed to the road conditions."

I knew that and didn't want to waste our time together discussing icy roads, tickets, or a woman named Veronica.

"I'll check on our steaks," I said, and Crane, having completed his safe driving lecture, went upstairs to shower.

I'd have to revisit the subject of the new deputy sheriff, Veronica, another time. For instance, was she an experienced law enforcer or a rookie? Was she single? Did she have a boyfriend or was she hoping to find one in the sheriff's department?

All legitimate questions, but I didn't want Crane to think I was jealous or insecure, even if I was. A little. It was just that he was so handsome, so infinitely desirable, and the world was full of pretty women. I trusted him, but he was a man, after all. I'd have to think of another way to find out everything I wanted to know about this Veronica.

On the other hand, didn't I have ample proof of Crane's love and devotion? I'd better trap the green-eyed monster in a bottle lest it turn on me, and steer our next conversation in a different direction. Toward coyotes or my search for Violet's survivors. Maybe not the search. Crane didn't understand why I hoped to solve the mystery of Violet's murder.

You'd think a deputy sheriff would be interested in a cold case, especially a killing that had taken place so close to our home. I supposed it was all part of his ongoing campaign to steer me away from delving into the past. He was afraid it might lead to danger.

In my mind there was a difference between what I planned to do, which was passive, and taking part in a bona fide criminal investigation.

After school I'd done an internet search for Viola Randall and found a woman with that name who appeared to be the right age for Violet's aunt. She resided in Silver Oaks Retirement Village, located in Oakpoint. That was easy. Almost too easy. At any rate, I could visit her some day after school, perhaps take her a bouquet or a plant, and explain my interest in her niece's death.

First, though, I'd have to call her. It wouldn't do to appear unannounced, and I'd have to decide how much to tell her. Certainly not about my time slip and that I had met Violet. What could I say then? That required thought.

Maybe I could use Brent's purchase of the Randall family home and his plan to open it to the public as an inn. I'd tell her that he'd come across the names of previous owners and was curious.

All true. Wasn't there a law requiring a seller to disclose information about a crime associated with the house before it was sold? I wasn't sure. Chances were Viola Randall wouldn't know either. Of course the crime hadn't been committed inside the pink Victorian but in the woods of Huron Court.

Close enough. Now, if Ms. Randall agreed to meet with me, I could move forward in my search. Perhaps a diplomatically worded note would be better than a phone call.

Crane joined me in the kitchen. "That smells good," he said.

"It's just steak."

"It still smells good. What kind of pie is that?"

"Apple," I said.

He kissed me, a more enthusiastic sign of affection than he'd given me on his arrival. The frost in his gray eyes had melted.

From the dining room, Candy gave a little yelp.

Please save me a chunk of steak, she might have said.

~ * ~

In honor of Thanksgiving, which was right around the corner, I showed a movie from the fifties, *The Plymouth Adventure*, in my America Lit Survey class, even though we had long since left the Puritan Age behind, as my students were quick to remind me.

I fielded a few objections to the film which Slade Johnston referred to as a product of the dinosaur age, but all in all, my students were happy to sit and watch the simulated waves and scenes of imminent starvation. Movie Day didn't require any particular effort on their part.

I responded to a few caustic remarks.

"That's just a model ship."

"I don't get it. Why did that lady jump overboard?"

And "Aren't there going to be any Indian fights in it?"

Well, thanks to Metro-Goldwyn-Mayer, I'd made the historic voyage come alive for them. Sort of. At least, *The Plymouth Adventure* was more palatable than Bradford's writing.

Happy Thanksgiving to all. A week early.

After school, Leonora and I took a detour to Silver Oaks Retirement Village, not to visit Viola Randall, but to get the lay of the land, as Leonora said. I hadn't written my note yet, but I wanted to see the place.

Tucked in a northeastern corner of Oakpoint, the development was relatively new. It consisted of look-alike one-story frame houses with small front yards. Plenty of young trees throughout the village would provide shade in the summertime. In its center, a man-made lake shimmered with ice floes.

"It's depressing," Leonora said. "I'd hate to live here."

"I think it's pleasant. Anyway, you're years away from retirement."

"I love my house. I never want to leave it. It's my ambition to grow old in Foxglove Corners."

"I hope you do. Does Jake feel the same way?"

"I think so."

If Leonora was considering marriage, she should be aware of Jake's living preferences. I didn't point that out, feeling certain that she knew it.

"For someone who is older and maybe alone in the world, this is a perfect place to spend the rest of your life. There's little maintenance and close neighbors."

"When are you going to talk to Violet's aunt?" she asked.

"I'll write her a note tonight," I said.

~ * ~

The *Banner* devoted an entire page to coyotes, a decision likely inspired by another pet who had been set upon in his owner's backyard. An outside cat, Ruffles, had fallen prey to a ravening coyote.

A sidebar gave an update on Pippa, the last known victim of a coyote. Although seriously injured, she had recovered and was available for adoption at the Foxglove Corners Animal Shelter.

What? Pippa had an owner. I remembered how broken up she'd seemed after Pippa's attack. I made a note to call Lila or Letty Woodville at the shelter. Curiosity again. But how could I help being curious when so many strange things were happening?

Another sidebar contained a timeline of coyote attacks in Foxglove Corners. I counted them. Eight in less than a month. The last complaint came from a sheep farmer, Dell Whitman, who had lost three of his animals to coyotes and vowed to kill all the thieving varmints.

Good luck with that, Farmer Dell, I thought.

Before turning the page, I checked the average height and weight of the coyote. Two feet at the shoulders and forty-six pounds, which wasn't especially formidable.

That didn't describe the large creature I'd seen hanging around our house. Perhaps that animal wasn't a coyote, but something else.

Like a wolf. I wondered if wolves had migrated this far south from the Upper Peninsula. That was all we needed— coyotes and wolves. Creatures that howled in the night and snatched the weaker ones away to their doom.

It seemed as if my peaceful country home was under attack, and that was unacceptable.

Thirteen

Trista Summer Thunder, the champion-sired tricolor, was still missing. I found the article on the third page of the *Banner*.

Reward Increased for Missing Collie

The paper had obtained a different picture of Trista in an elegant pose with blooming lilacs in the background. The accompanying story alluded to three Trista sightings, none of them verified.

Trista's owner was offering a fifteen hundred dollar reward for her safe return. No questions asked. The amount surprised me. Certainly if a well-intentioned rescuer had decided to keep Trista, that generous sum would guarantee a happy outcome to the incident. And with so much money, a person could purchase a show prospect puppy as pretty as Trista.

I wondered if Jennifer and Molly were still looking for her. They must be. The girls were determined and resourceful, and a collie doesn't just vanish from the face of the earth.

Remember, I told myself, *this is Foxglove Corners.*

What if Trista had wandered onto Huron Court and been swept away into another time?

Come now. That is so unlikely.

But if she had, a person in the past could have come across the beautiful tri and taken her in. To a dog, one time would be as acceptable as another as long as a loving human provided comfort and food. In that case Trista would never be found.

I had to stop speculating before I created an entirely fanciful scenario and, worse, began to believe it.

If a person living in our time hadn't adopted Trista, she had most likely found a home in the woods.

With the coyotes.

And how would that play out?

I set the paper aside and gently pushed Trista out of my mind until the next day when I met Molly, Jennifer, and Ginger while walking on the beach at Sagramore Lake with three of my collies.

The temperature hovered slightly above freezing, and the water was smooth and bright, like glass. We were all bundled up, Ginger looking a little sissified in her red coat.

As the collies sniffed their welcomes and pranced around one another with unbridled enthusiasm, I asked the girls about their search.

"We've looked all over," Molly said, shivering in the wind. "We found a collie, but it wasn't Trista."

"Are you sure?" I asked.

"Wrong color," Jennifer said. "She's pretty but scrawny, and her coat was a mess. She wasn't wearing a collar. We took her to Ms. Appleton."

Sue would remedy that. A good brushing and bath, and we'd have another stray collie to place in a foster home.

"Where all have you looked?" I asked.

"Mostly in the woods around here," Molly said. "We can't cover every inch of woods, though. No one could do that. We tried calling her name, and we always take treats."

"I'm starting to think somebody took her away," Jennifer added. "Too bad. We could really use that reward money, and Trista needs to go back to her owner."

"Don't give up hope," I said.

"We won't. If no one's taking care of her, she'll be cold and lonely, and what will she find to eat?"

I thought of Sue's River Rose rescue, Icy, who had survived in the wild during a brutal winter.

"Dogs are resilient," I said. "It looks like Trista has a thick coat. She'll find food somewhere."

"Something yucky," Jennifer said.

Molly leaned down to give Misty a pat. "And raw," she added. "Roadkill. Ugh."

It was too cold to stand near the water talking. Wishing the girls luck, I walked on, giving Huron Court a wide berth.

At least someone was looking for Trista, and fifteen hundred dollars was a powerful lure. I suspected that someday soon the *Banner* would announce Trista's recovery.

~ * ~

The next day after school, Leonora and I decided to take a break from cooking with take-out dinners from Clovers. We were hoping with Thanksgiving so near that Mary Jeanne would have something special on the menu.

"I have plans for Thanksgiving this year," Leonora said as we pulled into the lot.

"Are you taking a trip?" I asked.

"Sort of. I'm having Thanksgiving dinner with Jake and his family at their home in Ellentown."

This was a milestone in their relationship. She sounded happy, but also tense. Well, that was understandable. Jake meant a lot to her.

"Have you met them before?" I asked.

"No, and I'm a little nervous."

"Just be yourself. They'll love you. Everybody does."

"I offered to bring pies," she said. What kind should I make? Pumpkin or pecan? And how many?"

"For how many people?"

"There'll be five of us. Jake's mom and dad and his sister."

"One of each," I said. "You're a master baker, and I know you'll make a good impression on them."

We found a parking place, not difficult as the dinner crowd hadn't arrived yet, and opened the door. The winterberry wreath offered a bright red welcome, but at the rate its berries were dropping, it would soon be a brown grapevine circle.

Ironically, Clovers' dessert carousel featured pumpkin and pecan tarts. In anticipation of the holiday, the day's specials were roast turkey and West Virginia ham, both with sweet yams.

"Ham," Leonora said. "Just what I was hoping they'd have."

Annica came out of the kitchen carrying a tray of red tarts. Her earrings were tiny gold acorns dusted with crystals that brought out the gold in her red hair.

I needed more glitter in my jewelry box— and in my life.

"What are you ladies doing for Thanksgiving?" she asked.

"I'm having dinner with a friend," Leonora said.

"And I'll cook a small turkey for the two of us. Crane will be on duty."

"I wonder where Brent will go on Thanksgiving," Annica murmured.

"Did you ask him?"

"No. He didn't mention it. He'll probably spend the day at the house."

"The pink Victorian you mean?"

"He's always there," she said. "I was thinking about asking him to have dinner with my mom and me."

"Well, invite him. There're only a few days left."

Brent could eat at the Spirit Lamp Inn, which he owned, or the Hunt Club Inn, but he liked home cooking, as evidenced by his frequency at our dinner table. On the other hand, dinner with the family implied serious intentions. Freedom-loving Brent might balk at the mere suggest of strings.

"All he can do is accept or decline," I added.

It wasn't like Annica to be so hesitant. She shook her head slowly to the accompaniment of a tiny jingling sound. Every pair of earrings she owned had the capacity to jingle.

"What if he says no?" she asked.

"Good heavens. Then he says no. You and your mom have a nice holiday dinner and Angel has turkey giblets."

"He might say yes," she said. "I'll do it. He's been coming to Clovers for breakfast. I'll ask him tomorrow."

As Leonora and I placed our order for ham and yams, I remember the first time I'd invited Crane to dinner. I'd cooked a Virginia ham then, and everything had turned out well with the food and our developing relationship.

"Good luck," I said.

I was eager to learn the outcome of Annica's dinner invitation. Every holiday needs a bit of suspense to give it sparkle. Thanksgiving was no exception.

Fourteen

The next evening Brent invited us to be his guests for dinner at the Hunt Club Inn. Although I had never felt comfortable with the inn's hunter's décor and traditional fox head wreath, it was a pleasure to wear my black knit maxi dress, crystal teardrop earrings, and three inch heels on a week night. And a double pleasure not to have to cook. And a triple pleasure to bask in the compliments from Crane and Brent.

As usually happened, we'd been seated at a table close to the fox wreath. The fox's eyes seemed to be fixed on me, appeared to be filled with reproach. I was supposed to be an animal activist, for heaven's sake, although my energies of late were centered on collie rescue.

This always happened when I dined at the Inn: this vague sense of guilt, of the need to be doing more for the animals than I was.

The men ordered prime rib, and I decided on rainbow trout. I tried to look anywhere but at the fox. When the waiter set a basket of rolls on the table, I had something else to concentrate on. I was ravenous, as we usually ate an hour or so earlier.

Brent wanted to talk about the pink Victorian. I noticed he'd stopped referring to it as his inn or the Gingerbread House. He now called it Violet's house.

With Annica's help, he had finished decorating the living room. It had a purple, rose, and green color scheme, and he'd found three turn-of-the-century paintings of young girls and collies at the Green House of Antiques, as well as a two-tier Duncan Phyfe table.

"Thanks for the tip, by the way," he said. "I wish you could see the room."

"She'll be happy to see pictures of it," Crane said.

I glared at him. "Hey! I can speak for myself. I wish I could see it, too, Brent, but that's not going to happen. Did you take pictures of the living room?"

"Just a few. I'm waiting for the rug to be delivered. It's black with flowers in the middle and at each corner. They're yellow and pink roses."

"That's funny," I said. "The rug I remember was like that. Mostly black with cabbage roses. The same colors. It was very old-time looking."

"You didn't describe the rug to me."

"Well, no. It slipped my mind until just this minute."

Now that I thought about it, I could almost see Violet's rug with its border and the splashy roses. A large spray in the center, smaller ones at each corner, as Brent described the new rug.

What a coincidence! It was a coincidence, I assumed.

Images came tumbling back into my memory, images I'd just as soon forget. Misty and Violet's collie, Ginger, lying in the middle of the floor. Violet with her long chestnut hair and glittering sapphire earrings. And more…

The too-sweet taste of the strawberry-flavored soft drink Violet had served me. The scent of violets. Emotions as strong in this moment as they had been at the time. Confusion. Fear. Despair.

How would I ever find my way back home?

"I've been by the house just about every day," Brent said. "There's always something I have to do there. I don't remember the Spirit Lamp Inn taking up so much of my time."

"Your contractors and landscapers did all of the work," I pointed out. "And you didn't have to fill all the rooms with furniture."

We fell silent as the waiter served our entrees. Thick slices of prime rib with fresh green beans and steak fries, each on plates of their own. Fresh green garnish. And my fish. Well it looked good, and I was hungry.

Darned that fox. Although I didn't know why I let him influence me. Nobody ate a fox steak or fox chops, and with a houseful of carnivores, I was used to cooking meat.

When Brent spoke again, I had the feeling that this, the subject he introduced without a word of preamble, was the purpose of the invitation.

"Sometimes I wonder if there isn't something unwholesome about Violet's house," he said.

Unwholesome? That was almost as evocative an adjective as evil, and it didn't sound like the kind of word Brent would use.

"That's why I won't let Jennet go back there," Crane said.

For the second time this evening I glared at him. He was oblivious, intent on cutting his beef.

I said, "That's why I decided, all by myself, to stay away from the house."

"I guess I told you that a few times I thought I heard voices in the house," Brent said.

Ah! The heart of the matter.

"You did, and we thought it might be the wind."

"The wind doesn't sound like voices whispering."

Crane said, "Sometimes it can."

"What I heard was human whispering."

"Just those few times?" I asked.

"More than that. When Annica's with me, I don't hear anything. It's when I'm alone. And the wind isn't always blowing. Like yesterday."

"Is this why you say the house is unwholesome," I said.

"Maybe. I'm just wondering."

"What are the voices saying?" Crane asked.

"I can't tell. It's like hearing a conversation but not being able to make out the words. We all experience that, right?"

"Can you tell where this whispering originates?" I asked.

He took a long drink of his wine. "In another part of the house. Maybe upstairs? Never in the room I'm in. But always inside."

"I wonder who's doing the whispering," I said.

"I think you should stay away from that house, too, Fowler," Crane said.

"How can I? I've gone too far."

"Too far?" I asked. "What do you mean?"

"With the inn," he said quickly. "I've invested too much money and time in Violet's house. I can't walk away from it."

He couldn't? Or didn't want to? At this point, only he and Annica appeared to be interested in Brent's expensive project. He could bring it to a stop at any time and put the house and property up for sale.

What he wanted, I suspected, was encouragement to keep it. I tried to see the situation from his point of view, keeping his millionaire status in mind.

"As long as all you hear is whispering, I wouldn't worry. Not too much. Now if at some future time you can make out what these voices are saying or if you notice something else disturbing, that would be the time to step away from the inn."

"What you're saying is 'Wait and see'?"

"I guess I am. Maybe nothing else will happen, and maybe one day you'll decide it was just the wind, after all."

"Or, you can cut your losses," Crane said. "Spend more time with your horses. Go hunting. Take some of your lady friends out to dinner."

Because of whispering? I thought.

No, because of evil. Or, in Brent's words, unwholesomeness.

I almost said, "Brent, I changed my mind. Listen to Crane. Get rid of that house."

But I didn't, and Crane and Brent began discussing coyotes.

~ * ~

The next time I went to the library, I walked over to the old white Victorian next door where the Woodville sisters, Lila and Letty, managed a no-kill animal shelter for the stray dogs of Foxglove Corners. I hadn't visited them in a long time, and I was curious about Pippa. Why was a dog who had an owner available for adoption?

I knocked on the door, setting off a cacophony of barking and high pitched yelps. Some of the dogs were in the yard, others in the house. It didn't matter. The Woodville sisters could always count on their four-legged burglar alarms.

Lila's surprise at seeing me reminded me that I'd neglected my old friends. She whisked off her voluminous apron and patted the few strands that had come detached from her silver French twist.

"Why, Jennet, what a wonderful surprise! Come on in."

"I hear voices," Letty announced, coming down the hall.

You could tell Lila and Letty were sisters. Lila was a trifle heavier than Letty, and Letty wore her hair, also silver, in a short, stylish bob.

I stopped for a moment in the vestibule, glancing at the portrait of Caroline Meilland, the slain animal activist who had drawn me into her cause, the now defunct organization, Militant Animal Rights Activists or M.A.R.A. Whenever I visited the shelter, I was aware of Caroline's spirit pervading every room, as alive as she had once been. In her honor, her good friend, Major March, continued to support the shelter from his home in Colorado.

It all seemed so long ago.

"I was in the neighborhood," I said. "Well, at the library. I was curious about one of your dogs. Pippa."

"She isn't a collie," Letty said.

"Even so."

"Pippa," Lila said. "Poor little mite. She's well, dear, nicely recovering from her ordeal, and she seems happy."

"That's good to know, but why is she here? Did something happen to her owner?"

Lila scoffed. "Pippa had to be shaved because of her injuries. When her owner saw her, she called Pippa ugly. She decided she didn't want her."

"That's incredible," I said. "A coat will grow back. She's the same dog."

Lila shook her head. "Mrs. Goode wants a dog she can be proud to be seen with."

"Wretched coyotes," Letty said.

"No, wretched owner. Do you think you'll be able to place her in a home?" I asked.

"Probably, when her fur grows in, but Lila and I think we'll keep her. She's a little charmer."

"May I see her?" I asked.

"Just a minute. She's outside."

Lila opened the door, and three golden retriever puppies dashed in, their little bodies bouncing, followed by a small dog who resembled a cocker spaniel. Her shorn hair made her look like a puppy. Yelping, she made a dash for the new person in the room. If she remembered her ordeal or her rejection, it didn't show in her snapping brown eyes.

"But she's so pretty," I said, trying to understand.

"Some people…" Letty let her sentence trail off.

"They shouldn't be allowed to own a dog," Lila finished. "They don't understand that a dog has feelings. They shouldn't lose their home because of an accident that wasn't their fault."

I gave Pippa a pat on the head— no, several pats— and wished I had stopped at the new dog bakery. If only I had something to give her.

The puppies began to tear around the living room, and Pippa left my side to find a small red ball.

She dropped it at my feet. I rolled it for her into the hall and watched as she and the puppies scampered after it.

"She'll be okay," I said.

"Can you stay for a while and have coffee with us?" Lila asked. "I baked an apple walnut coffeecake this morning."

Two of my favorite ingredients. But I had to hurry home and make dinner.

"Just for a while," I said, following the sisters through the hall to the kitchen. "And just coffee."

Lila plugged in the coffeemaker and joined us at the table. "What have you been up to these days, Jennet?" she asked.

"Well…"

What could I tell them? Not about my time slip. That wasn't a secret, but not too many people knew about it, and I didn't feel Lila and Letty would deal well with the concept of time travel. Coyotes were a safe subject, along with school and Star.

Choose one.

"Have you seen any coyotes around the Corners?" I asked.

"There's a pack that lives in the woods across the street," Letty said. "Sometimes they come out and stand in the park. The little kids don't play there so much anymore. I'm glad. It makes me nervous to think a coyote could just grab one of them."

I nodded. "They're taking over Foxglove Corners."

"They have to live too," Lila said. "They get hungry just like we do."

"But our dogs and children shouldn't be on the menu."

"No, of course not. That reminds me, Jennet. Are you sure you won't have a piece of coffeecake?"

In the kitchen of the animal shelter, resistance was futile.

"Just a sliver," I said.

Our dinner was two hours away.

Fifteen

Viola Randall's answer to my note arrived in the next day's mail. She agreed to meet with me in her home at my convenience, adding that she had been thinking about Violet lately and half expected to receive news about her.

Oh, no. I hadn't said anything about news. I'd only told her about Brent's acquisition of the family home and his interest in information about the previous owners.

I hoped she wouldn't be disappointed.

Also, the wording of Ms. Randall's response bothered me slightly. Rather, it made me wonder. After all these years, she had been thinking about her niece and anticipating a message? Violet Randall had had the ability to know future events. She'd had foreknowledge of the tragedy that was about to befall her, but not its nature. Could this so-called talent run in the family?

Probably not, but it was strange nonetheless.

Wanting to make the connection before the Thanksgiving holiday, I called the number on the note and arranged to visit Violet's aunt after school. Leonora and I drove separate cars that day, and I spent my conference hour at school jotting down questions I wanted to ask.

By the time the last bell rang, I was eager to keep our appointment but at the same time nervous about it. Would I come across as a morbid busybody and alienate her? I hoped not, but there was so much I couldn't tell her.

For instance, if I mentioned Huron Court, a road that led to yesteryear, she would dismiss me as a lunatic.

If only I could tell her that, though, how much easier our conversation would be.

Silver Oaks Retirement Village was a ten-minute drive from the school. On the way I stopped at a flower shop and bought a dozen pink carnations.

Ms. Randall's unit, if that was the correct term, was within walking distance of the man-made lake. Occupying a corner lot, her house would have a glorious view in the summer. It was pleasing in November with a dusting of snow on the trees and a silver cast on the water in the fading light.

A last minute attack of nerves puzzled me. Why was I apprehensive? Perhaps because I suspected this meeting might be significant in ways I hadn't yet fathomed? Well, apprehensive or not, seeking out Viola had been my idea, and here I was.

I knocked on the door. It opened. The die was cast.

Viola Randall was a slender, attractive woman dressed in black. She was possibly in her sixties, with silver streaks in short chestnut hair. It was almost the same shade as Violet's hair, and to my dismay, she wore sapphire earrings. I was happy that they weren't similar to Violet's earrings or I would start thinking about implausible matters like reincarnation. As it was, Viola had the look of her niece.

She's Violet's aunt, I told myself. *You should see a resemblance.*

"Ms. Randall?" I said.

Her smile was warm and inviting. "Call me Viola. And you're Jennet."

"I brought you some carnations."

She took them. "How sweet of you. I love carnations. Come in out of the cold. Have a seat, and I'll put these in water."

The house appeared to be larger than it looked from outside. It had a breezy open floor plan with a combination living and dining room and a view of a spacious kitchen toward the back. A large picture window gave a view of the lake.

The focal point of the room was an upright piano. On its top, three collie figurines kept company with about a half dozen photographs, one of a smiling, happy Violet. She looked as I remembered her.

I chose a chair, a blue floral print on a cream background, sat, and slowly became aware of a light fragrance wafting through the cool air.

The spicy carnations, of course, with their hint of cloves...

No, that wasn't it.

It was the scent of violets, a fragrance that had lingered in the pink Victorian decades after Violet's passing. Her perfume of choice, obviously shared by her aunt.

Viola had given her niece the perfume as a gift and liked it so well that she bought a bottle for herself. That's all it is. Don't freak out.

"You wanted to talk about my niece," Violet said.

"Yes, if it won't upset you."

"There was a time when I was heartily tired of being asked about Violet. Now, so many years later, I want to talk about her. All of a sudden it seems so immediate to me."

Strange, I thought. *Why now?*

"Would you like something to drink?" Viola asked. "Coffee or tea?"

"Tea would be nice, if it's no trouble."

"None at all. I took Violet to a tea room for her seventeenth birthday. She loved it. That was the last time I saw her."

While Viola filled a teakettle and opened a package of cookies, I told my story about Brent buying the house on Huron Court.

"That's how I first became interested in Violet's murder," I said, telling a sliver of the true story. "Afterward, I read old newspaper stories and wondered if they ever found out who killed her."

"Never. That house was so isolated." She paused, looked away, and brought teacups down from a shelf. "There were no witnesses. The police had no clues."

"I visited her grave in Old Resurrection Cemetery," I said.

"She told her mother she wanted to be buried there. We thought it was an odd request at the time."

I'd read that in Violet's diary, but, of course, I couldn't tell her that.

Viola rejoined me in the living room. "We were a small family. Violet's mother was my older sister. Violet was an only child, and I never married. So now I'm alone. It could have been so different if they'd only stayed in Oakpoint, but my sister fell in love with that old house. For years they were all happy in Foxglove Corners."

She pulled a tissue from her pocket.

In spite of Viola's willingness to talk about her niece, I felt as if I were invading her privacy, stirring to life unbearable memories. I had to remind myself that Viola had wanted to talk.

"Did they ever find Ginger?" I asked. "The articles I read didn't mention her."

She stared at me. "How did you know the dog's name?"

Uh oh. A major slip.

"I came across it somewhere," I said.

She seemed to accept that, although the newspaper accounts had simply referred to a collie.

"Ginger came home a few days after Violet disappeared," Viola said. "She didn't have her leash on. If only dogs could talk. She could have told us what happened."

I often had the same thought, but dogs were able to communicate in other ways. I saw evidence of that every day in my own home.

"I'm not criticizing Ginger, but I read that it was a whole month before Violet was found. Wouldn't you think a collie would have led the searchers to her?"

She smiled faintly. "Lassie would have. After whatever happened, after what she'd been through, Ginger was traumatized. She wasn't the same dog. She lost her will to live."

Because she had lost Violet. I remembered my last rescue, Star, grieving for the family that didn't have time for her.

"Ginger wouldn't eat and didn't want to stay inside," Viola continued. "I took her home with me. At the time I had a large house in Oakpoint with a fenced-in yard. In time she might have adjusted to a new home, but she passed away a few weeks later. The vet thought she'd had a heart attack. Ginger was only about a year old."

It was my turn to reach for a tissue.

Poor Ginger. Poor, poor Violet. Dog stories with unhappy endings always made me cry, and I'd taken a small part in this one.

Unbidden, an image of the sable collie took shape in my mind. Reddish-gold fur blowing in the wind, eyes shining with joy, dashing after a ball... Forever running for that ball on the plane where it was always playtime, happy time, for the girl and her dog.

I felt a shiver, the kind that always accompanied memories of Violet and Ginger.

"Are you all right, dear?" Viola asked.

"It's all so sad."

"It is that."

Viola couldn't know the images that flashed on and off in my mind. As far as she knew, I was reacting to a heart wrenching tale. It was time to turn the talk in a different direction.

"I read there were no suspects," I said. "None at all?"

"No official suspects. There was a vagrant named Clancy who used to hang around the Corners, but he was questioned and cleared. I always wondered if Violet knew her killer. There were a few boys, one in particular, David... I shouldn't say anything. He was questioned, as we all were, and released."

"Why did you suspect him?" I asked.

"Because Violet didn't like him. My sister told me that Violet went out with him a few times, then decided not to see him again. He wouldn't accept that and kept calling her and turning up in places he thought she'd be. Today we'd call it stalking."

"It *was* stalking," I said. "As a rule, people don't take rejection that far, but there are exceptions."

"David claimed he was just trying to get her interested in him again."

"What happened to him?" I asked.

"I have no idea."

I filed David away for future reference. Perhaps he was still alive, still living in Michigan.

"Then there was a girl from her high school, Bettina. She was incredibly bossy. But I always thought the killer was a man."

"It might well have been a stranger passing through town who wanted to kill someone."

"That's what the police thought. I do hope it wasn't anyone she knew."

I took a sip of tea. It was too cool. I'd forgotten about it while we'd talked and completely forgotten about the plate of gingersnaps on the coffee table.

I had one more question for Viola. In a sense, I hated to ask it, but it could be relevant.

Should I risk undoing the rapport we'd built up?

Go ahead.

"Are you aware that over the years some people have claimed they saw the spirit of Violet and Ginger walking on Huron Court?" I asked.

Sixteen

"I've heard the stories," Viola said. "And I have the book."

"*Ghosts and Other Oddities Among Us?*"

"That's the one. I have a few others that mention her."

"Do you think the stories are true?" I asked.

"There are more things in heaven and earth, Horatio, than are dreamt of in your philosophy."

That was true but not a proper answer.

"I wish I knew," Viola said. "For so long, so many years, I've wanted to know if Violet was all right. One time I even consulted a psychic. All I know is that I've never seen her. Well, one time… No, not really."

What did that mean? I waited but Viola didn't elaborate on her answer, and I didn't feel I could ask her to explain.

"According to the accounts in the ghost book, Violet has been seen walking on Huron Court," I said.

"Yes, and not in Oakpoint. I've only lived here for two years. Violet wouldn't know where to find me, and I have no intention of returning to Foxglove Corners. Not ever. So we'll have to wait until I pass to meet again."

I glanced out the window. It was dark and I had a long solitary drive ahead of me, but I didn't want to leave yet. Crane was bringing a pizza home, so I didn't have to worry about dinner.

I said, "I believe that the spirits of our loved ones know where to find us."

"Then you think the stories are true?"

"I do."

"What I don't understand is why I never saw Violet," she said. "We were very close. I was her godmother."

"Would you *want* to see her?" I asked.

She hesitated. "I want to know for certain that she lives on somewhere. That she's happy and maybe has Ginger with her. I want to tell her how much I love her and miss her and wish we'd had more time together when she was on this earth. I keep reliving her birthday celebration in the tearoom. That was my last memory of us together."

She dabbed at her eyes. In a moment, I would be crying with her.

"So the answer to your question is yes, I want to see her," she said. "Wherever and whenever I can."

~ * ~

The drive home wasn't as stressful as I'd feared. It was dark, yes, but the freeway was well lit, traffic was light, and the pavement was dry. Myriads of stars sparkled in a clear sky. I missed Leonora's company, though. I rarely drove this way without her.

The scene changed when I exited the freeway. I was on a dark country road watching for leaping deer and other wildlife. I thought about what Viola hadn't said. What had she meant by not seeing Violet? Not really?

Well, I might still find out. We had parted on good terms, and she'd asked me to keep in touch with her. There would always be another day.

Not always, though. Not for Violet, when she set out on what was to be her fateful walk with Ginger.

At last and without incident, I turned onto Jonquil Lane. Good timing. It had started to snow. Before getting out of the car, I scanned the area for coyotes.

All clear. The yellow Victorian was dark. Camille and Gilbert had taken the dogs and driven to Tennessee for the Thanksgiving weekend.

The lights in our house were on. Crane was waiting for me, and the dogs were barking. Raven bounded out of the darkness to greet me. Inside the collies outdid themselves to give me a boisterous welcome. You'd think I'd been gone for days instead of a few hours.

"How was your visit, honey?" Crane asked when the furor died down.

"Good, but sad. Viola Randall is a charming lady. She still misses her niece. She likes violet perfume," I added.

"How is that relevant?"

"So did Violet. If you remember, that was the scent I smelled in the pink Victorian."

He didn't comment.

"It was a coincidence," I said.

I filled the teakettle, and Crane brought the pizza out of the oven, whereupon the dogs switched their focus to him.

"It smells delicious," I said.

He cut me a large slice and one for himself. "Some people can't accept death."

"She told me she consulted a psychic. She wants to know if Violet is okay."

"That's going overboard."

"But it's understandable when death is so sudden and senseless. Viola had some otherworldly contact with Violet. She started to say something about it, then apparently changed her mind."

"That's an unusual family," he said. "But now it's over."

I nodded. "For me, it's over. But not for Viola and not for Brent."

~ * ~

Out in the cold night, the coyotes were howling.

I woke up, fell asleep again, and...

entered a snowy forest where thick-growing trees trapped the icy air. The trees seemed unnaturally tall. I couldn't see their tops.

I was so cold. Had Crane opened the window? I'd better get up and close it. I turned over and dropped into a deep slumber.

I made my way to some murky destination, hampered by twisting branches and blowing snow. Icy shards stung my face, and sharp wood jabbed my sides. I was chasing an animal. Or an animal was chasing me. I wasn't sure.

Abruptly the scene shifted. The trees thinned out. The ground sloped upward, and I came out of the forest to find myself on a snow-covered road.

Not just any road. Huron Court, the one road I'd sworn never to traverse again.

Misty was with me, a white collie bounding out of a wave of snow. We had to reach Sagramore Lake. Once we did, we would be home free.

Suddenly Misty barked. Another dog answered. Dog or coyote? Ginger?

Through swirling snow, I saw a curve in the road.

Not again. Dear God, take me home.

The dream ended abruptly, as dreams do. It had been an insane jumble of memories and images. My mouth was dry. My breasts and shoulders were damp. I lay still until my breathing returned to normal. Then I sipped water from the bedside carafe.

Why couldn't I ever have a pleasant dream? Crane and I on a second honeymoon, walking under a southern sun, all well with our world and all the world shining on our love?

I turned on the small flashlight I kept on the nightstand and aimed it at the clock. Midnight. The witching hour. Time for unwholesome dreams to surface.

Shining the light on the doorway, I saw our nighttime guardians, Halley and Misty, lying close together on the threshold. Halley didn't stir, but Misty lifted her head, dark eyes bright and questioning.

Did dogs dream? Did Misty ever dream of her time on Huron Court?

"Go back to sleep, puppy," I whispered. "You were in my dream. Do you ever dream of me?"

~ * ~

The next time I woke, the dream had dissolved, no more substantial than a fleeting memory.

It was morning, and it was going to be a good day with school dismissed for Thanksgiving recess after third period. Leonora was going shopping for pumpkins and pecans, and I planned to visit Lucy Hazen as everything needed for our dinner was safe in the refrigerator or the pantry.

Crane poured coffee for us as I scrambled eggs.

"I heard the coyotes howling last night," he said

"So did I."

I swirled the fork through the eggs. "It's getting to be a nightly occurrence. They're too close to the house for comfort."

"Think of it as a little night music," he said.

I thought of Trista. If she were living in the wild, sooner or later she'd encounter a coyote. What would happen then?

Suppose it had already happened?

I knew Trista was champion-sired, and I was sure I'd recognize her from the pictures in the paper, but her personality was an unknown. Was she intelligent, courageous, aggressive, capable of being led astray by a wily cousin?

I might never know, but I wished for a happy outcome. For Trista, for Jennifer and Molly, and for Trista's owner, who was willing to part with an enormous amount of money for her return.

The eggs were ready. Perfect. The bacon was crisp, the toast done. I always liked to start the day with a good breakfast.

Crane raised his orange juice glass. "Here's to a peaceful co-existence."

"I'll drink to that," I said.

Seventeen

Lucy Hazen, Foxglove Corner's renowned horror story writer, lived with her blue merle collie, Sky, in Dark Gables, an atmospheric house on Spruce Road. In a pleasant sunroom filled with green and flowering plants, she wrote novels that enchanted and terrified her young readers. One of her books, *Devilwish,* had been optioned for a movie. We hoped that movie would become a reality and would be made in Foxglove Corners.

In the meantime, Lucy wore her black dresses and skirts, kept writing, and read tea leaves for her friends. When the need arose, she warned them of personal danger.

Lucy and Brent were unlikely friends, and I wanted to discuss with her my concern about his obsession with Violet's house.

"I'm worried, too," Lucy said as she handed me a plain white teacup, plain being the best kind of cup for tea leaf reading. The Zodiac charms on her bracelet jingled a note of alarm in the quiet house.

Lucy pushed back a strand of her glossy black hair that had escaped from its French twist. "Unfortunately," she added, "in this matter, he won't listen to me. He's gone so far overboard we'll never be able to pull him back."

Lucy was given to gloom-and-doom rhetoric, usually peppered with phrases commonly seen in Gothic novels.

In this instance, I felt it was appropriate.

"What do you make of the whispering he hears?" I asked.

"It could be conversations from the past trapped in time and imprinted on the present."

That seemed complicated.

"But why whispers?"

"Perhaps the words lose volume as they come through."

I didn't always agree with Lucy's interpretation of events. This particular one seemed far-fetched.

"Or people from the past might simply have been whispering."

"Who all lived there again?" Lucy asked. "Besides Violet Randall?"

"Her parents, and after they left the house, a couple named Gardener. Any number of people might have come by to visit."

Even I, although my time in the pink Victorian had been short, less than an hour.

"Could Brent be hearing whispers from the future?" I asked.

"Mmm. It's possible but not likely. Drink your tea, Jennet, before it cools off."

Unintentionally I poked Sky in the face with my elbow. She sat next to me on Lucy's wicker sofa, her eyes fixed on the slices of cranberry nut bread I'd brought for Lucy. The plate was on the coffee table, near her nose, but she was polite, not a bit like my food thief, Candy.

I wiped a spot of drool from my sleeve and broke off a piece of bread for her.

Lucy took a sip of her own tea. "That's good. Just a touch of cinnamon. I've been writing all morning." She gave Sky a pat on the head. "I assume Brent told you about the mirror."

"He didn't. What happened?"

She paused. "Well, it's no secret. I'm sure he wouldn't mind you knowing. He found an antique mirror in one of the trunks and hung it in that room with Violet's possessions. He stepped back to make sure it was level and saw a face looking at him."

I felt the familiar press of cold wrapping around my body. It occurred at times like this when I came face to face with the inexplicable. I knew what Lucy was going to say next. Still, I said, "Whose face was it?"

"A pretty girl with long chestnut hair. She was wearing sapphire earrings and a lacy white top."

"That's how I described Violet time and time again."

"The face was only there for a second. He blinked, looked again, and saw his own reflection. He swears he didn't imagine it."

I was certain that he hadn't and wondered why he hadn't told me about it.

"You'd think he'd take that mirror down and pack it away in the trunk," I said.

"That's what I would have done. Not Brent, though. To him, that house is a challenge, and I think he wants to see Violet, even though he won't admit it.

"He may get his wish," I said. "That house is haunted."

"I'll go further. The house is evil."

I was in the mood for a little levity. "I guess Violet got tired of walking up and down Huron Court. I'll bet she's tired of wearing the same outfit and those earrings, too."

"Ghosts don't worry about having a variety of clothes," Lucy said. "Anyway, there's no prying Brent away from his inn. He wants to open it for Christmas."

"I wonder what will happen between now and then— if anything."

She glanced at my cup. "Let's see what the tea leaves have in store for you."

My favorite part of having tea with Lucy was having my tea leaves read. I took one more sip, drained the excess liquid in the saucer, and turned the cup toward myself three times, while making my wish.

Intriguing patterns formed inside the cup. They meant nothing to me, but Lucy could see future events and sometimes warnings in the formations.

Did I believe it? Well... Not really. Not always. It was an amusing parlor game, always fun. That was what I said if people asked for my opinion. On the other hand, Lucy had many remarkable talents. What she'd told me had often come true. So I did believe. A little.

Lucy held the cup away from her and studied it. Her frown told me she saw a problem or something unpleasant.

"I see a viper close to your home," she said.

"You mean a snake?"

"A snake. Yes. Look."

She pointed to an arrangement of leaves that did indeed resemble a coiled snake.

"I hate snakes," I said.

"This isn't a literal snake," she pointed out.

I knew that much about tea leaf reading.

"It's a symbol of someone with snake-like qualities. A poisonous individual. I don't like to see this person so close to your home."

"Do you see an initial around it?" I asked.

"I can't say that I do."

"Nothing that looks like a V?"

For Veronica?

She handed me the cup. "You look."

I did. "There's no initial," I said and gave her the cup back. "What else do you see?"

Lucy saw my wish, three little dots, and pointed it out to me. She saw confusion, but that was my life, in school and out. Finally she saw a road that forked in two different directions.

Huron Court.

Get out of my teacup, I wanted to say.

Lucy set the cup down on the tray and helped herself to a sliced of cranberry bread. "That's all for today, Jennet. A mix of good and bad."

"More bad than good," I murmured. "What are you doing for Thanksgiving?"

"Working," she said. "Christmas is my only holiday. I bought a frozen turkey dinner with mashed potatoes and stuffing," she added.

"Don't do that, Lucy. Have dinner with Crane and me. I have a small turkey, and it's only us this year."

"Well, I don't know… If you're sure."

"You can take home a doggie bag for Sky," I said. "We'd love to have you."

She smiled. "Okay then. I guess I can have two holidays."

"That's settled then."

I wished I knew if Brent had accepted Annica's invitation to dinner— if she'd even invited him. I decided not to mention it. I didn't know the nature of Brent's and Lucy's relationship and wasn't about to ask.

One way or the other, Lucy's company was going to enliven our day.

Eighteen

With the snow falling steadily and the yellow Victorian across the lane steeped in darkness, a sense of uneasiness slowly crept up on me. At first I was so busy getting the turkey ready for the oven, preparing relish trays, and doing whatever I could ahead of time that I was scarcely aware of it.

The house was too quiet. The dogs were drowsy, rousing only to bark at a family of deer that wandered out of the woods.

My other near neighbors, the Lintons, were also away. I might have been the last person on earth, living alone in a yellow Victorian farmhouse on Jonquil Lane.

It was just that this day, this holiday, was so different from a normal Thursday. At this time on an ordinary weekday— I glanced at the kitchen clock— I would be waiting for my fourth period American Literature class to come storming into the room. I would be hungry and apprehensive about their behavior and would be worried about a snowy commute home on the freeway.

Did I want to exchange a quiet day at home for an ordinary Thursday?

Not a chance.

Noting the dogs' interest in the pumpkin pies, I moved them from the counter to the top of the refrigerator.

All right. The turkey was stuffed and in the oven, the dining room table was set with my best linen, silver, and china, and Rebecca Ferguson's candlesticks gleamed with a fresh polishing and new white tapers. The dogs had been out, and I could relax for a while with a Gothic novel Miss Eidt had found for me at an estate sale.

Misty followed me into the living room and flattened herself out near the rocker. I brought my tea with me and let my book transport me to Victorian England and a heroine whose husband was trying to have her committed to an insane asylum.

How was that for a major problem?

The uneasiness followed me and intensified. I tried to concentrate on the perils of the beleaguered Arabella, but my mind insisted on replaying the conversation with Lucy. I kept imagining Brent looking into an antique mirror and seeing Violet's face.

Why hadn't he told me about his experience? It wasn't like him to be secretive. Not about the pink Victorian.

If I were to look into that mirror— which wouldn't happen, not in a million, billion years, would I see Violet again?

Why did I keep thinking about her?

You know why.

Because she couldn't rest in peace. Wasn't that one of the reasons ghosts walked? And because she thought I could help her. Somehow. Once I hadn't even been able to help myself.

What would Violet's aunt say if she knew about the mirror? Which she wouldn't, not from me.

I wondered if Brent had accepted Annica's invitation for a wholesome family dinner with Annica and her mother? I hoped he hadn't decided on a solitary visit to the pink Victorian today instead.

He wouldn't. Or would he?

Finally I closed the book and contemplated cutting into one of the pumpkin pies and having another cup of tea. That would drive the malaise away.

The silence hanging over Jonquil Lane like an ominous storm cloud reminded me unpleasantly of Huron Court, that other quiet road, the accursed country thoroughfare that refused to let travelers reach its end.

Oh for heaven's sake. This was a holiday, no time for morbid thoughts.

In another few hours, Crane would be home, and Lucy would arrive any minute. I hoped two more bodies in the house would chase this unsettling feeling away.

Somewhere in the woods across the lane, the coyotes began to howl.

~ * ~

"I have the strangest feeling," Lucy said. "There's something in the air tonight. Besides snow. Something evil."

I took her long black coat, brushed the snow onto the door mat, and hung it in the closet. She'd brought us a box of candy, an assortment of chocolates decorated in festive colors for the holiday. I thanked her and set it on the mantel. The dogs had become increasingly interested in the smells of cooking that wafted from the kitchen. The chocolates had quickly caught their attention.

"I feel it, too," I said. "It's the isolation. This is a particular lonely part of Foxglove Corners."

"It's more than that," Lucy countered. "But it isn't here. The house looks lovely, Jennet. So warm and bright."

It was, with a minimum of effort on my part.

Flames danced in the fireplace and pillar candles in harvest colors throughout the rooms added their light. I'd added bouquets of dried flowers and a basket of gourds to the décor.

"Everything is ready," I said. "Crane will be home soon. Let's have some tea while we wait."

I'd hoped that once I had company of the human kind, the feeling would subside, but it didn't. Well, when Crane came home, he'd bright the light with him. In many ways, Lucy and I were too much alike, both of us touched with a Gothic wand.

Lucy drank her tea quietly with Misty lying close to her long black skirt. "It's like the calm before the storm," she said. "Something is going to happen. The very earth is waiting for it to begin."

A sentiment like this would be enough to unnerve anyone. I, however, was used to Lucy's way of talking. If you thought about it, something was always going to happen. Unless you were like Lucy or Violet, gifted with the ability to glimpse into tomorrow, you simply had to wait until it did.

The clock struck six. Crane was late. A whole ten minutes late. The roads must be hazardous. As always, I sent out a prayer for his safe return.

"Does this something have to be bad?" I asked.

"I'd say so."

Great.

"But nothing we can't deal with," she added.

As if on cue, a distant howling broke into the silence. Candy gave a high mournful howl in return. From her dog house, Raven joined her. For the next few minutes, the dogs were restless, pacing and looking out the windows into the darkness.

Was it Thanksgiving or Halloween again?

"I hear the coyotes in my woods, too," Lucy said. "I saw one yesterday when I was out with Sky. It watched us for a few minutes, then ran away. They don't like us humans."

I told her about my stand-off with the coyote-like creature that was larger than any coyote should be.

"I haven't seen it since that night. At times I wondered if I imagined it."

"I'm sure you saw some animal. Maybe one of those coywolves I read about. They're part of it, I think," Lucy said.

It? The coyotes, I assumed. If only she would be specific. I was about to ask her to explain what she meant when the collies flew to the kitchen door in a blur of multi-colored fur.

"That's Crane," I said rising. "I'll be right back."

Be thankful, I thought.

For the imminent end of the disquietude. The main light source of the house was even now coming through the door.

~ * ~

While Crane showered and changed out of his uniform, Lucy helped me bring the dishes to the table. Shrimp salad on crisp lettuce leaves, cranberry relish, yams whipped with miniature marshmallows, pickles and olives. All the trimmings. Then, supervised by my collie pack, I took the turkey out of the oven and begin carving it while Lucy put the rolls in the oven.

When Crane joined us, it truly felt like a holiday. He wore his special Thanksgiving shirt with its rows of turkeys strutting across a leaf-strewn field. He filled the goblets with sparkling grape juice, I lit the candles, and we sat down to eat.

"It looks like Old Man winter has us in a death grip," Crane said. "I dealt with three accidents today."

"You should spend the night with us, Lucy," I said.

"That's sweet of you, Jennet, but what about Sky? She'll be alone. I fed her before I left, and she has water, but…"

"The snow is supposed to stop around midnight," I said. "The roads will be better in the morning."

"I think I'd rather risk it. I'll be careful."

"How about if I drive you home?" Crane said. "Jennet can pick you up tomorrow so you can get your car."

"That would be better, but it's so much trouble for you both."

"It's no trouble," he said. "That's what we'll do then."

I glanced at him, thankful for a gallant husband and good friends. Oh, and good collies. I couldn't forget them.

This might be a quiet Thanksgiving, but it would go down in our history as a good one.

Nineteen

When dinner was over and the kitchen restored to a pristine state, when Crane left to drive Lucy home, the feeling of unease returned in full force. Earlier in the day I had thought of it as a cloud hovering over the house. By now, it had burst, spreading a layer of anxiety over everything in its path.

Sated with turkey, and sleepy, the dogs were oblivious of weird feelings. I was alone in the house, the lone human, that is, and Lucy's words came back to haunt me.

"There's something in the air. Something evil."

Not since my early days in Foxglove Corners had I been so aware of country darkness and quiet.

Rein in those disturbing thoughts, I ordered myself.

As the wife of a lawman, I was used to Crane being away from home. Sometimes he was gone for entire weekends. Before my marriage, I'd lived alone and prided myself on my courage. After all, I was a tornado survivor. Was I going to let a little ambiguous emotion unnerve me?

Ha! I was already unnerved.

It's dark, I told myself. *It's the country. Everything is as it should be.*

And the coyotes were howling.

The disturbing thoughts rushed back. I checked my watch. By now Crane would have dropped Lucy off. Would he make it home safely? Would the Jeep slide off the road into a ditch or, worse, down one of those deep slopes where treetops were level with the ground? Would I be alone again?

I hastened to reassure myself. Crane was a match for any weather. He would be home soon, and we could end Thanksgiving on a romantic note by the fireside.

Even so, I was jittery, and my thoughts soon settled on the familiar. The old mystery of Violet's murder and the current one of the antique mirror through which Brent had seen Violet's face. And always, always Huron Court.

What had made a country road in Foxglove Corners, on the surface no different from any other country road, a direct route into the past? At least for me.

That, too, was a mystery. Why could others travel on that road and remain in their own time?

I might never know the answer to that question. And if I did, it certainly wouldn't be tonight.

Trailed by Misty, I moved silently through the rooms, blowing out candles and turning on lamps. I needed strong light to break up the darkness.

A sudden scream scattered my thoughts.

What on earth?

It had originated outside, somewhere in the snow-begotten night. Not too far from the house.

My heartbeat sped into an uncomfortable rhythm. At my feet, Misty stirred. Candy came rushing in from the living room, hot on the trail of the disturbance.

"It's all right," I murmured, not believing my own words.

Could that ghastly sound have come from a human throat? Or, and this was more likely, had a predator just pounced on a hapless weaker animal?

I let the thought die, unwilling to dwell on a hypothetical bloody scene.

Don't let a typical night sound unnerve you.

It was quiet then. I stood at the window, trying to see outside. Impossible, with all the snow falling.

Something in the air. Something evil.

Finally I took control of the situation. Crane would be fine. He had driven in all kinds of weather and never yet had an accident. I dropped into the rocker, promising myself to wait for him calmly, to be there, a welcoming presence when he came in from the storm.

Misty padded into the living room and lay beside me. Of all the collies she seemed to be the one who wanted to stay by my side whenever possible, usurping Halley's place. My even-tempered Halley never pushed her away. Halley knew she was my heart dog.

Thank heavens for good dogs and Crane, I thought. *Rest and be thankful. It's a night for thanksgiving.*

The refrigerator hummed, one of the dogs yelped in her sleep. From the pattering on the windows, I suspected the rain was turning to sleet, which wasn't good. Time passed slowly.

To-day will die to-morrow,
Time stoops to no man's lure.

The lines reminded me of Violet.

Don't think about time.

I could hear every individual tick of the clock, most likely because I was sitting so close to it. Outside, the coyotes continued their mournful keening. Safe and warm inside, I said a prayer for Crane to hurry home and bring the world's brightness with him.

~ * ~

He stamped the snow from his boots and gave his furry welcome committee a round of vigorous pats. It was almost eleven o'clock.

"It's bad out there," he announced. "I'm glad we didn't let Lucy drive home alone."

"How does a cup of cocoa sound?" I asked.

"Perfect."

He shook the snow off his jacket and draped it over a chair. "Then we can go to bed. It's been a long day."

"But a good day." I brought the cocoa tin from the cupboard. "I thought I heard a scream a while ago."

"The coyotes again?"

"I don't think so."

"They're vocal tonight. What else could it be?"

I found two large mugs and the package of mini marshmallows I'd tossed into the yams. Milk. A pinch of salt. I hadn't meant to mention the scream. My tongue had a will of its own.

"I suppose if anyone were in trouble, we'll know about it tomorrow," I said.

He seemed happy to dismiss the scream. "What are you going to do tomorrow, honey?"

"Plan next week's lessons and try to come up with a new way to use our turkey leftovers."

Slowly the cocoa came to a boil. I gave it one last stir.

"I'll call Leonora," I added. "I'm dying to know how dinner with Jake's family went. Oh and whether Annica had Brent over for dinner. Whatever I do, it won't be Christmas shopping in the mall."

~ * ~

The next morning I stared at the *Banner* headline, not wanting to believe what I was reading. *Search Underway for Missing Teen.*

I scanned the story and glanced at the picture of the long-haired blonde girl with the wistful expression. Jillian Cranbrook, returning from a Thanksgiving get together at her college roommate's house, had disappeared on her way home. Apparently she'd had car trouble on Squill Lane, and for some reason, left her car on the side of the lane, to be buried in the snow. Her purse and cell phone were on the passenger's seat, together with black leather gloves, a scarf, and a pair of four-inch heels.

The snow had obliterated any tracks.

Jillian was nowhere to be found. It seemed an obvious case of abduction, although what abductor would wait in a snowstorm to snatch his victim?

Shades of Violet Randall. This was the same kind of story in virtually the same place, only decades later. There were differences, beside the seasons. There was no dog in this story, and the girl was driving, rather than on foot. Well, of course. Who would go walking in the snow? Unless she had no choice.

Once again Lucy had sensed the encroaching evil.

Only, please God, let there be a different ending to Jillian's story.

I left the rest of the paper unread and thought about the bizarre mood that had gripped me yesterday. The scream hadn't been a coyote or a coyote's prey, then. Nor my greatly overworked imagination. A young girl had been in distress and whatever happened had taken place close to our home.

Squill Lane was even more isolated than Jonquil Lane. To the east, a charming yellow cottage, usually untenanted, stood next to a cornfield. To the west, Sue Appleton's farm overflowed with horses and collies and activities. But no activities were scheduled on a holiday and none at night.

Situated on Jonquil Lane, the infamous unfinished construction shadowed the landscape. It had been the first area the police had searched. Of the missing girl there was no sign.

And all around us were woods, dark, silent, and forbidding with endless places to conceal a body.

In last night's treacherous weather, who could survive for long without gloves and a scarf? I didn't like to think of that answer. If it were an abduction, though, she would have been removed from the scene.

At this point, who knew?

It appeared that Foxglove Corners had another mystery. Possibly a deadly one

Twenty

By mid-morning of the next day I was bored with schoolwork and hungry for any kind of sandwich except turkey. Bright sunlight shone on the fresh snow, and the call of the outdoors was impossible to ignore.

I took Misty, Sky, and Gemmy for a walk to Squill Lane, hurrying them past the unfinished construction, although after the search for the missing girl, I didn't think the ruins held any menace.

The abandoned vehicle had been removed from the side of Squill Lane, leaving an ominous imprint in the snow.

What had happened here last night? I hoped the *Banner* would have an update. According to the latest newscast, volunteers were still combing the woods for evidence— or a body.

At any rate, perpetrator and victim appeared to be long gone from this picturesque snowbound lane. And it was indeed picturesque, with snow that sparkled as if it had been mixed with diamond dust or frozen tears for the lost traveler. Nature reveled in her beauty no matter what befell a member of the human race.

Feeling depressed, I led the dogs back home and drove to Clovers for lunch.

It didn't look as if the restaurant was busy, judging by the half dozen cars in the lot, one of which was Annica's. People were probably shopping at the mall, chasing bargains.

The culinary spirit of Thanksgiving lived on in the restaurant. Pumpkin pies and tarts in the dessert carousel and the day's special, turkey pot pie, leftovers perhaps, but glorious ones.

Annica was working alone. Her black sweater and skirt were striking with her red hair, and gold horn earrings gave her attire a bright accent. The apron tied around her waist depicted a turkey on a platter.

"Hi, Jennet," she said, leading me to my favorite booth with its view of snow-heavy woods of Crispian Road. "Breakfast or lunch?"

"Lunch. Let's see..." I perused the hanging menu board. "Ham salad on white with sweet pickles and a large ginger ale."

When she brought my sandwich and a cup of coffee for herself, she sank into the chair opposite mine with less than her characteristic verve.

"Did Brent come over for Thanksgiving dinner yesterday?" I asked.

"No. He said he already had plans and asked if he could have a raincheck. What the heck does that mean? An invitation for *next* Thanksgiving?"

"You'll have to ask him," I said, hoping those plans hadn't included a visit to the pink Victorian.

"Did you hear about that girl who disappeared last night?" Annica asked.

"Yes, and I might have heard her scream."

"No kidding."

"I'm not sure. I heard something. It could have been a cry for help or an animal. Either way, I couldn't investigate."

"Jillian Cranbrook is in some of my classes at Oakland. I don't know her well, but when something like this happens, you feel like you've lost a friend."

"She's one of our own," I said. "The women of Foxglove Corners."

Annica stirred sugar into her coffee and added a double measure of half and half. "I drive alone all the time, to and from school and Clovers. I'm on the road when it's dark more often than not."

"And it gets dark so early at this time of year."

Once again I was grateful that Leonora and I carpooled to Marston. Not so much because of the freeway but the long miles of country road that made up the second half of our commute were fraught with danger of all kinds.

"Well, what are we going to do?" I said. "We can't stop living."

"I talked to her friend, the one she was with yesterday. Ronda is in my Chaucer class. She heard there's nothing wrong with the car. It had a half tank of gas."

"So she was kidnapped."

"That's what the cops think. I read about something like that happening a few years back. A woman left her things in her car and simply disappeared. She was in a wooded area. They never found a trace of her. You don't think… No, that's impossible."

"What?" I asked.

"That Squill Lane is like Huron Court?"

"Are you saying that Jillian Cranbrook stepped out of her car and into the past?"

"It happened to you. What do you think?"

"That some pervert saw an opportunity to grab a young girl and took it."

"But why would she get out of her car? That doesn't make sense. She could have run him down. Surely she wouldn't stop to pick up a stranger."

"We won't know until they find her," I said, choosing to be optimistic.

Annica made no such choice. "I don't think that'll ever happen."

~ * ~

I didn't see Brent until late the following afternoon when he showed up at the dinner hour and agreed to sample my first turkey casserole.

"Where did you have Thanksgiving dinner?" I asked.

"I had a quick sandwich at the Spirit Lamp Inn. They were packed."

"Why quick?"

"I had to stop at Violet's house. A holiday is prime time for break-ins."

That was his excuse?

"Was everything okay?"

"You could say that."

I just had. Was Brent going to tell me about the face in the mirror? I waited while he engaged Sky in a game of tug of war with a stuffed duck until it became obvious that he wasn't going to elaborate.

I said, "Did you hear any more whispering?"

He shrugged. "I might have. It was hard to tell with all the wind and snow."

"But surely you can tell the difference."

"Usually."

He wrestled the duck from Sky's mouth and threw it into the dining room. Candy grabbed it by the tail feathers and scampered back to Brent.

"I wish you could see what I've done with the place, Jennet," he said. "Could I give you a little tour sometime? The sheriff doesn't have to know."

"Know what?" Crane materialized at the foot of the stairs. He had mastered the art of moving quietly. Candy dropped the duck at his feet. He picked it up and sat next to Brent.

"That I'd gone inside Violet's house," I said.

"What are you up to, Fowler?" Crane demanded.

Always a quick thinker, Brent said, "I've turned that old Victorian into a show place. I'm eager to show it off."

"Then take pictures with your phone," Crane countered. "I don't want Jennet anywhere near that time-trap."

The autocratic deputy sheriff was back again.

That was my signal to speak up. I could make my own decisions. Only I didn't want to view Brent's improvements. Not really. Crane's word choice, time trap, reminded me of my seemingly endless walk on Huron Court.

Would Brent tell us about seeing Violet's face in the mirror? It didn't seem so until later while we ate dessert he said in an offhanded manner, "I wanted an inn with a ghost story attached to go along with the Spirit Lamp Inn. I never bargained on a real live ghost."

Crane splashed another spoonful of whipped cream on his pie. "Is there such a thing?"

He shrugged. "Sometimes it seems there is."

Now, I thought, he'll tell us about seeing Violet's face. Instead he said, "Objects move around in that house."

"Such as?"

"The other day I found an old mirror in the attic and hung it in Violet's room. Sometime after, it fell off the wall. Luckily it didn't break. There's no rug in that room yet."

"Did you use the right kind of nail?" Crane asked.

"Sure."

"Did you pound it in to a piece of rotting wood?"

"My walls aren't rotting," he said. "I hung it the right way. I'm no amateur. Then it fell again. This time I left it."

I waited.

"The next time I checked, the next day, it was on the wall again."

"That's impossible," Crane said. "Unless you have a vagrant camping out in the house."

"That was my first thought, so I checked every door and window. There's nothing to suggest anyone had been inside except Annica and me."

The mystery deepened. Intrigued, I pushed away my growing desire to investigate the phenomenon. It wasn't worth the risk.

"Did you see any signs of an intruder?" Crane asked.

"Nothing. Annica left a picnic basket in the kitchen with apples and a bag of chips. Everything was there."

"And this is the place you want to take Jennet?" he demanded.

"It should be safe."

"Safe isn't good enough with a mirror falling down and hanging itself up again. You must have overlooked something," he added. "I'll stop by if you like, but Jennet isn't going within a mile of Huron Court. Quit trying to tempt her."

I felt invisible. I had to say something. "I'm incapable of being tempted."

How lame. Try again.

It turned out I didn't have to.

The dogs created a noisy diversion, falling over one another to reach the window. Three deer stood in the yard, as still as lawn ornaments. Then they were gone.

When the dogs settled down again, Crane and Brent were discussing the Thanksgiving abduction, as the *Banner* called it, and the likelihood that Jillian Cranbrook would never be found.

It was a somber end to our evening.

Twenty-one

The mirror in the house on Huron Court occupied my thoughts for the rest of the weekend. Any mirror or painting can fall off a wall, but it takes a human hand to hang it up again.

I thought of one possible explanation. A supernatural manifestation would require a burst of energy. What was the appearance of Violet's spirit in the mirror if not a supernatural manifestation?

In most circumstances, this might be considered a ludicrous theory, but this was a happening in the pink Victorian, center of all things strange and fearful. I thought it unlikely that a vagrant had found his way into the house, mainly because of the undisturbed contents of the picnic basket. Vagrants usually don't leave food untouched.

I was still waiting for Brent to be completely forthcoming and couldn't understand why, when he had been comfortable sharing the tale of the moving mirror, he hadn't mentioned that he had seen Violet's face reflected in its surface.

Lucy probably knew. She was Brent's confidante, and we all flocked to her when confronted with an inexplicable occurrence. I couldn't wait to talk to her again. But Thanksgiving recess was over. The week ahead promised to be busy with a staff meeting and an in-service day. I'd have to wait.

On Monday, Leonora and I bought our lunch in the cafeteria. On the menu were spaghetti and meatballs, one of the cafeteria ladies' specialties. While we ate, I told her about the mirror.

"Brent has gone off the deep end," she said. "I didn't think he was the type."

"He never seemed to be. That house has changed him."

"I've never known you to leave a mystery uninvestigated," Leonora said. "Are we going to tackle this one?"

"I'll admit I'm curious, but I promised Crane I wouldn't go near Huron Court again. That includes the house."

"Not even when Brent turns it into an inn?"

"I don't think that'll happen."

"If he plans to open it by Christmas, he'll have to hurry," she pointed out.

"He doesn't seem to be in much of hurry."

We ate silently for a few minutes, our eyes on the clock. The walk to and from the cafeteria had sliced several minutes off our eating time.

We'd said all we could about Brent, and the disappearance of Jillian Cranbrook was too distressing a subject for lunchtime. I decided to ask Leonora about her Thanksgiving. So far, all she'd said was that she'd had a nice time. Come to think of it, she had been uncharacteristically quiet on our drive to school this morning.

"Did you like Jake's family?" I asked.

"Oh, definitely," she said. "They were very welcoming. I had the impression that Jake doesn't invite girls to his parents' home often."

"That's good. Were your pies a success?"

She nodded. "They turned out well."

Obviously I wasn't going to hear any more details. Oh, well, we were almost out of time. I finished the last meatball as the bell rang. Leonora's student assistant, Sylvia, stood in the doorway, ready to take our trays back to the cafeteria. It was back to work and all mysteries on hold.

~ * ~

"I don't know what's going on at Brent's house," Crane said that evening as we sat in front of the fireplace with Misty lying between us. "Nobody broke in, that's for sure. Do you think there's another key floating around?"

"What does Brent say?" I asked.

"He's positive there isn't. He reminded me he had the locks changed when he bought the place. He kept all the keys."

I didn't tell Crane about my 'burst of supernatural energy' theory. It no longer seemed feasible.

"Well, I don't think Violet hung her own mirror back on the wall," I said.

"Maybe Fowler did it himself and forgot."

"Unlikely."

Misty nudged me with her nose. She felt that she was being ignored, which was true at the moment.

"How long did you stay at the house?" I asked.

"About a half hour. Why?"

"I don't want to wake up one day and find out that you vanished into the past."

His smile was half-hearted. No doubt we were both thinking of the time that had happened to me.

"I promise not to do that," he said.

"I don't suppose you heard the whispering Brent keeps talking about?"

"Not a sound, except the ordinary noises. I wonder if someone is playing a trick on him."

"He says Annica is the only one he's taken to the house. She'd never do anything like that."

"I don't know then," Crane said.

Misty leaped down from the sofa, found her toy goat, and dropped it into my lap.

Play with me, play, play, play.

I tossed it into the dining room.

"When there's no natural explanation for a mystery, look to the supernatural," I said.

"I can't see it being a problem unless it happens again. In that case, I'd advise Fowler to take the mirror back to the attic and forget about it."

"And wait for whatever happens next," I said. "This being Foxglove Corners, I'm sure some new mystery will come along."

~ * ~

The case of Jillian Cranbrook was an ongoing mystery. She seemed to have vanished in the Thanksgiving snowfall. Interviews with her family and friends went nowhere. She'd loved her classes at Oakland University, was looking forward to a ski trip to Colorado over the Christmas holiday, and when she graduated, to a career as an elementary teacher.

She was a happy, sensitive, caring young woman.

Something had happened to derail her life.

I kept thinking about Violet's murder and the invisible perils of living in Foxglove Corners. Huron Court, Squill Lane, and Brandymere, that storied road on which an unwary traveler reached the end of the earth and fell off, never to be seen again.

That was an obvious legend, pure local color, but it accounted for several unsolved disappearances.

"We live in a haunted town," I told Lucy when I managed to squeeze in an hour for a visit.

She handed me a cup of steaming tea. "I wonder why that is. People disappear all over the country. They're abducted, they're murdered, they die in hundreds of different ways. In that respect, we're not unique."

"Then there's the pink Victorian," I said. "Has anything besides the mirror happened to Brent there?"

"There was something else."

Ah! Enlightenment at hand.

"Brent claims that shadows move. Maybe they're not shadows. He says that sometimes they look dimensional. I want him to get out of that house before…" She frowned, took a long sip of tea.

"Before what?"

"Before he can't," she said.

~ * ~

I was more concerned than ever about Brent. Why wouldn't he be able to walk away from his investment? To be sure, he regarded the pink Victorian as a challenge. Brent loved a challenge, whether it was chasing the fox or keeping one step ahead of the myriads of beautiful women who pursued him.

The next time I saw Annica, I asked her if she had ever had an unnatural experience in Violet's house.

"There was that scream we all heard," she said. "It turned out that Violet and Ginger had stepped into the future for just a second."

I remembered. That mystery had been solved through an entry in Violet's diary.

"I meant recently. One of the times when you've been in the house alone with Brent."

A puzzle frown creased her brow. "I don't think so. It's been windy. You can hear the wind blowing from every room in the house. It's scary."

"But you haven't heard voices? Whispering?"

"No."

"What about the antique mirror?"

"Brent said it fell and hung itself back up. Or should that be hanged?"

"Hung is correct."

"I've been in the room a few times, putting finishing touches on it. The mirror never moved an inch. I'm beginning to think he's imagined it."

Annica wasn't the kind of person to leap immediately to a supernatural explanation, and Brent wasn't a fanciful man.

Correction. Brent had never been a fanciful man.

When it came to Brent and the pink Victorian on Huron Court, all bets were off.

Twenty-two

It wasn't easy for me to stand on the sidelines while all sorts of supernatural goings-on played out in the pink Victorian. Mirrors with fantastic powers and shadows with dimensions cried out to be investigated. In the past I'd have been a part of the action.

But I couldn't do anything to change the situation. I had promised Crane I'd stay away from Violet's house. I'd also promised myself.

It bothered me that Lucy knew more about Brent's affairs than I did. After all, Brent had been my friend before he'd met Lucy.

I supposed it didn't matter, as long as I learned what was happening—eventually.

On a weekday stopover at Clovers, Annica and I shared a cup of coffee on her break.

"Brent isn't talking about opening a second inn anymore," she said, "but he wants every room in the house historically accurate. He plans to give tours and invite groups of psychics for special weekends or something. Did you ever hear of anything nuttier?"

So much for the Inn's Christmas opening.

"How much does he have to do before it's finished?" I asked.

"Most of the bedrooms need wallpapering and furniture. I've been helping him with coloring schemes and decorating ideas, but it's not leading anywhere."

I smiled at the thought of Annica's ulterior motive, the one I knew existed. Still I asked, "Where do you want it to lead?"

"To a relationship," she said.

I'd expected her to say "to a date." Obviously she'd gone beyond that modest goal.

"Give it time," I said. "But remember, this is Brent you're dealing with. In the meantime keep your eyes open."

"For what?"

"For anything out of the ordinary."

~ * ~

Jennifer and Molly were still looking for Trista, and they thought they had found her. But there was a problem. There always seemed to be a problem.

They came over one blustery day after school to ask for advice. They sat around the oak table in the kitchen, their bright parkas over their shoulders, while I made them cups of cocoa and naturally one for myself. The one-time lemonade girls were growing up at an alarming rate.

"There's this lady in Lakeville," Jennifer said. "She has a tri who looks like Trista in the picture, but she says she's had her since she was a puppy. She calls her Melody."

"What makes you think she isn't telling the truth?" I asked.

"Melody doesn't know her name."

"Where did you see Melody?"

"The lady owns a craft shop in Lakeville," Jennifer said. "It's called the Busy Bea Craft Shoppe. I went in with my mom to buy a Christmas stocking kit for Ginger. Melody is there every day."

Molly spooned miniature marshmallows into her cup. "Here's our evidence. Jennifer called the dog Trista, and she tilted her head and raised her paw to shake hands."

"That's pretty flimsy."

"She looks exactly like Trista in the picture," Jennifer repeated.

Unfortunately none of us had seen Trista in real life. So many tricolor collies resembled one another. Not my two, though. Halley and Candy had distinctive looks.

"What should we do?" Jennifer asked.

"I can't think of anything offhand," I said. "You certainly can't challenge this craft shop owner. Nobody could do that except for Trista's owner. Or her breeder."

There was the answer. A quiet suggestion to either one of them that it would be in her best interests to visit the craft shop. Trista would know her owner… Or maybe it should be the breeder, as Trista had been lost before reaching her new home. The girls could then collect the reward, Trista could go home, and the story would have a happy ending.

It might be as I had suspected. The owner of the Busy Bea had come across Trista running free and given her a home. Perhaps she hadn't known about the reward. Perhaps she didn't care. I was eager to know the truth.

I explained the plan to Jennifer.

"You're amazing, Jennet," Molly said. "We knew you'd know what to do."

"Maybe I'll visit this craft shop myself," I said.

"They have all kinds of stuff for Christmas. Do all your collies have stockings?"

"Well, no."

Neither did Crane or I. I hadn't grown up in a home where Christmas stockings were a tradition. Also, I wasn't a lover of crafts. Who had time for them?

No one had to know that. The first chance I got, I was going to the Busy Bea Craft Shoppe. In the meantime I jotted down the breeder's contact information for the girls. It was a relief not to worry about Trista struggling to survive in the wild.

~ * ~

The coyotes were in the news again. They had become scapegoats suspected of every vile deed in Foxglove Corners. A cat, Chessie, had gone missing. Who to blame but a hungry coyote? A neighbor on Jonquil Lane had an experience similar to mine in which a large coyote had stood in her walkway, daring her to leave the car until several horn blasts drove him off. Dell Farmer had lost two more sheep.

Closer to home, Camille discovered the remains of a slaughtered deer on the edge of the woods next to her house. Sometimes I heard the pack howling at night, and on occasions Raven answered their call.

On Saturday morning, Camille invited me over for coffee and apple muffins. Also she'd brought us a basket of homemade strawberry jam from Crane's Aunt Becky in Tennessee.

It was a pleasure to relax in her blue and white country kitchen where I'd brought so many problems in the past. Somehow Camille always knew how to shine a ray of hope on the direst situation.

"Gilbert found a company that traps coyotes and takes them away to be euthanized," she said. "We're going to hire them."

Euthanize?

"I hate that word," I said. "Couldn't they just march them out of town?"

"If they relocated them, they would become somebody else's problem. And with our luck, they'd find their way back to Foxglove Corners."

That made sense. I forced myself to think about the latest victims. The cat, Chessie, who was the sole pet of an elderly woman. The sheep, who should have been safe on their farm. And a deer, one of the graceful animals who still delighted me even after living in the country for so long.

Well, kill or be killed. Eat or be eaten. Nature was beautiful and cruel.

"Did you see the article in the *Banner* about the Cranbrook girl?" Camille asked.

"No. Is there anything new?"

"They have a person of interest, a homeless man who's been living in the abandoned construction."

Thank heavens for the dogs, especially Raven, who by her own choice lived outside. She was an alert and vocal guardian.

"That's near Squill Lane, where Jillian Cranbrook left her car," I said. "I thought the police searched the ruins."

"They did. I guess he wasn't there at the time."

"I remember one of those houses is still in fair shape," I said. "I noticed it once when I had to go in there after Misty."

"Oh, Jennet. Please stay away from that place."

"I don't like it either, but I needed to find Misty."

"Those dogs will be the death of you," she said.

"Just Candy and Misty, and Crane walks Candy. Sometimes I think Misty must have taken lessons from Candy. Then Misty was with me when..."

I let my sentence drift away and concentrated on Camille's muffins.

"When I was trapped on Huron Court," I said. "I'm so tired of having to stay away from places," I added. "First Huron Court and the pink Victorian, now the construction. Where next?"

"Wherever the coyotes nest."

Which seemed to be on our doorstep.

"I'll talk to Crane about the exterminator," I said. "I don't like the idea, but we can't have them outnumber us. We'll pay half their fee."

Camille refilled our coffee cups. "That won't be necessary. I just hope they're successful."

Twenty-three

The coyotes were howling. They were so close it seemed as if they had broken into the house. At the moment I could have cheerfully clobbered them with a hammer.

Tomorrow was going to be a long and tedious day at school, and to make matters worse, it was Monday. I had to be rested and alert, which meant I didn't need to be kept awake by the wild pack.

Crane slept beside me, solid and reassuring, undisturbed by what he referred to as a little night music.

I should try to fall asleep again.

I closed my eyes and drifted into a dream of a dense forest. Shivering in my long nightgown, I was trying to move through trees, but low-growing branches grabbed at my arms and long vines trailing on the ground did their best to trip me.

I knew that forest. I had been there before, struggling with branches and vines, either running away from some vile thing or pursuing it. Hot breath propelled my body toward a sliver of light in the distance. Ahead was sanctuary, but I knew I wasn't going to reach it in time.

I tried to call Crane but couldn't make a sound. It was as if my vocal chords were frozen.

The howling of the pack pulled me out of the dream. I lay still, listening. In a perfect world, the coyotes were the ones who wouldn't be able to make a sound. From the doorway Misty whimpered. She'd gone to sleep beside Halley.

"Hush," I whispered.

Another dog was barking. That sound was outside the house. It had to be Raven, who rarely barked at night unless an intruder, usually a four-legged one, strayed into her territory.

I shone my small flashlight at the clock. I could sleep for another half hour or get out of bed now and start breakfast. A mild throbbing behind my right eye made the decision for me.

Get up.

At that point, I was counting on aspirin and determination to get me through the day.

Weren't nights supposed to be restful?

~ * ~

I set a plate of fried eggs in front of Crane and added six strips of bacon.

They looked delicious. So did he, as always so handsome in the morning with his uniform freshly pressed and his badge shining as if newly minted. I wished we could both stay home. Someday...

"How can you sleep through the night with all the noise?" I asked.

"I didn't hear any noise."

"Coyotes howling. Raven barking. Misty whining. So much for country peace and quiet. When I lived in Oakpoint, I slept through cars racing down the street, sirens, and sometimes my neighbor's parties. These disturbances are different."

"Let's hope the coyote traps work," he said. "Then you'll have your country quiet back."

"As annoying as those varmints are, I don't like to think of them being killed."

"Should we hold back on the exterminator?"

"Can't we look for a company that will move them to a wild animal preserve where they won't bother anybody?"

"I can ask around," he said.

"I'd go along with that. Camille and Gilbert can do what they like. Camille felt terrible when she saw the remains of that deer practically at her front door."

Crane nodded. "I'm sure she did. Pass the orange juice, honey."

He wasn't unsympathetic to Camille's feelings, but he looked at life and death in a different way. So many deer died during hunting season. When I first met Crane, he had been a hunter and even had a hunting partner. Then there was Brent, my good friend, a dedicated fox hunter. I liked foxes too, but they never bothered me. In fact, I rarely saw one. The coyotes were all around me, invading my space and ruining my rest.

Kill or be killed. It was a harsh way of living.

Maybe I wasn't a country girl at heart. It didn't matter, though, because Foxglove Corners was my home. I had to adapt.

I reminded myself that coyotes were wily. Remember that cartoon character, Wily Coyote? Maybe they'd evade the traps.

Such thoughts were incompatible with enjoying breakfast. The two aspirin I'd taken were beginning to work. I felt as if I could face the day, whatever it brought. I dipped a strip of bacon into my egg yolk. Yes, delicious.

~ * ~

After school, Leonora and I took a detour to Lakeville to visit the Busy Bea Craft Shoppe.

"You can see the collie and question the owner while I look for Christmas presents," she said.

The Busy Bea was a pretty little store in a familiar location. Soon after moving to Foxglove Corners, I had met animal activist, Caroline Meilland, whose shop, The Fox's Den, had occupied the same space. She'd kept a winterberry wreath on the door. It kept dropping blood red berries.

The current proprietor had hung a Christmas wreath festooned with cloth candy canes and miniature toys. A happier welcome. Merry brass bells rang when I opened the door, and we stepped inside waiting for someone to acknowledge our entry.

For a moment it seemed as if I'd travelled back in time. I half expected to see fox paintings and figurines displayed inside. Caroline would be smiling behind the counter, eager to tell me about her animal rights organization.

The moment passed. From a room toward the back, I heard a high-pitched bark. A middle aged woman in jeans with waist-length black hair emerged from the back room. Her nametag, framed in holly berries, identified her as Beatrice. No doubt she was the shop's owner. At her side, a tricolor collie strained on a loosely held leash, ears flattened against her head.

Trista?

It could be. The collie's black fur had a blue cast in the light of the hanging lamp. She had a narrow white collar and a mark that resembled a star on her head. Just like Trista.

"Are either one of you afraid of large dogs?" Beatrice asked. "If you are, I can put her in her crate."

"Not at all," I said. "We both have collies. Your dog is a beauty. What's her name?"

"This is Melody," she said.

"Did you find her at a local kennel?"

"Melody was a rescue," Beatrice said. "I have no idea who her breeder was."

That wasn't the story she'd told the girls. Unless she'd rescued Melody when she was a puppy.

"Did you adopt her from the Lakeville Collie Rescue League?" I asked, knowing she hadn't.

"Mmm. No, she came from a rescue in Ohio."

"Well, she's breathtaking," I said.

"I like her." Beatrice dropped her hand to the collie's head.

I wished I could say, 'She looks like that dog who went missing a while back— Trista Summer Thunder.' But I sensed that wouldn't be in anyone's best interest in case this really was Trista and Beatrice knew it.

"I love those shadow boxes," Leonora said, pointing to a wall display. "How hard is it to put them together?"

"Not hard at all," Beatrice said. "A child could do it. The instructions are pretty straight forward."

"Think about it, Leonora," I said.

She could assemble a prize-winning Halloween witch cake but wasn't handy with tools or reading instructions, for that matter.

"I thought I'd give one to Jake for Christmas," she said.

"How unromantic."

"It will be if I fill it with pictures of us. Could I see the sample?" she asked.

Beatrice walked over to the wall with her, leaving Melody loose but still attached to her leash.

Leonora said, "I don't suppose I could buy the sample?"

"It's not for sale."

Left alone, I held out my hand for the collie to sniff. "Good Melody," I murmured, moving my hand to her head. "Melody is good."

She wagged her tail.

She knew 'Melody' and 'good.'

I lowered my voice, keeping my hand on her head. "Good dog, Trista."

I was hoping for a sign, for Trista to indicate in some canine fashion that she recognized her real name. Perhaps her dark eyes had a particular shine. Maybe I was imagining it. She tilted her head, that endearing collie gesture that never failed to melt my heart.

I held out my hand. "Can you shake? Will you shake hands with me?"

She waved her paw in the air. I grasped it. Her nails were sharp; they needed trimming.

"I'll have one," Leonora was saying.

"If you have any trouble assembling it, bring it back and I'll help you," Beatrice said.

They began walking toward the cash register.

I lowered my voice. "Trista."

She raised her paw again. If only dogs could talk.

My suspicions were strong, but only Trista's breeder would be able to tell if this rescue from Ohio was the dog she'd lost after the accident. I could also check the Ohio rescues' websites to see if they'd ever had a tricolor collie with a star on her head for adoption.

I didn't think I'd find one.

Twenty-four

Later that afternoon the dogs began to bark. They headed for the front door. It wasn't Crane, then. We had a visitor. Through the bay window I saw Brent's vintage yellow Plymouth turning into our driveway. I also saw snow flurries dancing through the air.

Brent hadn't visited us in a while. I smiled, wondering how he knew I was cooking an especially tasty meal—pot roast with potatoes and carrots. Everybody's favorite. Whatever had brought him to our door, I could use the company. It had been a strange day.

Raven dashed out of her house to intercept him and danced excitedly around him, sniffing at the package he held. It was the forest green shopping bag from Pluto's.

Well, no wonder.

I opened the door. Raven surprised me by blasting inside, scattering her way through the house collies.

"Welcome, stranger," I said. "I thought you forgot us."

He brushed a dusting of snow from his dark red hair. "Never happen," he said. "I've been busy."

"At the house?"

"Mostly. And at the barn. It's a busy time of year."

I took his heavy jacket and ordered the dogs to fall back, a command which they, of course, ignored.

"We're going to get more snow," he said, peeling off his leather gloves.

"Well, it's the season. Come in and get warm. I just built a fire."

I took the shopping bag and considered. The collies had switched their attention to me, with pleading looks that I'd never been able to resist. Relenting, I spread a pool of multi-colored flavor bones for them on the rug. I could vacuum later if there was anything left to clean.

"What's for dinner?" Brent dropped into the rocker and patted his leg. Misty needed no additional encouragement. She leaped into his lap and settled down happily, licking crumbs from her muzzle.

"Pot roast," I said. "You'll stay." It wasn't a question.

"I haven't had a decent meal in days," he said.

That was strange for a man who owned the Spirit Lamp Inn and frequented Foxglove Corners' Hunt Club. He could afford to have a prime rib dinner with all the trimmings every day of the week.

"Why not?" I asked.

He waved his hand in the air. "I've been busy with the house."

"I was talking to Lucy the other day," I said. "What's going on there?"

"Weird stuff. I'm thinking of hiring an exorcist."

"I don't think that's how it's done."

"One of those ghost hunters then."

He stroked Misty's head. "I keep telling myself I wanted a haunted inn. They say to be careful what you wish for."

"Lucy told me about the face in the mirror and the shadows."

"She's going to write a book about it. She has a title already: *The Ghost in the Mirror*."

"Did it come down off the wall and hang itself up again?" I asked.

"So far, no. That one time was a fluke. I still think I had an intruder in the house. The sheriff says no, but he doesn't know everything."

"What about seeing Violet's face?" I asked.

He looked uncomfortable. In fact... I took a good look at him. There was an unaccustomed wariness in his eyes, and he seemed pale. Maybe it was just that his dark summer tan had faded.

"I came to the conclusion I imagined it," he said. "When Annica's with me, nothing happens. When I'm alone, it's like a different place. All whispers and shadows. It's funny. It wasn't that way when the house was empty. You remember..."

I nodded. Unfortunately I remembered only too well. I hadn't seen shadows or heard whispers, but I'd smelled the scent of violets and once, when I'd looked out the window, the season had changed.

"Now that I have the place almost furnished, it's kind of coming alive," Brent said.

In spite of the fire which was making the room quite comfortable, I felt a chill.

"You're speaking figuratively, I hope, because that's impossible."

I felt uneasy making that statement because, deep down, I didn't believe it.

"The sheriff doesn't want me talking to you about the house," he said.

I bristled. "Why not?"

"He says it'll upset you. So when he gets home, we'll change the subject."

"Crane is over-protective," I said. "The pink Victorian has nothing to do with me anymore. I'm worried about you, though. You're taking this so much to heart. I never thought opening a haunted inn was a good idea."

"You may be right. Anyway it won't be ready by Christmas. I wish you could see how we've fixed it up," he added.

"You know I can't."

"I guess not. That whole area isn't safe for you."

"You can make it a real showplace, but if you don't get a handle on these phenomena, you won't be able to attract regular guests," I pointed out.

Apparently he wasn't ready to capitulate yet.

"So far, it's just those incidents with the mirror and the whispers which could still be the wind. Maybe there's something in the way the house was constructed that attracts and traps sounds," he said.

"I'm not an architect, but that doesn't sound right."

"It would explain a lot. Then there are the shadows. Sometimes they seem substantial. Like real people. But they're dark like shadows should be and they move— kind of quickly. They leave you wondering if you've even seen them."

Lucy had told me about Brent's shadows, but hearing him talk about them, seeing how serious he was, alarmed me.

"Good grief, Brent," I said. "Cut your losses. Find another enterprise. Maybe a few new horses."

"I might do that. Not yet, though."

I moved closer to the fire, suddenly aware of shadows. You never thought about them. They were just there. Always there.

Shadows of collies moved in and out of the lamplight, searching the rug for the last crumb. I rose to sit closer to the fire and glanced down at my own shadow, walking across the room. The credenza in the dining room cast a shadow.

None of these shadows had what Brent referred to as substance. How was that even possible? Had he seen real people?

I was about to ask him to elaborate on the shadow experience when he said, "By the way, Jennet, I ran into the sheriff at the

Lakeside Diner this morning. He was having coffee and doughnuts with another woman."

Another woman? All right. Keep calm. Don't overreact.

"Was she pretty?" I asked. "With black hair?"

"A real looker. Super shapely, even in a uniform."

"That must be the new deputy, Veronica something-or-other. I don't like her. She gave me a ticket when I was only driving a few miles over the limit."

And told Crane about it. Who had been unhappy with me.

And now she was sharing coffee with my husband. The Lakeside Diner, or Grill as it was then called, used to be our place a long time ago before we were married. Crane had taken me there on one of our first dates.

Would Crane tell me about his coffee companion? More to the point, why had Brent told me? Didn't I have enough to worry about with that accursed house wrapping its tentacles around him?

Some of the old Brent's animation returned to his face. "She could give me a dozen tickets. I wouldn't mind."

"Spoken like a man," I said. "The world is full of pretty women."

And Marston High School had its share of handsome men. Ned in the Business Department, for one. Coach Adam Barrett. You didn't see me having coffee with one of them in a secluded Oakpoint restaurant.

Whoa, Jennet, I told myself. *Rein in that thought. You're not jealous, I hope.*

It occurred to me that I was entertaining Foxglove Corner's favorite bachelor, a man sought after by scores of women, among them my own friend, Annica. Crane had never indicated that he was jealous of Brent.

Because Brent was just a friend.

Wait a minute. That wasn't true. Before Crane and Brent had become friends, Crane had indeed been jealous of Brent.

And Veronica something-or-other was a co-worker of Crane's and possibly a friend.

The collies flew to the back door, ready to welcome the master of the house. Even Misty, who leaped down from Crane's lap.

"Remember," Brent said. "Sheriff's home. New subject."

Twenty-five

By the light of the candles in Rebecca Ferguson's candlesticks, I passed the dishes around the table. The roast on its own large platter, potatoes and carrots cooked with the meat, salad, the relish tray.

"It looks too good to eat, honey," Crane said.

Brent raised his water glass. "To Jennet. She's is a gem."

"You'd better taste it first," I said.

I was being modest. I knew my dinner would be delicious, and a pie cooled on the kitchen counter out of reach of the ever-curious collies.

One question remained: Would we be a congenial party?

I was afraid that, because the pink Victorian and Huron Court were off limits, conversation would limp to a standstill. Fortunately, there were other matters to discuss. For example, the possible discovery of the missing collie, Trista, in the Busy Bea Craft Shoppe, Brent's Christmas plans to drive his sleigh through Foxglove Corners and deliver toys to needy children, Lucy's movie option. All happy topics except for the one that wasn't happy at all, the disappearance of Jillian Cranbrook, which remained a mystery.

Crane was an affable host. Brent appeared to have cast off his malaise, and all sorts of stories kept the conversation flowing smoothly. Neither Brent nor Crane mentioned Veronica. Well, why would they? Perhaps after Brent left, Crane would mention his coffee date. If he didn't, I could always ask him about it, explaining that Brent had seen them in the Lakeside Diner.

But had Crane seen Brent? I'd forgotten to ask.

You're blowing this all out of proportion, I told myself

"What are we having for dessert?" Brent asked.

"Apple pie."

"Great! That's my favorite," he said.

"I thought your favorite was chocolate peppermint," I countered.

"Can't a man have two favorites?"

A sudden howl broke through the deep night stillness. My heart skipped a beat even though I should be used to the coyote's call. The collies barely stirred. They appeared to accept the howling. They knew they were safe in the house with us—and the leftover roast beef.

"It sounds like it's right outside," Brent said.

I couldn't help glancing out the window. All I saw, of course, were our reflections, sitting companionably around the table.

"They're close enough," I said. "This is the first year there've been so many. One of them is particularly large and bold. He almost kept me from getting out of my car one evening."

"That sounds like a cross between a wolf and a coyote," Brent said. "Coywolves, they call them. I wish someone would come up with a better name."

"I don't understand about those crosses. We have plenty of coyotes around here, but what about wolves? They're not in the lower peninsula, are they?"

"Not as a rule," he said. "There may be some."

"Then you wouldn't think there'd be much mating going on."

"All it takes is one," Crane pointed out.

"Don't you mean two?"

"One wolf."

"Most of the ones I've seen are small and scrawny," Brent said.

I rose, blew out the candles, and began collecting plates. "We can have our pie in the living room."

"Want some help, honey?" Crane asked.

"I have it covered."

In the kitchen I fed the collies, spreading toppings of beef over their kibble, and almost took Raven's dish out to her when I realized she was in the house with us. I stacked the plates, cut the pie, and rejoined the men who were discussing the Cranbrook case which they both thought would end badly.

I feared it had already ended.

Coffee and pie in front of a cozy fire in the Victorian farmhouse I'd fallen in love with at first sight. Not everyone was so fortunate. I spared a thought for Jillian Cranbrook, hoping that some miracle would bring her home.

Brent seemed relaxed and in a hearty good humor, more like the Brent of old. I hoped he would go straight home when he left our house and not stop at the pink Victorian. There would be no reason for him to go there at this hour. No reason that made sense.

In all, it was a pleasant evening, and at its end, Brent issued an invitation of his own for dinner at the Hunt Club Inn on Saturday.

"Not that their food is better than Jennet's," he added. "But she won't have to cook that night."

"I'm right here," I reminded him. "You can tell me."

Accompanied by all the collies, Crane walked Brent to the door and turned on the outside light.

When he came back, I'd have a chance to ask Crane about his coffee break with Veronica.

"I guess I'd better take the girls out for the night," he said.

Hearing that, they rushed to his side.

While they were outside, I cleaned the kitchen and rehearsed what I'd say to him. In the end I had three versions, none of which made me sound like a jealous wife.

But when he came back, when the dogs gathered around their water bowl, and I turned to him, he took me in his arms and kissed me. He always seemed more romantic after one of Brent's visits. Why, I wondered, was that?

No matter. Only a fool would break that mood with a question about another woman. So I didn't say anything.

I could always bring up the subject of that blasted female deputy another time. Maybe. Maybe not. In all probability, their encounter was an innocent coffee-and-doughnuts interlude between fellow deputies.

That was what I told myself.

~ * ~

I was eager to know what had transpired at the Busy Bea Craft Shoppe. Had the girls contacted Trista's breeder, and had she identified Melody as Trista? Jennifer and Molly had searched so diligently for the missing collie. I wanted them to have their reward money, and I wanted Trista returned to her rightful owner. If the collie at the Busy Bea was Trista, that is. I was ninety-five percent sure she was.

But I didn't hear from the girls and didn't run into them while walking with the dogs on Sagramore Lake Road. I resigned myself to wait. There was nothing in the *Banner* about Trista's return and hardly anything about Jillian Cranbrook. Her family was still hopeful, even though they were given no reason to hope. They wore yellow ribbons and held a candlelight vigil for Jillian on Squill Lane.

All the ribbons and candles in the world wouldn't help.

In the meantime, snow fell, turning Jonquil Lane into a winter wonderland and the freeway into a skating rink. It piled up in all the county's dark and secret places, quite possibly burying a body deeper with each passing day.

Of course no one said that.

Life went on. It always does. And the coyotes continued to howl.

I looked forward to Saturday night and dinner at the Hunt Club Inn. I had a new black dress with a square neckline that would show off my sparkly rhinestone necklace. It would be heaven not to have to think about school or time travel or the miscellaneous travails that befell other people.

On Thursday, after a meeting of the English Department, Leonora and I stopped at Clovers for take-out dinners. Annica was there. Even though she was waiting on a table toward the back of the restaurant, I could tell she wasn't her usual easy-going self. There was something in her forbidding body language, and in the frantic tinkling of her silver bell earrings when she moved her head.

We decided on beef stew and rice. As Annica prepared our orders, I said, "Is anything wrong?"

"It's the snow," she said. "I've had enough of it."

"It isn't even officially winter yet," Leonora pointed out.

"Tell that to the weatherman."

"Better still, tell it to Mother Nature," I said.

"That isn't funny, Jennet."

She rang up our orders and poured three cups of coffee, one for herself. "I'll take my break now," she said.

"What else is bothering you?" I asked.

"Kids," she said as she led us to my favorite booth with a woodland view. "People who take their little angels out to dinner and let them scream and run all around disturbing everyone."

"That is annoying, especially for other diners."

I scanned the restaurant but didn't see any misbehaving children. The crowd seemed unusually sedate, enjoying their meals, talking quietly.

"Anything else?" Leonora asked.

"Men," she said. "They're useless."

Leonora stifled a laugh. "Sometimes. Not always."

The silver bells rang in agreement as Annica shook her head. "I've reached the end of the rope. I'm going back to my Victorian novels. I'd rather spend my days with Heathcliff or Mr. Rochester."

"I've often had the same thought about Jake," Leonora said. "Do we really need men in the world?"

"The Amazons didn't."

"But weren't they myths?" Leonora asked.

I thought of Crane. "The right man can add a certain zest to life."

Annica stirred sugar into her coffee with a vengeance.

"Are you going to tell us what's really wrong?" I asked. "It might help to talk about it."

She lowered her voice. "I was stood up. Me. That doesn't happen to me."

"Who's the guilty party?" Leonora asked.

"Brent. I invited him to dinner. I went all out. Well, I *did* bring a few dishes from Clovers. My mom went over to my aunt's so we could have privacy. Then he never showed up. He didn't even call."

"That doesn't sound like Brent," I said.

Annica wasn't finished. "After all I did for him. I thought he liked me. All that time I wasted helping him decorate his house. I could have been studying."

Her voice broke. She stopped talking and took a sip of coffee. I'd never seen her so emotional.

"Like I said," she repeated. "Men. Who needs them?"

Twenty-six

While we were in the restaurant, it had started to snow again. I turned the car's heater on its highest setting, and we both brushed the windows clean.

"Annica didn't mean it," I said as we pulled out of the parking lot. "She's crazy about Brent."

"That wasn't nice, him not showing up to dinner when he accepted her invitation."

"No, but he must have had a good excuse."

What that excuse was I couldn't imagine. But I knew Brent cared for Annica. He would never hurt her deliberately.

"A man did that to me once," Leonora said. "The next time I saw him, we were at a party. He called me Lorna. The rat couldn't even remember my name. I guess my dinner invitation was a bit premature."

"This happened yesterday," I said. "Maybe Brent will call her today."

The condition of the country roads claimed all my attention. This day had seemed never ending. My classes had been civilized, more or less, but the English meeting had dragged on. Then to add more stress to my life, the freeway was busy and slippery. At this point my energies were at their lowest ebb.

I was glad I had our dinner in the trunk. I'd make rolls and a salad, and we had leftover apple pie. I hadn't brought any school work home. It should be a pleasant evening.

As it turned out, it was lovely and restful. I didn't think about Brent again until the next day. Usually if we had plans, he called to confirm them. When I didn't hear from him, I began to wonder if I'd misunderstood the date.

"Brent *did* say this Saturday, didn't he?" I asked Crane.

"Right. At the Hunt Club Inn."

Recalling Annica's experience, I wondered if Crane and I would be the next ones to be stood up.

"I'm going to call him," I said. "Just to be sure."

I tapped in his number. When it went straight to voice mail, I left a message.

"No answer?" Crane said.

"He must be out and about."

But the hour grew late, and finally, it was time for bed. When Brent didn't return my call, I started to worry.

"Fowler can take care of himself," Crane assured me. "You know that."

"In most cases," I said.

But not if he strayed into that twist on Huron Court, the one that flung an unsuspecting traveler into another time.

Not if the house on Huron Court had him in its clutches.

As we might not be dining at the Hunt Club Inn tomorrow night, I began to plan a substitute dinner. We had plenty of roast beef and gravy left and half a pie. I'd make hot sandwiches and mashed potatoes. That prosaic meal happened to be one of my favorites.

I could still dazzle Crane with my new black dress and sparkly necklace. I'd take his mind off a pretty woman in a deputy sheriff's uniform which, incidentally, looked much better on Crane than it did on her.

That's right, I scolded myself. *Think about fashion and food and another woman when Brent may be in trouble.*

There. I'd said it. Rather, thought it. Brent would never fail to show up for an engagement he had initiated unless he was prevented from doing so.

"Something is wrong," I said.

As if to reinforce my statement, Misty appeared at my side and stared at me. Her eyes were dark and soulful, and she didn't look happy.

Yes, wrong, she might have said. *Help him.*

Crane looked up from the *Banner.*

"It's that horrible house," I said. "Something happened to Brent."

"Don't borrow trouble," Crane said. "He's probably involved in something with the Hunt. Maybe he met a new girl."

And forgot about Annica and his good friends?

I shook my head. "You don't know Brent at all."

He folded the paper slowly. "I'll check on him tomorrow, honey. Don't worry. It's probably nothing. We'll all laugh about it at dinner."

I couldn't see that happening.

"I'll leave it to you, then. How would you like hot beef sandwiches on Saturday night?"

"That'll be fine," he said, "but let's see what tomorrow brings."

~ * ~

Saturday morning came and still there was no word from Brent. I did the week's grocery shopping in a series of snow squalls and stopped at Dark Gables, needing to share my growing concern with Lucy.

A gust of wind blew her long black skirt around her legs as she stood in the doorway with a subdued Sky at her side.

"This is about Brent," she said.

"How did you know?"

"I had one of my premonitions. Come in out of the cold."

I gave Sky a 'hello' pat as I stepped inside.

"Brent is in trouble," Lucy said. "I can't reach him on his cell. I can't reach him in any other way either. I've been trying."

I didn't ask her to explain. "Neither can I. We had dinner plans tonight with him."

"That's not going to happen," she said. "Come back to the sun room. I only wish I could offer you sunlight."

"I'll settle for a cup of tea," I said.

I made myself comfortable in the wicker sofa next to Sky while Lucy put the kettle on with a jangling of her many bracelets that was louder than it should be in the quiet house.

The view through the French doors was breathtakingly beautiful and at the same time chilling. Snow-draped woods seemed to hold secrets. Nearer to the house, Lucy's fountain, stilled and silenced for the season, appeared to have a secret of its own. From out of the woods came a mournful howl.

"The coyotes have been vocal lately," Lucy said. "It's like they know something we don't."

I hoped that wasn't so.

She wrapped an ivory crocheted scarf over her shoulders, although the temperature in the house was comfortable enough, for me anyway.

"Brent is in trouble," Lucy said again. "But the circumstances are vague. I sense loss and confusion and fear. Wherever he is, it's dark and cold. So cold..."

"He was supposed to have dinner with Annica at her house yesterday," I said. "She thinks he stood her up."

"He wasn't able to keep that commitment."

"The house did something to him," I said. "I know it."

"It's possible. We all tried to warn him, but he refused to listen to us. He had to have his haunted inn. What could we do?"

The teakettle whistled.

I said, "The question now is, what can we do to help him?"

Lucy sighed. "I don't know, Jennet. Nothing, I'm afraid."

~ * ~

There had to be something.

My teacup readily revealed its secrets. A pattern suggested turmoil in my home with the initial 'V' at the center.

I'd never told Lucy about the new female deputy sheriff in Foxglove Corners. Somehow she knew. The teacup knew.

But it didn't know anything about Brent.

"Crane is going to try to track him down," I said.

Lucy set my teacup back on the wicker coffee table. "He won't be able to."

"He's going to stop at Brent's barn and the pink Victorian, probably his house on Wolf Lake Road, too."

"Brent isn't in any of those places. I can say that for certain."

"Can't you do something, Lucy?" I asked.

"Whip up a spell?"

"Something."

"Whatever powers I have don't work that way," she said.

I knew that, but after talking to Lucy, I was even more concerned about Brent's safety than I'd been before. Who knew what Brent was going through while we sat around and talked about it?

"When I was missing last month, Mac Dalby found my car and the remains of the deer I'd crashed into," I said.

Lucy nodded. "And they said you were in the hospital with a concussion and other injuries."

This led to an ominous thought. After Jillian Cranbrook had failed to arrive at her destination on Thanksgiving, searchers found her car on Squill Lane in perfect condition. There couldn't possibly be a connection. Could there?

Unlikely. Jillian was a young woman stranded in a snowstorm. Like Crane, Brent was strong and resourceful. I'd say almost undefeatable.

So, lose that idea. Where was he, then?

Twenty-seven

The only clue to Brent's whereabouts was the car, his prized vintage Plymouth Belvedere.

"It's parked in front of the house," Crane said later that day. "There's about a half foot of snow on it."

"You found him then. Thank heavens."

I gave the gravy a stir and glanced at the plate of sliced beef on the counter. It was still there. So was Candy, her eyes fixed on the bounty so heartbreakingly out of her reach.

"Not him," Crane said. "Just the car. When I knocked, he didn't come to the door. I don't have a key, but it turns out it was unlocked."

That was something else Brent would never do, leave the house open to invasion from burglars and vagrants. Especially after the mirror incident.

"I looked all around inside," Crane said. "Searched the whole place. I found an empty bag in the living room from the Lakeside Diner. Also a can of root beer, half full."

"So he was there. Or someone was."

"It was Brent. I saw that dark green leather jacket he wears tossed over a chair."

Lucy's words drifted back to me. "Wherever he is, it's dark and cold. So cold."

"He went back in time," I said.

"Or forward."

"No, back, I think. Violet Randall called him."

"Violet's dead and buried," Crane reminded me. "You thought she was a ghost."

"She was alive back then. Back in time."

Perhaps I was making too many assumptions. If Brent had been whisked back to the past, he wouldn't necessarily be in the year I'd visited or even in the same place.

"Then I stopped at his house and his barn," Crane went on. "The house is locked, and he hasn't been at the barn in three days. That isn't unusual. He leaves a young man, Ben, in charge."

"Can we report him missing?" I asked. "It's been forty-eight hours since he's been gone."

"I did."

"He must have stopped at the pink Victorian on the way home," I said. "That was a fateful decision. And he never made it home."

"I don't think so, Jennet. He'd just had dinner with us. Why would he have a bag from the diner and a root beer?"

"Okay," I said. "He went to the house the next day."

I stepped away from the stove and began tossing a salad. If only Brent would be at the door, arriving unexpected at the dinner hour with a bottle of wine or a bouquet of flowers. If only his prized Plymouth were parked in front our house.

"Mac doesn't know about the house or time slips or any of that," Crane said. "All he knows is that last month you had an accident on Huron Court, killed a deer, and landed in the hospital."

"Shouldn't you tell him?" I asked.

"What difference would it make? Mac isn't the Time Police. Besides, he wouldn't believe me."

"I never thought this would happen, not in a million years. Not to Brent, of all people. Can't we do something?

I hoped Crane would have a better answer than Lucy. Ironically he repeated her sentiment, only in different words.

"I can't think of anything, honey, other than to keep looking."

~ * ~

Life went on in Foxglove Corners. The coyotes continued to wake me with their incessant howling. No one came forward with information about Jillian Cranbrook's disappearance. In a surprising twist, the tricolor collie no longer spent her days in the Busy Bea.

I met Jennifer and Molly while walking Misty, Halley, and Sky on Sagramore Lake Road. As we were all bundled up against snowy wind gusts, the conversation was short and shouted.

Molly said, "Trista's breeder, Mrs. West, went to the shop. Beatrice said she didn't have a dog. She was just babysitting a collie for a friend."

"That's the third version of the story she's told. I'm more convinced than ever that the dog she called Melody is Trista."

"It doesn't look like we'll be getting that reward," Molly said.

"Don't give up. Didn't you girls want to be detectives?"

"But what can we do now that Trista isn't there?" Jennifer asked.

"Did Beatrice mention the friend's name?"

"She just said a friend."

"You need to talk to this friend. That's your first step. If she exists."

It was possible that Beatrice simply kept the collie out of sight, probably at home. Now that I thought about it, she'd taken a risk by bringing Trista to the Busy Bea. People would admire the beautiful collie and remember the one who had gone missing. Someone would be sure to remember Trista's star shaped mark.

"I don't see how we can do that," Molly said.

"Let's see. You bought a Christmas stocking kit for Ginger. Develop an interest in crafts. Christmas is coming. You can buy presents for your moms or aunts at the shop. That'll get you in the door."

"Then what?"

"Make friends with Beatrice. Ask for help. Ask questions. Look for clues."

"Like a dog's dish with a name engraved on it?" asked Molly.

"She wouldn't leave something like that in the shop," Jennifer said.

The girls looked baffled. I didn't know what sort of clue to suggest they search for.

"I guess we can try," Molly said.

"That's the spirit. Good luck."

To the dogs' disappointment, we went our separate ways. Their reunion had just begun. Unknown to them, I'd decided to cut the walk short. The wind had a sharp bite, and the snow that hit my face felt more like hail.

I was glad the girls were looking into the mystery of Trista. It sounded like a particularly baffling one. In any event, I had enough on my plate worrying about Brent.

~ * ~

Realizing that Annica didn't know about Brent, I stopped at Clovers to tell her about our suspicions. She took a break, and we sat at the booth with cups of steaming coffee and the view of the Crispian Road woods.

"Brent is now officially a missing person," I said.

"He didn't stand me up, then?"

"Not deliberately."

"That's good then, but where is he? Men like Brent Fowler don't go missing." The color seemed to drain from her face in an instant. Her voice trembled as she said, "You don't suppose he's dead, do you?"

That thought had never occurred to me.

"No, but he might be somewhere else. On a different plane."

"You mean he might have had one of those time slips?"

"It's possible."

"That isn't good. He'd never abandon that car, would he? And he wouldn't leave the house without his jacket unless he had no choice."

She appeared to be on the verge of tears. I longed to find words to comfort her, but I felt like crying myself.

I tried to create a possible scenario. Brent had been inside the house when he'd slipped out of his own time. He hadn't had a chance to dress for cold, snowy weather. I didn't know whether he had landed in December or in a different season. Whether he had stayed in the house or been flung outside onto Huron Court.

I didn't know anything for certain, and my speculations were disheartening.

I remembered what Lucy had said. Wherever he was, it was dark and cold.

Where did you go, Brent?

"We have to help him," Annica said. "What can we do?"

No one, not even Lucy, could answer that question.

"Wait," I said. "And hope."

"Maybe there's a clue in that old house."

"Besides the drink and his jacket?"

"There could be."

"Well, I can't go near the place. I don't want Crane to spend any time there either. What if he disappeared, too?"

"Nothing in life is certain, is it?" Annica said. "It can all end at any time without warning, between one breath and the next."

"That was always true, even without those crazy time slips."

Annica dabbed at her eyes with a napkin. "I… That is, we… We can't lose him, Jennet. He's such a good man. Who'll drive his sleigh through Foxglove Corners with presents for the kids this Christmas?"

"Let's hope he'll be back by then."

"Let's do better than that," she said. "We can pray."

Twenty-eight

I was busy at school and more often than not harassed by my students, especially in my fourth period American Lit class. I didn't mind as much as I would have before Brent's disappearance. Sparring with smart alecks kept my mind off Brent and Huron Court and the vagaries of the pink Victorian. At least temporarily.

In the occasional quiet moment, thoughts and fears would come flooding back. During lunch, for example, when Leonora and I were alone in our part of the building.

For once I had an appealing sandwich, ham and Swiss cheese on rye bread, and Leonora had brought brownies for our dessert.

"Did you hear the latest in the Cranbrook case?" she asked. "It was in yesterday's *Banner*. Just a short article."

I hadn't looked at the paper in two days.

"What happened?" I asked.

"The police arrested an elderly vagrant, Kevin Clancy. He's been camping out in the abandoned construction."

Which was too near our home for comfort. Once again I was thankful for our guardian collie, Raven, who lived outside.

"His name sounds familiar," I said. "Didn't they question him at the time?

"They did but couldn't hold him. Now they found something that belonged to Jillian Cranwell in his possession."

"What was it?"

"They aren't saying. They refer to it as an object. Clancy claims he found it on Squill Lane."

"Clancy. I know I've heard that name before," I said. "But where?"

"That's no mystery. You probably read it in the paper. He was a person of interest in the early days of the investigation."

I frowned. That name was associated with another memory, but my mind refused to yield up any more information at the moment.

Let it go, I thought. *For now.*

I glanced at the clock. I had ten minutes to finish half a sandwich and a brownie. It seemed as if I'd only taken the first bite.

I said, "If this vagrant killed Jillian, what was his motive?"

"Who knows? Not money. Remember her purse was in the car. A thief would have taken it."

"What then?"

"That's what they have to find out."

"I wish I knew what that object was," I said. "Something she had on her person? Like a watch?"

"Maybe Crane can tell you," she said.

"I can ask him, but..."

He rarely discussed police matters or sheriff's business with me. He had made one exception. I knew that Lieutenant Dalby had conducted a search of the house on Huron Court and taken possession of Brent's green leather jacket and the remains of his snack from the Lakeside Diner. He'd also found a small black notebook with Brent's name on the first page, evidence Crane had overlooked.

"It was a record of furniture he purchased for each room," Crane had said. "No prices. Just lists."

"How will that help find him?"

"Mac talked to Annica. She said Brent always carried that notebook with him. It's proof that he was at the house."

"But we knew that already."

"It's additional proof," he'd said.

The memory of that conversation brought Brent and his plight rushing home to me. The investigation was proceeding at a snail's pace, and this latest discovery seemed irrelevant.

"Brent has been gone for four days," I told Leonora.

She handed me a brownie, mopping up the spill of powdered sugar on the table with a napkin. "Do you still think he experienced one of those time slips?"

"I'm almost certain of it," I said. "I keep seeing him wandering on Huron Court, trying to reach Sagramore Lake and running into that weird barrier that sends people in the opposite direction."

"That's what it was like for you."

She broke her brownie in two as the bell shrilled an end to our quiet time. I sighed. Our twenty-minute lunch period was never long enough. The teachers never stopped complaining about it, and it never changed. I'd have to eat my brownie during my conference hour.

"Brent will come back," Leonora said. "He'll find the way. After all, you did. Hold on to that thought."

"I will," I said. "But what if it doesn't work that way?"

~ * ~

The coyotes of Foxglove Corners were a wily lot. Camille and Gilbert had hired an exterminator who had set his traps in the nearby woods and collected what I considered an exorbitant fee. To date not one animal had been caught. Crane and I decided to suspend our search for a humane trapping company.

"One trapper on the lane is enough," Crane said, "and he doesn't seem to be having any luck."

I should be used to their yips and howls, as I'd grown used to the wail of the wind over time. But, too often in the night, I woke to the call of the pack. Sometimes I was grateful to them for cutting a nightmare short. Since Brent had vanished, I'd had the same unnerving dream with variations on different nights.

I dreamed of Huron Court. At first I was watching Brent stumble along the misty country road. Then I was the traveler going forward, being inexplicably turned around to retrace my steps, never reaching Sagramore Lake, although I could see a glimmer of blue lake water in the distance.

In the light of many a morning, I attempted to understand it. Brent's experience had brought my own back to me, and it seemed as fresh and real as if it had happened only yesterday.

Often lying in bed, trying to go back to sleep, I remembered something Lucy had said in passing— that the howling coyotes might know something we didn't. As if the pesky varmints were unearthly creatures.

She often talked like that with chilling allusions to the unknown. The coyotes had been filling the night with their infernal racket long before Brent's misstep.

Misstep. Yes. That was it. He had stepped out of time into the past.

A soft whimper insinuated its way into my wandering thoughts. Misty had left her place in the doorway. I felt her breath on my arm, then her paw.

"Do you have to go out?" I whispered.

Silence.

"Then lie down. Go back to sleep."

She listened to me, scrunching the rag rug beside the bed before settling down on it.

Sometimes— all right, I was no different from Lucy— I wondered if Misty could read my thoughts and had come to comfort me.

Uncanny, perhaps, but Misty was, after all, a collie, and we'd shared what I'd come to think of as 'the experience.'

Yes, Misty could read my disquietude.

~ * ~

I didn't like walking the dogs when it was cold and blustery. I did, of course. Providing exercise in all kinds of weather was an integral part of dog ownership, a chore Crane and I shared.

Ever mindful of the coyotes, I never just opened the side door and let them roam at will, although I knew they'd stay close to the house.

All except Candy. And Raven. And Misty. They were my rovers.

After school the next day, I wrapped a scarf around my mouth and plowed up the snow-covered lane, into the wind, with Halley, Sky, and Gemmy, the easy ones. Even though I knew the vagrant Clancy was in custody, the abandoned construction was still a frightful place to me, a place to hurry past without a single curious glance.

No matter what mysterious sounds emanated from its depths.

The dogs found the area enchanting. Most likely the scent of coyote hung heavily on the encroaching vegetation and crumbling walls.

"Hurry," I said, quickening my pace. "Heel."

I almost slipped on an icy patch of gravel.

Something glittered on the snow at the edge of the woods that lined the lane. Something green. I bent to retrieve a thin bracelet of green stones held together with scrolls of gold.

The gems looked real, like emeralds. The owner must be devastated to have lost it. Perhaps I could find her and return it.

I slipped it into my pocket. As I did, I recalled the conversation I'd had with Leonora at lunch about the unnamed object found in the possession of the vagrant Clancy.

Could this be another one of Jillian Cranbrook's belongings? If so, it was evidence, and I had to turn it over to the police as soon as possible.

I did what I swore I'd never do—looked at the abandoned construction, wondering what secrets it held.

The emerald bracelet might be one of many possessions that would lead to the solution of the Cranbrook case. I had one question, though. No casual driver would have seen the sparkle of green and gold in the snow, but supposedly the police searched the woods thoroughly.

Why hadn't they spotted it?

Twenty-nine

Through a veil of falling snow, an unfamiliar car pulled up in the driveway. It was as blue as a summer sky and sleek in design, obviously vintage, although about a decade younger than Brent's Plymouth Belvedere. I'd guess it was another Plymouth, possibly a Duster.

The collies were already storming the door, and Raven dashed out from her house, tail wagging madly.

Brent flung open the car door and allowed Raven to jump on him, unmindful of his brown suede jacket.

It was a scene I was afraid I'd never see again. For a moment I wondered if I was imagining it, believing what I'd so ardently wished for.

Brent wasn't dead. He didn't appear to be hurt. He was real.

Raven escorted him to the porch while I stood at the bay window spellbound.

How? When? And why hadn't I'd known he'd returned?

There was only one way to find out.

I opened the door and flung myself into his arms, along with a pack of yelping, tail wagging collies. Snow flew in every direction.

"This is what I call a real welcome," he said.

"Come in. Don't mind the snow."

Sky and Misty especially were wild with excitement. I took Brent's jacket. Studying his face as he roughhoused with the dogs, I detected a subtle difference, an absence of the 'Lord of the Manor' spark which he invariably presented to the world.

Absurdly I felt like crying, now that Brent had resurfaced.

I pointed to the rocker, where Sky waited demurely for him. "Have a seat. I'll get you a cup of coffee and you can tell me everything. What happened to you? Where have you been? How long have you been back?"

"Whoa! One question at a time. As to what happened, I wish I could tell you. I don't know."

Mulling over that strange utterance, I poured two cups of coffee and joined him in the living room. Misty had already claimed her place on his lap.

"How can you not know?" I asked. "You've been gone for five days."

"That long?"

"That long. Crane reported you missing. The police are looking for you. Mac had your Belvedere towed."

"So that's what happened. I thought it was stolen."

"You'll have to check with Mac. Where did you get the Duster?"

"It's mine," he said. "I bought it last month."

"I'm lost. Start at the beginning."

"That's the trouble. I don't know where the beginning is. All I remember is walking down one of those country roads without a name."

"Huron Court?"

"No, another one. I think. I was freezing. Luckily an old farmer picked me up and drove me home. I had a feeling that I was supposed to be here, at your house. That I was late."

"That was last Saturday night," I said. "You were taking us out to dinner."

"I had my house key and my wallet— everything but my jacket. So I got the Duster out of the garage and drove right here."

"The police have been looking for you," I repeated.

"I don't know what to tell them. Where I was. How I got there. How I got back. Nothing. I'm so hungry," he added. "I grabbed a few slices of bread from the freezer and let them thaw."

"I'll make you a sandwich."

He spilled Misty out of his lap to her chagrin and followed me into the kitchen where I assembled a turkey and Swiss cheese sandwich for him and found an unopened package of potato chips.

"You went back in time," I said. "Back to the past."

"What? No. I'd remember that. As far as I can tell, I had a blackout."

"You couldn't have been wandering around on country roads all that time," I said. "Someone would have seen you. Especially since they're looking for you."

"What can I say? I don't remember."

Between gulps of coffee, he had wolfed down his sandwich. It seemed as if he hadn't eaten for five days. Could that be true? He didn't look as if he had lost weight. Quickly I made him another sandwich while Candy waited patiently for a slice of turkey or cheese to come her way.

"You were in the pink Victorian," I said.

"I don't remember that."

"That's where the Belvedere was parked. Your jacket was inside, along with your black notebook."

He frowned. "I have no memory of that, but if the car was there, it must be true."

"I'm going to text Crane," I said, while he began demolishing his second sandwich. "He'll be home soon but I don't want to wait. We'll notify Mac that you're returned, and oh... You should go to Emergency."

"Naah," he said. "I feel fine. All I needed was food."

"It won't hurt to have a doctor check you over," I said. "You can't have been outside that long. You must have found shelter somewhere."

He rubbed his forehead. "I wish I could remember. Nothing like this has ever happened to me before. I'm as healthy as a horse. Just hungry."

"There's always a first time," I said. "What's your last memory?"

"Having dinner here with you and Crane."

"At some point after that night, you must have been driving on Huron Court or stopped at that accursed house."

"I guess so, but if I traveled to the past, you'd think I'd remember what life was like back then, what year it was. You'd think I'd have come across Violet, but it's all a blank screen. You can see why I'd rather not talk to the police."

"Yes, but you have to. You have to let them know you're no longer missing."

"Is there any more turkey?" he asked.

"A little. You can have it."

He glanced at the stove. "What's cooking in that pot?"

"A nice beef stew. You can have some when it's ready."

I refilled his coffee cup. As for my own, it was full. I'd been so engrossed in Brent's tale, I'd forgotten about it. As unusual as his disappearance had been, this reappearance was even stranger.

He divided the last bit of sandwich between Candy and Misty. Not wanting to slight the other dogs, I spread a generous serving of Camille's homemade biscuits on the floor for them.

When I looked up, I noticed a change in Brent. That devilish spark that had been buried under the confusion and angst was back.

"Did anyone miss me?" he asked.

"Oh, yes…"

Lucy! Annica! They had to know Brent was back and I assumed unharmed. Quickly I sent two more text messages, one to Annica, one to Lucy.

Answers flew back. From Lucy, "Thank God," and from Annica "Yes!"

~ * ~

Crane was incredulous, repeating questions I'd already asked Brent.

"You've been gone five days, Fowler. Where the devil were you?"

To which question, Brent gave his anticipated reply. "I have no idea."

"He wasn't in this time," I said. "Wherever— no, make that *whenever*— he was, it couldn't have been this cold, or he'd be in worst shape."

A change of seasons seemed to be a feature of time travel. During my brief foray into the past, I'd been thrust back into the early part of the season when autumn color was at its peak.

"I'm in good shape," Brent pointed out. "Still hungry, though."

"We'll all have some good beef stew in about fifteen minutes," I said. "While we're waiting, let's recreate the scene, using the facts we know. You drove up to the pink Victorian with takeout from the Lakeside Diner."

"A burger and a drink," he said. "Funny. It's coming back."

Encouraged, I continued. "You got out of the car, went into the house, and turned the heat up in the house."

"Yeah, I leave it on fifty-eight when I'm gone," he said.

Good. It was working, but my scenario was fragile, made of air and supposition. At any moment, it could shatter.

Crane was listening intently, but I couldn't tell from his expression what his thoughts were.

"You took off your jacket and tossed it over a chair, ate your burger, and pulled your notebook out of your pocket."

"That's right," he said. "I want to buy another lamp for the living room. Annica found one she thought would work at the Green House of Antiques."

"Did you go to the Green House?

"No, that was part of the next day's plan."

"So you left the notebook in the kitchen where Mac would later find it."

"I wanted a drink of water," he said.

"You took one of the new glasses down from the cupboard and turned on the tap."

Water running. Tepid at first. Then cold enough to drink. It was as if I were there watching him.

"That's what happened," he said, "but I don't remember if I had my drink. That's where memory stops," he said. "It's like the lights went out. Then they came on again. I was walking down that country road. I saw a rusty old truck behind me and flagged it down."

"Unbelievable," Crane said.

I frowned at him. "No, Crane. Just the opposite."

Brent was the first one to believe my fantastic tale after I woke up in the hospital. I owed it to him to have unconditional faith in his story. What little there was of it.

"We have to take Brent to the hospital, Crane. Just to make sure he's okay."

"Not until we eat," Brent said.

Ah, yes. He was back indeed.

Thirty

The next day over salad and pizza, we continued our discussion of Brent's otherworldly experience. I had asked Annica to join us, but she was working at Clovers and afterward had to rush to her class.

The Emergency Room doctors had subjected Brent to a battery of tests and found that he was in good condition with no apparent reason for his blackout. They believed that in time every lost memory should come back to him. Five days' and nights' worth of memories. I wasn't a medical expert, but I doubted it, as this was no ordinary blackout.

"It's wonderful being together like this," Lucy said as I served the pizza. "For a while I was afraid this day would never come."

"It's all in the past," I said. "No pun intended."

With a blazing fire and a roomful of playful collies, we could ignore the blustery weather outside. Brent was the life of the party. Fully recovered, he masked his angst with his characteristic show of bonhomie.

He had brought home with him a seemingly insatiable hunger.

"I can't get enough to eat," he said. "It's like I didn't eat for those five days."

We had established that Brent's last memory was standing at the kitchen sink in the pink Victorian filling a glass with water.

"I remember being so thirsty," he said, "but I don't remember drinking. I went straight from the kitchen to that country road. The first sound I heard was an engine behind me. It was like coming out of the anesthesia after surgery. One second, they're wheeling you through the door. The next, someone says, 'It's over'."

"You must have turned off the faucet," Crane pointed out. "Otherwise you'd have flooded the house."

"I guess I did."

Five days of darkness. In the interim, Brent could have been anywhere— the past, the present, or the future. Or? It was frustrating for all of us not to know. But Brent was with us again. That was all that mattered.

He had already demolished one slice of pizza and was halfway through his second. I was glad I'd had the foresight to triple our usual order.

Brent was eager to return to the pink Victorian as soon as possible.

"I don't think you should, Brent," Lucy said. "You had a narrow escape. Don't tempt fate. The next time you might not find your back to us."

Brent had a stubborn streak, though, and wouldn't be persuaded. "I have to get to the bottom of it. We still don't understand what's going on there."

"Nothing good, I'm sure."

"It would be different if I'd been looking through that crazy mirror," he said. "All I did was pour a glass of water and whoosh! The lights went out. I disappeared."

"There wouldn't be anything supernatural about a glass," I said.

"No, they were ordinary acrylic glasses. Annica bought them at Macy's on sale. Leftover summer stock."

"Maybe the glass wasn't the trigger."

"What was then?"

"I don't know, but remember Violet's diary? She was sitting in a chair, doing her mending, when suddenly she was thrust forward in time."

"It would be nice if we'd have a warning," Brent said.

"Oh?" Lucy leaned forward in her chair. "How would you prepare yourself for a time trip?"

"I'd have taken my phone, for one."

"You could have taken pictures of the past," I said. "Don't you carry your phone with you?"

"It was in the car."

"The next time you get a hankering to visit that house, make sure someone goes with you," Crane said. "Anyone but Jennet."

"I'll do that. Nothing happened all those times when Annica was with me."

"Take her then and you should be safe. Or take Lucy."

"Not on your life," Lucy said. "I'd do almost anything for you, Brent, but I know enough not to flirt with evil incarnate."

"I have to solve the mystery," Brent said.

"Why?" I asked.

"Because if I don't, I'll always wonder about it. And what if I never remember what happened?"

I sympathized with that. In his place I'd have felt the same way. Still there was a time to exercise caution.

"You might end up in another dimension," I said. "Years from now, if the house is still standing, people will be talking about the red-haired fox hunter who disappeared within its walls. You wanted a haunted inn. You'll be the ghost."

"I won't go right away," he said. "I have things to do. There's a new horse at the barn. I have to buy Christmas presents for the kids, and I want to make it up to Annica for not showing up at her dinner."

"That should keep you busy."

We stayed together, talking and exchanging time travel theories until every leaf of lettuce in the large salad I'd made was gone and the dogs had gobbled the last of the pizza crust. Lucy declared she was exhausted, and Brent rose to drive her home in the yellow Belvedere, which he'd ransomed from the police.

I was sorry to see the evening end. Throughout the visit, I'd felt as if nothing could touch us, but when the blasted coyotes began their dark serenade, when Lucy seemed to shudder, a stray, unwelcome thought dropped into my mind.

A night like this was one to cherish. We would never be exactly like this again.

~ * ~

Like Brent, I had matters to attend to. I'd given the emerald bracelet to Crane to turn over to Mac. From Mac, Crane had learned that Jillian Cranbrook had been wearing an emerald bracelet when she disappeared. It was her favorite piece of jewelry, a birthday gift from her mother.

I was eager to learn if the discovery would aid in solving the mystery. Later, I was surprised to find an update on the case in the *Banner* that included a reference to the bracelet, without the name of the person who had found it. Lucky for them. I thought the police would want to keep 'the emerald clue' as the reporter referred to it, a secret.

Perhaps they had their reasons for publicizing it.

Now that Brent had been found, although strictly speaking he hadn't been lost, maybe Jillian would come home, too.

Not for the first time I wondered if she had disappeared into the past.

Leaving her bracelet in the snow?

Squill Lane was nowhere near Huron Court or Brandymere, Foxglove Corners' other 'Twilight Zone' thoroughfare. Also, Clancy, the vagrant, had an object belonging to Jillian in his possession. The two cases were worlds apart.

I had to admit, that in spite of my resolve to give the pink Victorian the widest berth possible, I shared Brent's desire to solve its mysteries. His memory loss was only one more hurdle to overcome, and perhaps it was temporary.

Sometimes I wondered why our two experiences had been so different. I'd give anything to know.

Don't even think about it.

I couldn't investigate that mystery without risking my life and everything I loved. I'd simply have to make peace with unsatisfied curiosity.

~ * ~

The very cold case of Violet Randall's disappearance and murder was a different story. All the research in the world couldn't hurt me. Unfortunately, the case seemed to be unsolvable. Any clues had long since vanished with the years, assuming they had existed in the first place.

I'd hoped to add to my knowledge about Violet and the time twist when Brent returned and had never anticipated his memory loss. I'd even hoped to encounter Edwina Endicott, self-proclaimed ghost hunter, on one of my visits to the library, but we were never there at the same time.

In school I concentrated on finishing my units and writing tests. Christmas recess was rapidly approaching. After our return in January, the first semester was virtually over.

In Foxglove Corners, snow continued to fall off and on, making a white Christmas a certainty. In the quiet of the night, the coyotes howled, and in the midst of a long spell of boring sameness, I had a strange feeling which must be akin to Lucy's premonitions. Something was about to change.

For the better? Or worse? I didn't know.

All I could do was wait.

Thirty-one

I didn't think I'd hear from Viola Randall again. In fact, I didn't recognize the number on my phone. Barring an emergency, no one called me while I was teaching. Her call came when I was alone in my classroom during my conference period.

"Jennet," she said. "Could you spare a few minutes to swing by my house? There's something I need to discuss with you."

"Well…"

I thought of Leonora. I'd driven today, but she might want to leave as soon as the bell rang. As I did. The day had been trying and tiring, and the sky was overcast, hinting of snow.

"It's something I remembered," she added. "It's important."

"I'll check with my passenger," I said. "If she doesn't want to wait, I'll arrange to stop by tomorrow."

"Tell your friend this won't take long."

"I don't have to hurry home," Leonora said when I told her about Viola's request. We both had dogs to take care of and both had helpful neighbors.

"I'm interested in Violet's murder too," she reminded me. "That must be what this is about."

"Let's hurry then."

The bell's echo still lingered, but no one seemed inclined to stay in the building a minute longer than necessary. We hurried out, making our way through groups of chatting, shouting students—and Principal Grimsley, who had stationed himself in the corridor near the back exit. He favored us with his pasted-on smile and glanced at his watch. Technically teachers weren't supposed to leave the building with the students, but very few paid attention to that rule.

"There'll probably be a reminder about teachers leaving early in the next staff meeting," Leonora said.

"You'd think he'd understand some of us live a long way from Marston, and at this time of year, driving can be hazardous. He lives here in Oakpoint, about fifteen minutes from the school."

If challenged, Grimsley would say a rule was a rule, and that teachers who disregarded it would be subject to discipline.

~ * ~

Viola Randall wasted no time on pleasantries.

"When I read about the emerald bracelet that poor missing girl lost out in your neck of the woods, I remembered Violet's bracelet," she said. "It was a thin chain of sapphires held together with golden links. Her mom gave it to her."

I couldn't recall seeing a bracelet on Violet's wrist but remembered her sapphire earrings. She always wore them.

"The bracelet matched her earrings," Viola added. "The sapphire wasn't her birthstone, but she loved jewelry with blue stones."

I waited, somehow knowing that Viola's information was going to be important, perhaps crucial to at least one case.

"Violet wore that bracelet the day she disappeared, but when they found her body, it was gone. We figured that whoever killed her stole it."

"But left the earrings?"

"What else could we think?"

"Maybe she lost it in the woods," Leonora said.

"That could be. It was never found."

I could understand that. Once dropped on the forest floor, a small piece of jewelry would soon be buried under layers of autumn leaves. Years of layers. It might have sunk deep down into the ground.

It was a fluke that Jillian Cranbrook's bracelet remained at the edge of the woods and miraculous, considering the amount of snow we'd already had this season.

"I don't remember reading about a missing bracelet in my research," I said.

"Maybe no one mentioned it. Or didn't think it was important."

"And you just remembered it?"

A faint blush stole over her face. "When I read the article in the *Banner*. Yes."

Perhaps she sensed that I realized she was keeping back some of the story. She paused, her gaze focused on the French doors and the Christmas lights that illuminated the man-made lake beyond her property.

"I should explain. Sometimes I have feelings. Maybe flashes of understanding would be a better way to describe them. I hadn't thought about Violet's bracelet for years. At the time, there was so much else to deal with... So much sorrow. Then years later I read about Jillian Cranbrook's bracelet, and suddenly I saw a circle of sapphires as clear as if it were lying beside me on the sofa. It was so real I almost reached out to touch it."

Anyone else would be skeptical, but Viola had apparently passed on her powers, if that was the right term, to her niece. Violet had known her life was about to end. Then there were the time slips.

Did Viola know about the time slips? I wanted to ask her but thought it best to wait until I knew her better.

"There's something else," Viola said. "You may not believe this, but I want to tell you anyway. That article mentioned a suspect in the Cranbrook case, a vagrant named Kevin Clancy."

At that moment, I had a flash of understanding of my own. A fact that had long eluded me leaped into my mind. That name had cropped up in both cases.

"A young man with the same name was questioned in my niece's death," Viola went on. "He was released, but I wonder... Doesn't it seem odd to you that two men named Clancy were involved in two disappearances in the same area? Maybe in two murders? That's if Jillian Cranbrook is found dead."

"It's a coincidence," I said. "But I can believe it."

For the first time, I was hopeful that Violet's killer would be identified and punished.

"What should we do about it?" I asked.

"I can't very well do anything," Viola said. "I can't travel all the way to Foxglove Corners to talk to the police."

"All the way?" Leonora repeated. "We do it every weekday. Twice a day."

"You girls are young and energetic. And would that Lieutenant Dalby, who's in charge of the case, think it was significant? That's one of my concerns."

"All we can do is tell him," I said. "Let's examine the facts. Violet was killed about thirty years ago. This Clancy could be the same man, but Kevin and Clancy are fairly common Irish names."

"He was a young man at the time but a no good vagrant even then. He was an alcoholic who couldn't or didn't hold down a job. In those days, there was a drug store in Foxglove Corners with a soda fountain. He was a regular there. I remember hearing that he had a violent temper. They say a leopard doesn't change his spots."

How old was the suspect in Jillian Cranbrook's disappearance? I had no idea, but I could find out. He had been described as elderly. That would fit with the facts as Viola had related them.

"Is there anything else you want to tell us?" I asked, with a glance at the rapidly darkening sky.

"No, except that Clancy was part of my flash of remembrance. Clancy and my niece's beloved bracelet."

"Then it's worth looking into," I said. "Luckily, Lieutenant Dalby happens to be a friend of mine."

That was stretching the truth a bit. Mac was Crane's friend. He was my nemesis.

"I'll see that Lieutenant Dalby hears about the bracelet as soon as possible. He can make the connection, if there is one."

"You'll let me know what he says?" she asked.

"Definitely. And if he wants to talk to you, he can come to Oakpoint, or I can drive you to Foxglove Corners. It's not really the end of the world."

"It's just that I go so few places these days," she said. "And I never drive on the freeway."

"Don't worry about that," I said.

As we said our goodbyes, I felt a streak of exhilaration, a certainty that after all these years, something definitive was going to happen. I'd never anticipated this development. A dastardly double crime committed by the same person decades apart? If I'd read this in a book, I would have thought it an unlikely and unfair resolution.

Now to see if a long lost sapphire bracelet would make any difference in the case.

~ * ~

"Do you think the suspect could be the man who killed Violet Randall?" Leonora asked as I navigated the freeway through a mist of snow.

"It's possible. A vagrant with an obsession for pretty young women on their own and colorful, sparkling jewelry."

"It just seems so improbable. So much time separates the two cases."

"Maybe there were more women over the years that we don't know about," I said. "Victims in different places. I can't wait to tell Mac."

"Do you think he'll believe something so far-fetched?"

"Probably. The police are desperate for clues. If Viola leaves out the flash of understanding part. To me, it's believable that a missing necklace could have lain hidden in her mind all this time. What confuses me is that Violet still had the earrings when they found her body. Why steal the bracelet and leave the earrings?"

"Maybe he couldn't figure out how to get them off," Leonora said.

Clancy knows.

The thought seemed to come from nowhere.

If only I could interrogate Kevin Clancy. It wasn't possible, of course. But Mac could. He'd have to take my story seriously, have to believe that an item in a news story had jarred Viola's memory, because I couldn't breathe a word about premonitions or forebodings to him. Like Crane, Mac dealt in unadorned facts.

That sapphire bracelet would have to stand on its own.

Thirty-two

Crane listened to the story of Violet's sapphire bracelet quietly, his expression grim. At the end he said, "This cold case is beginning to look dangerous, Jennet. I'll pass the information along to Mac. He'll take it from there."

I looked at him. "Of course. Is Clancy still in police custody?"

"So far as I know."

"Then there's no danger to me."

"All the same. Leave it to Mac."

I didn't ask him to elaborate, hoping he'd move on to another aspect of the subject, and he did.

"Clancy admitted he stopped to help a young woman whose car broke down on Thanksgiving night. He claims she refused his help and walked off into the storm, not taking anything with her. That's the last he saw of her, and he found the emerald bracelet later."

"A likely story."

I could believe Jillian's first impulse would be to run from a stranger appearing in the snow, but wouldn't she realize she'd be safer in a vehicle with the door locked? Assuming she'd taken the precaution of locking herself in. What compelled her to open the door? Once outside, she'd be vulnerable. And surely, if she were going to flee, she would have grabbed her purse.

I imagined myself in a similar situation. What would I do?

Call Crane on my cell phone. Or Brent or Camille or Leonora. I had many people I could contact in an emergency, but then Jillian must have had friends as well.

I knew I'd never get out of my car and start walking in a snowstorm.

"Do you remember where her cell phone was?" I asked.

"In her purse."

In her purse, in the car. Whatever happened must have been fast, giving her no time to react sensibly.

"Where could she hope to escape to? That's a pretty isolated stretch of roadway."

There was Sue's horse farm and the yellow cottage at Lane's End, which was usually untenanted. The rest was farmland and woods.

But what was the saying? Any port in a storm? Anything better than falling into the hands of a possible rapist?

"I don't believe that's what happened either," Crane said.

"What I don't understand is why would Clancy say he'd seen her that night? It doesn't make sense. All it does is place him at the scene. He should have stopped with the bracelet story."

"He isn't bright," Crane said. "Possibly he felt trapped."

If Mac had questioned him, the suspect would indeed feel trapped. Mac could be intimidating.

"I hope Mac questions him about Violet Randall."

"He will," Crane said. "It's a stroke of luck that Viola read that article in the paper. It could be the break that eluded the police when Violet disappeared."

Thoughts of Violet went with me as I put the finishing touches on dinner. We were having steak and baked potatoes again, a hearty meal for a cold wintry night. I was safe and warm inside my home with my husband and our dogs. Violet lay in the frozen ground under a thick blanket of cold snow.

It appeared that she walked only in the fall of the year. Perhaps if her killer were apprehended and made to pay for his crime, she would be able to rest in peace. As for Jillian Cranbrook, I hoped she was still alive.

I wondered if I was the only one who did, aside from her loved ones.

"The steaks are almost ready," I said, joining Crane in the living room a few minutes later. "We'll eat in about ten minutes."

Candy licked her chops. Our dogs knew the words that mattered to them. 'Steak' and 'eat' were two of them. All of them gathered around me, even Star who hadn't been with us that long. But how long does it take for a dog to learn family traditions?

"Will you tell me what Mac does with the bracelet clue?" I asked.

"Which one?"

"Violet's sapphires."

"Yes," he said. "I'll do that, since it's your clue."

"They both are," I pointed out.

"Good detective work," he said.

I accepted the compliment, although I hadn't done anything except find Jillian's bracelet in the snow and listen to Viola's memories.

Sapphires and emeralds. How odd that bracelets played a part in both cases.

~ * ~

On the second to last day before Christmas vacation, Leonora and I stopped at Clovers for take-out and also— we hoped— to see Annica. I hadn't talked to her since Brent's return. We pushed our way through a robust wind gust and walked into a warm oasis of good cheer.

Annica was arranging freshly baked tarts in the dessert carousel. In her bright red dress and gold hoop earrings, she was as glittery as any one of Mary Jeanne's decorations. She was happy. That was obvious.

Clovers itself glittered with poinsettia plants in all the traditional colors, along with the unusual peach and purple variety, which I didn't care for. The menu reflected the season with dinners of turkey and ham and prime rib.

"Have you seen Brent?" I asked as we settled ourselves in the booth by the window for a quick cup of coffee. Annica, who always managed to have a break due when we arrived, had brought a cup for herself.

"Yesterday," she said. "He brought me a dozen red roses and took me out to dinner. He gave Angel a bag of bones, too. I think I should forgive him for standing me up."

"My," Leonora said. "Twelve separate declarations of love."

"Uh... What?"

"They say red roses symbolize love," she pointed out.

"Oh, yeah. Well, I'd like to think that, but he felt guilty for not showing up to my house for dinner. I know he couldn't help it. I'm just glad he's alive and okay."

"Not quite okay," I said. "Not until he remembers where he was."

"Shouldn't he have remembered by now?" she asked.

"There aren't any rules."

"He really wants to remember. He went back to the house and stood at the sink filling a glass with water, hoping it'd trigger a memory.

My heart skipped a beat. How could he take such a risk?

"Nothing happened," Annica said. "He wanted to take me with him, but nothing happens when I'm there. I just smell violets every now and then."

"That's good," Leonora said. "For myself, I wouldn't go within a mile of that place."

"I'm not afraid." She stirred an extra spoonful of sugar in her coffee. "It might be fun to have an adventure in time. If I could have it with Brent."

"Believe me, it isn't fun," I said, "no matter who you're with."

Annica tasted her coffee, apparently deciding it was sweet enough. "Oh, Jennet, that female deputy was in for breakfast yesterday.

Veronica.

I didn't want to hear this, but I had to.

"She wanted to know if law officers get to eat for free. I told her they didn't."

I took a sip of coffee. "So she's a cheapskate, too."

"She asked me if I was paying attention to the speed limits. I told her I always do."

I shook my head. "A cheapskate and a smart aleck."

"Then, get this. She was hinting for me to tell her about Crane. It was a real fishing expedition. She started by asking if the sheriff's deputies came to Clovers for breakfast. I told her they did, same as anybody. Then she asked if Crane had a wife."

I bristled. She knew that he did.

"Don't shoot the messenger, Jennet. I'm just reporting the conversation. She said she hoped his wife could cope with his job because it isn't easy being married to a lawman who puts his life on the line every day."

I set my coffee cup in its saucer with unnecessary force. Fortunately it didn't break.

"What possible business is that of hers? She doesn't even know me."

"Hold on, Jennet. I told her he had the prettiest, smartest wife in Foxglove Corners and was totally devoted to her. She said she hoped you appreciated him because he was a real treasure. Those were her words. Real treasure."

"You'd better watch out," Leonora said.

"I intend to. She's a snake. Lucy saw her slithering through the leaves in my teacup."

"Maybe I shouldn't have told you," Annica said. "But I thought you'd want to know."

"I do. Thank you."

Forewarned is forearmed. Especially with a reptile.

"We women have to stick together," Leonora said. "I'd sure want to know if some hussy set her cap for Jake."

"Is that what you think?" I asked. "That this— woman set her cap for Crane?"

"It sounds like it. Otherwise, what kind of weird conversation is that to have with a waitress?"

She was right. Annica's story reminded me of what Brent had told me, that he'd seen Crane and Veronica together at the Lakeside Diner. Crane never did mention the incident to me, and I had changed my mind about asking him.

It looked as if I'd have to pay more attention to what was going on around me.

Thirty-three

Whenever something unpleasant happened, it stayed with me for a long time. Nothing could be worse than the thought that some hussy was scheming to attract my husband.

I wanted to do something about Veronica. Annica's words played endlessly in my mind. I wondered if she knew that Annica and I were friends. Had she counted on Annica repeating their conversation to me? Without a shred of supporting evidence, I decided that was her plan.

Had she set her cap for Crane, while knowing he was married? If so she'd have a fight on her hands. The trouble was, she hadn't made a move yet, that I knew of. One could hardly call that trouble. Still it left me back at square one, floundering, feeling threatened but not knowing how to proceed. What could I do?

Not much except talk to Crane, not about Annica's revelation but about Veronica.

After a good dinner, when we were relaxing around the fireplace with our dogs, I said, "How's the new female deputy sheriff getting along?"

Crane looked up from the paper. "Okay, I guess. She's fitting in. She likes to be called just 'Deputy,' by the way. It makes her feel like one of the boys."

"I'll have to remember that. Is she from this part of the state?"

"From some place up north, I think."

"I wonder why she came to Foxglove Corners."

"You'll have to ask her."

This wasn't going well.

"Foxglove Corners *is* a wonderful place to live," I said. "Do you think she'll be able to handle herself in an emergency?"

"I don't see why not. She's a professional. It's been quiet lately," he added. "Just speeders and accidents. By the way, Clancy changed his story. Now he says the woman he offered to help couldn't have been Jillian Cranbrook. The lady he met was older, fifty or sixty."

"So there were two motorists in trouble on Squill Lane on Thanksgiving night? I don't think that road sees two cars a week."

"Like I told you, the man isn't all there. No one believes in this second stranded motorist."

"Did he say anything about Violet Randall?"

"He claims he never heard of her. It was before his time."

"What about Violet's sapphire bracelet?"

"He said the bracelet was green, not blue, and accused Mac of trying to trick him. Clancy was going to see if he could find the owner, hoping there'd be a reward, but then he lost it himself."

I sighed. "He'll be found incompetent to stand trial. He'll never pay for killing Violet and Jillian— if it turns out that Jillian is dead."

"Tomorrow he'll probably have another story. Well…" He signaled to the dogs. "Let's all go out before bed, pooches."

The dogs knew 'go out' too. They flocked around him, waiting for him to open the side door.

I sat alone in a quiet house, feeling lonely in square one. Crane had deftly switched the subject from the female deputy to the suspect. Had he done this deliberately? Probably not. I'd never known Crane to be devious.

I'd have to introduce the subject again. Not tonight, though, but in another quiet moment. In the meantime, I'd try to find out more about the female deputy sheriff, facts either Crane didn't know or didn't consider worth repeating.

And no matter what she preferred to be called, Veronica wasn't one of the boys.

~ * ~

On the last half day before Christmas recess, the atmosphere at Marston was festive. My fourth period American Lit class didn't meet, which in itself was cause for rejoicing.

In each of the three classes, half the students hadn't bothered getting out of bed for a half day of classes, especially as it was a snowy morning. The absence list was two and a half pages long. In my World Literature class, Lynn and Suzette began to take apart the table top tree I'd brought in to give the classroom a bit of color.

"Who wants to come back in January to see a Christmas tree?" Lynn asked as she wrapped the silver treetop in tissue paper.

For the first time in memory, I wasn't looking forward to the holidays. I hadn't bought a single present, hadn't even hung a wreath on the door of our house. I loved Christmas, but this year a myriad other matters combined to dim the traditional light.

First, I worried about Brent and his determination to recall his lost memories, even if it meant consulting a hypnotist. Meanwhile, he placed himself in constant danger by returning time and time again to the pink Victorian.

Also, I had a grim new concern. Would I somehow be swept into the house's clutches, as helpless as any swimmer trapped in a deadly tidal wave?

It didn't have to happen. Not if I continued to avoid Huron Court and Violet's house. No matter what. Not even if another one of my collies needed saving.

Well, wait. I'd do anything to help a collie in distress.

Even that?

Don't add a hypothetical case to your other concerns.

Still, what if the house managed to ensnare me in another way?

Then, Jillian Cranbrook's disappearance and Viola's revelations about Clancy had brought Violet's murder back into sharp focus.

As if that weren't enough, here was Veronica the Viper slithering through the grass— make that the snow—around my house.

Who could spare a thought for Christmas bells and balsam firs and peace on earth, goodwill toward man?

Toward the end of third period, the band began their traditional march through the halls, serenading us with carols and holiday songs. One of the girls, dressed in elf attire, delivered a present to each teacher from Principal Grimsley, a box of red, green, silver, and gold Post-it notes with matching pens.

Have yourself a merry little Christmas...

Well, I'd try. I owed it to Crane and to my sister, Julia, who had written to inform us that she was flying in from England to celebrate Christmas with us.

Ring, silver bells, ring joyful, ring...

However, a sinister foreboding insinuated itself into the merry notes. Somewhere, something was even now unleashing a plan to turn merriment to horror.

~ * ~

"Why so glum?" Leonora asked as we drove home. "There's no school till next year. It's Christmas. We're free!"

Just what I needed. One more cheerful person.

The snow that fell was like white powder, a powdered sugar snowfall that did no harm. It turned familiar scenery into a magical glittering world even before we left the freeway and traveled on country roads.

"It'll be nice," I said. "Sleeping in, no lessons to plan, no hassles with kids… But I can't get excited about Christmas this year."

"Where's your Christmas spirit, Ebenezer?"

"It hasn't made an appearance yet."

"Come with me to the mall this afternoon. It's beautifully decorated this year with fairy tale characters. We can have lunch in the North Pole. It's a new restaurant opened up just for the season."

I was hungry, but…

"I'm not in the mood for shopping," I said.

"Once you're there, you'll change your mind. You can help me find the perfect present for Jake. I have a feeling this is going to be a special Christmas."

"Some other day," I said. "I want to take the dogs walking in the snow and breathe fresh air."

"You can do that anytime. Let's take advantage of a few free hours."

"That isn't what I feel like doing today. I'm sorry, Leonora. I won't be a good companion."

"This isn't like you, Jen. Are you coming down with something?"

"I don't think so. I hope not. The past months have caught up with me. Before, I was too busy at school to notice."

I resolved to conjure the mood. I would tie sleigh bells to the dogs' collars. I'd bake Christmas cookies for tonight's dessert and listen to the *Nutcracker Suite* which always reminded me of happy Christmases in the past.

"Call me when the mood appears, and we'll go Christmas shopping," Leonora said.

I agreed to do that.

Because Christmas was coming, whether I wanted it to or not.

Thirty-four

Before we reached the lane, my green parka had turned white, and Halley, Sky, and Star looked like snow dogs. We weren't going far, only to the lake and back, only far enough to enjoy the fresh, sparkling landscape.

I breathed in the cold, pure air. It smelled different in the country. It *was* different. It was better, as was everything in Foxglove Corners. I'd known that from my first days in the house on Jonquil Lane.

I turned on Sagramore Lake Road and spied Jennifer and Molly in the middle of the block throwing snowballs for Ginger. Their laughter and Ginger's barking were contagious. My trio tugged on their leashes, desperate to join in the fun. I would have been tempted to throw a snowball of my own if my hands hadn't been full of wet leather.

When we caught up to them, Star intercepted a snowball, looking surprised when it melted in her mouth. Although she was the oldest of my canine brood, she didn't seem to know how to play. As she'd come from a family that had no time for her, that wasn't surprising. Just heartbreaking.

The girls and Ginger came together in a bouncing, multi-colored group, and we all sheltered under an enormous tree with low-hanging branches.

"How is the detective work going?" I asked, as the dogs sniffed and play bowed, wanting the fun to continue.

Molly brushed snow from Ginger's head. "Real good. We found out where Beatrice lives and saw Trista in the back yard, lying in the snow. It was snowing on her."

"Collies love the snow," I said. "They have thick coats."

"Yeah, but her toes had icy wads in them."

I glanced at my collies. They were in the same condition. In fact, Star was nibbling at her right foot at the moment.

"I think it's all part of the fun for them as long as they don't stay outside too long," I said. "How did you find out where Beatrice lives?"

"That was a lucky break," Jennifer said. "We kept going back to the shop, like you suggested, and one day we ran into our neighbor, Mrs. Brier. She went to school with Beatrice— a long time ago."

"So Jennifer's mom drove us to her house," Molly continued. "There was Trista all alone in the yard. She was tied up."

"We called her Trista, not Melody," Jennifer added. "She remembers her real name."

Molly said, "We're sure she's Trista. That isn't a nice place for her to live. She should be in her own home."

So Beatrice was lying. That she was keeping Trista tethered while she worked at the Busy Bea was a crime in my book. Collies flourished in all kinds of weather, but they were happiest when they lived in a house with their humans.

"Did she have water?" I asked.

"There was a pail, but from where we were standing, the water looked like it was frozen," Jennifer said.

If she got thirsty, she'd have to lap up the snow.

"What now?" Molly wanted to know.

"You turn the problem over to Trista's owner," I said. "She'll know what to do."

Two young schoolgirls couldn't accuse a grown woman, a businesswoman, of stealing a dog. Well, they could, but I suspected Beatrice would be ready to override them with a logical story.

Still, she couldn't supply proof of ownership, and while many tricolor collies were similar in appearance, Trista had that distinctive star mark on her head.

Trista's breeder would surely have pictures of Trista with that marking.

The girls had done their part; enough, I trusted, to earn the generous reward. I hoped they received it in time for Christmas.

"We can't really talk outside," I said. "Stop by my house when you have news or any time. We're all home from school. I'll make cocoa— and cookies. Christmas cookies."

Their eyes lit up, and Ginger licked her chops. Like my dogs, she knew the words that mattered to her.

Wishing one another a merry Christmas, we parted company. The girls went back to their game, and I walked on with the dogs to the lake.

Fun in the snow with a promise of young guests for cookies and cocoa. I found myself looking forward to it.

The Christmas Spirit took a few tentative steps forward. Maybe my malaise would melt away like the girls' snowballs.

~ * ~

Brent insisted on taking us out to dinner at the Hunt Club Inn that evening.

"I feel bad about not showing up the last time I invited you out. I want to make it up to you."

"That wasn't your fault," I said quickly, thinking of my black dress and the necklace I'd planned to wear with it.

"They have the place all decked out for Christmas."

I said a mental goodbye to the pork chops defrosting in the refrigerator. "It'll be a nice change."

"What are we waiting for?" Crane asked.

"I can't think of anything," I said.

Maybe a change of scene and good company would encourage the Christmas Spirit to come out and play.

At the Hunt Club Inn, they would have changed the decorations on the fox head wreath. Holly, ivy, perhaps tiny ornaments. I hoped that tonight I'd be seated in some obscure corner where I wouldn't have to look at it, feel sad, and remember that Brent was a fox hunter, which was the reason we would be in that particular restaurant.

"We don't let the dogs kill the fox, Jennet," he'd told me once. "It's all in the fun of the chase."

"Fun for whom?" I asked. "Not the one being hunted."

I remembered that conversation as if it had just taken place.

"It's good sport," he said. "Horses, dogs, friends in all kinds of weather. It's tradition. Come hunting with us one day, and you'll understand."

"I haven't been on a horse in years," I said, "and I managed to fall off that one time. Don't ask me how. But even if I were the country's best horsewoman, I wouldn't terrorize a little fox."

I didn't believe Brent's romanticized version of the Hunt. After all, if the hunters let the fox escape, how did the fox at the Hunt Club Inn become separated from his head? But I wasn't going to dwell on that and allow it to cast a shadow on our evening with Brent. There was no hope for that particular fox anyway.

As we followed Brent to his vintage Belvedere, Crane stole a quick kiss. "You look beautiful tonight, honey."

"Thanks. And you look exceptionally handsome."

He always did, but I was used to seeing him in his uniform and in jeans and the colorful shirts he liked. Tonight he looked as he had on our wedding day.

I wasn't going to let the specter of Deputy Sheriff Veronica Whatever-Her-Last-Name-Was intrude on our evening. I could assemble the weapons in my arsenal tomorrow.

~ * ~

I couldn't escape the fox head. It wore a collar of tiny blinking lights, and its eyes seemed to follow me as I walked beside Crane to our table. The Inn's focal point was a gigantic white pine decorated in a hunt motif with jaunty foxhounds, miniature hunters, and, of course, foxes in a variety of colors and materials.

What else had I expected? Candy canes and gingerbread stars?

"Finally," Brent said, "a place that looks like Christmas. I'm in a mood for a good prime rib dinner."

He seemed like the Brent of old— hale and hearty, a good companion for any season, but when the waiter had brought our wine and taken our order, he grew somber.

"This makes me think of my own inn," he said. "I was going to have a grand opening on Christmas Eve. I wanted to give the house one more Christmas."

What a strange sentiment. As if the house cared about a holiday.

"I guess you've given up your idea of turning the house into an inn."

"For the time being." He took a big gulp of wine. "Ah, that's good! Right now I'm waiting to remember what happened when I was gone. It's still a blank screen. That's five days of my life that I didn't live."

"You *did* live, somewhere," I reminded him.

"I'd like to go back, and this time I want to be aware of everything."

"You can't just chart a course to the past," I said. "There's no time machine in the house or anywhere else that I know of."

"My advice is to enjoy the life you have," Crane said. "That's what I'm doing."

He reached across the table and laid his hand over mine.

"I'm doing that," Brent said. "I've been Christmas shopping for my kids. Hey, Jennet, would you wrap the presents for me again this year?"

"Sure." I liked playing a small part in Brent's Christmas Eve tradition of traveling through Foxglove Corners with his gift-laden sleigh. "Give me enough time, though. I want to do a good job."

Christmas cookies, a visit from Molly and Jennifer, and now wrapping a hundred plus toys and dolls and books for children who wouldn't have gifts of their own under the tree, who might not even have a tree.

By the time I finished creating bright and appealing packages, the Christmas Spirit should be well entrenched in my home and my heart.

Wrapping multiple presents was an enormous task, though. I intended to ask Leonora or Annica to help me.

Thirty-five

That night I dreamed about Christmas. Transitioning abruptly into wakefulness, I lay in bed trying to remember the fragile strands that were already slipping into oblivion.

I was in a large bright room with myriads of clear blinking lights strung along the crown molding. A fir tree dripping snow lay on its side in a corner waiting to be decorated. The air was frigid. It was as if a window were open, allowing dangerous cold to pour inside.

A heady scent of balsam mixed with violet perfume anchored me to the dream. I was in the pink Victorian, the one house I should never, ever enter.

Along with the scents came sounds. A barely audible tinkling, like wind chimes trembling in a winter wind. Merry, robust sleigh bells drowned the wind chimes out. Louder ringing, discordant and horrible, overrode both chimes and sleigh bells. In minutes the cacophony had gone from pleasing to painful.

I wanted to escape the assault on my hearing, but I couldn't move.

Then another sound obliterated the bells. Out in the night, the coyotes began to howl. They were so near I felt as if they were in the room with me.

I heard Lucy whisper, "Their howling is unnatural. It's a harbinger of disaster."

And Brent's booming voice: *"I want to give the house another Christmas before it dies."*

Before it dies?

To my knowledge, Brent had never uttered those last three words.

But how could a house die?

Easily. It could be demolished to make way for a new structure— or catch fire. I couldn't think of a third possibility.

It's all right. It's only a dream.

I turned on the bed, hoping to touch Crane, my real anchor, and came in contact with a cold, crumpled sheet. His pajamas lay across our bedroom rocker.

Misty, who had slept at the foot of the bed, and Halley who kept vigil in the doorway, were gone.

And why not? Another scent from the waking world wafted up the stairs. Apple-smoked bacon had lured the dogs to the kitchen.

Oh, no! Now that I didn't have to go to school, I'd intended to make Crane a special breakfast every morning. Something with bacon.

I swung out of bed and into my slippers. By the time I reached the kitchen, the last of the dream had evaporated, along with its sounds and scents.

Crane, already in his uniform, stood at the stove scrambling eggs. The bacon, crisp and enticing, lay on a cake platter next to a stack of toast. He'd squeezed oranges for fresh juice, too.

I couldn't resist grabbing a piece of bacon to nibble on.

"Morning, honey." Crane gave the eggs a vigorous swirl. "I was just about to send Candy upstairs to get you out of bed."

"I've been awake, thinking about a dream I had."

"A good one?"

"Not exactly. It was about Christmas." I tried to remember. It seemed far away, but the images came.

A balsam-and violet-scented Christmas. Lucy casting one of her dark comments as if it were a spell. Brent making an unsettling declaration.

Crane scooped the eggs onto our plates. "Did the coyotes keep you awake last night?"

I frowned. "I heard them. I thought I was dreaming."

"They woke me up," he said. "That's a first."

"I was going to make breakfast for you this morning."

He tousled my hair. "You were tired. I wanted to let you sleep."

We'd both had a late night, but Crane had a long day ahead of him. I had no commitments and no plans other than vague ones to buy extra flour and sugar and bake Christmas cookies. Tomorrow I'd set the alarm clock.

I tasted the eggs. They were perfect, light and fluffy, a goal I often failed to meet.

"You're getting to be a good cook," I told him. "Should I let you take over in the kitchen?"

"I'll never be as good as you are. By the way, I fed the dogs and they've been out."

"You'd never know it."

Seven pairs of eyes were fixed longingly on our repast. Anyone would think they hadn't eaten in days. As usual, Candy had commandeered a spot closest to the bacon.

Who could resist a begging collie?

"Later," I said. "If there's any left."

"I'm meeting with an interesting man today," Crane said. "Detective Vernon Jasperson. He worked on the Randall case."

"He must be old."

"Vernon has been retired for years, but he remembers every case he ever had." Crane paused to spill more bacon onto his plate. "He interviewed Clancy."

Ah! There was news. Clancy could claim that Violet's murder was before his time, that he had no knowledge of it, but records don't lie. A detective familiar with the case was a godsend.

"Maybe he can tell you why they couldn't hold Clancy," I said.

"I can tell you that. They didn't have enough evidence to charge him. Vern always thought he was guilty."

"You can ask if he knows anything about Violet's sapphire bracelet."

"I'll do that."

"Did you ever find out what object Clancy had that belonged to Jillian Cranbrook?" I asked.

He paused, then said, "I guess you can know. It's a watch, a fancy, expensive one with a diamond studded band."

A disturbing image of the vagrant removing glittering jewelry from a lifeless wrist took form in my mind.

"I wonder if Clancy has been living here in Foxglove Corners all these years."

"He's says he's been down south, recently in New Orleans. He only came back to Michigan this fall."

"In time for a northern winter?"

"Around Thanksgiving," Crane said.

In time to intercept Jillian Cranbrook as she drove home in a snowstorm.

~ * ~

Having most of the day free was a novelty. I could have baked Christmas cookies, called Leonora and gone shopping, or visited with Camille or Lucy. Possibilities were endless, but along with freedom had come a rare inertia that was akin to malaise. The Christmas Spirit deserted me for greener pastures.

I walked Gemmy, Sky, and Misty to the lake, hoping to see Jennifer and Molly with Ginger, but Sagramore Lake Road was deserted. Young people know how to make the best of a vacation from school.

I used to have that knowledge. Once upon a time.

When it started to snow, I gave Huron Court a wide berth and led the dogs home.

Dinner was a beef and potato casserole, already prepared. I didn't have any new Gothic novels to read. If I cleaned house today, it would need cleaning again for Christmas. By noon, the snow tapered off and I was bored with staying inside. I'd read somewhere that interest follows action and decided to treat myself to a trip to the library

Everyone on Jonquil Lane had decorated their houses for the season. At the Hometown Bakery, I bought a coffee cake sprinkled with red sugar and proceeded to the library.

It was especially festive with blue and white lights strung in the evergreens. For the door, Miss Eidt had found or perhaps crafted an unusual wreath of real balsam decorated with old time cut-outs of Christmas trees, stockings, sleds, and Victorian ladies and children in vibrant period attire.

Breathing in the scent of balsam, I stepped inside and almost collided with Blackberry as she skittered across my path en route to some private corner.

This was where the Christmas Spirit had taken refuge when she fled from my presence. The library was awash in red and green. In front of a window, Miss Eidt had set up her childhood dollhouse, the magnificent antique fashioned to resemble the old white Victorian itself. The Halloween cauldron and rats had been replaced by miniature Christmas figures and decorations.

Miss Eidt stood at the cardboard carousel adding holiday books to the collection. As Annica often did, she wore red, a long dress with a three-strand pearl necklace.

I presented her with the bakery box, glad I'd had the idea to come to the library and happy that I'd thought to stop at the bakery.

She looked as happy as if I had given her a priceless antique. "Oh, my. It smells delicious. What are they? Doughnuts?"

"It's a Christmas coffee cake," I said.

"You'll have some with me later."

"I can be tempted."

She set it on the counter next to a dark red poinsettia. "We haven't seen you in ages, Jennet. What have you been up to?"

"Well, I've been busy at school, but now we're on vacation, and I'm out of reading material."

"I can remedy that. I found a few good Gothics for you. Well, about a dozen."

"Who could ask for a nicer Christmas present?"

"An old friend of yours is here," she added. "It's Edwina Endicott. She's been back in the supernatural section for the last half hour."

Edwina Endicott, Ghost Hunter. All of a sudden, my enthusiasm that had been on hiatus came bouncing back. While Edwina wasn't one of my favorite persons, she was definitely a favorite source for otherworldly news.

"I'll go say hello to her," I said.

Thirty-six

I found Edwina Endicott where Miss Eidt said she would be, in the Supernatural section leafing through a thin paperback. A slender woman in a shapeless brown coat, she had arranged her grayish-brown hair in a high bun with long curling strands on either side of her face. A gaudy Christmas tree pin lent a flash of color to her appearance.

"Hello, Miss Greenway." Her eyes lit up when she saw me, making her look almost pretty. "I was hoping to run into you again one of these days, and here you are."

"It's Mrs. Ferguson."

"Oh, yes, the deputy sheriff's wife."

She couldn't have forgotten that. Some weeks ago when we'd first met, she'd known my marital status and the name of my husband before I'd even introduced myself, claiming that she'd read about me in the *Banner*. That fact had made me a bit wary of her as I wondered what else she knew.

In all likelihood she was harmless, although Miss Eidt, always kind, had described her as out of touch with reality.

"Did you find a good book?" I asked.

"It's a new one," she said. "*All About Cryptids*. There's a chapter about a Michigan creature in here, the Dogman. They say he has the body of a man and the face of a dog. He's elusive, but lots of people have seen him over the years."

"I've heard of him."

"Monsters aren't my main interest, if you'll remember." She lowered her voice, although we were alone in this part of the library. "Last week I saw the girl and her collie dog walking in the snow on Huron Court. I remember you were interested in her, too."

Violet!

I hadn't expected that. "I thought she only appeared in the fall."

"She must have changed her habits. It was freezing cold, but she was dressed for a summer stroll in blue pedal pushers and a sleeveless top. That alone told me she was our hometown apparition. That and the collie, of course. They were several yards ahead of me. Then they went around a curve in the road and vanished."

The apparition was Violet. Of that there could be no doubt. Ghosts had no need to shield themselves from rain or snow. I recalled another ghost, the spirit of Rosalyn Everett, who had walked the snowy fields of River Rose dressed only in a long white gown.

Here I'd been thinking of Violet lying in her grave in Old Resurrection Cemetery. Lying, but obviously not at rest.

I wondered, though. Why would Violet haunt Huron Court at a different time of the year? Could it be that she knew we were closing in on the truth of her murder and wanted to influence the events in some manner? Did that make her restless? You'd think she would have been happy to lie still and wait for the man who had stolen her life to fall into a trap of his own making.

Yes, she knew about Clancy and probably knew the location of her lost bracelet as well.

We were on the right track with him.

I couldn't wait to tell Lucy about Edwina's sighting. And Crane. I could take Crane into my confidence, but never Mac.

"You know, I've been watching for her, so I had my phone with me," Edwina said. "Imagine my disappointment when I saw a view of the road but nothing else. Not even a shadow or a flash of light."

I smiled. "Ghosts don't like to have their pictures taken."

"That isn't always true. Did you ever hear of spirit photography?"

I had an experience of my own, not that I'd relate it to a relative stranger. Once I thought I'd taken a picture of the pink Victorian in all its glory, only to see the falling apart version of the house in the photo that emerged.

"I've seen some strange pictures on the Internet," I said. "For example, a family portrait with the image of a dead child standing among the living. I always thought they were fakes."

"Some may be. Not all. I think I'd die if I saw a stranger or, worse, a nebulous form, in a picture I took. From now on, I'll have a better camera with me when I go walking."

"Are you still going to try to catch their image on film?"

"Of course. After all, I *am* a ghost hunter." She replaced the cryptids book on the shelf, adding, "I'll let you know if I see the girl and the collie again."

I wished Edwina a Merry Christmas, wondering how she would do that unless we met again in the library. She didn't ask for my cell phone number, and I didn't offer to give it to her. I was still a little wary of her.

~ * ~

Edwina's reference to the Michigan Dogman steered my thoughts about coyotes in a different direction.

That giant coyote I'd thought was a coywolf... Could he (or it) be the Michigan Dogman? I didn't think the creature had ever been sighted in our part of the state. Which didn't mean he couldn't have wandered downstate into Foxglove Corners. If he were real, that is.

The animal I'd seen had walked on all four legs, not two. It had come and gone without fanfare. I'd wondered if I'd really seen anything.

I'd rather believe in the coywolf or the Dogman of Michigan legend than in Lucy's harbinger of evil.

Miss Eidt's young assistant, Debbie, was at the main desk looking bored. I rapped on the office door before opening it. Miss Eidt was brewing tea. She'd found a dainty Christmas plate for the coffee cake and cut it into slices.

Also on the table I saw my Gothic novels. Some were in excellent condition, others somewhat the worse for wear with creased edges and yellow pages. But all had enticing covers depicting the requisite damsel in distress posed against ancient castles, crumbling ruins, and stormy cliffs.

"I don't have a present for you, Miss Eidt. I haven't gone Christmas shopping yet."

"Oh, my dear. I don't need a present. I have everything I could ever want."

She might not need anything, but I wanted to give her something special and pretty. She usually wore pearls. Perhaps a new necklace. Maybe a pendant attached to a rope of pearls. I'd really have to start my Christmas shopping, whether or not I was in the mood.

"Sit," she said. "Tell me everything you've been up to. You have such an exciting life."

I'd never told Miss Eidt about the pink Victorian, Violet, or my time slip. She was impressionable and tended to worry excessively. All she knew of my recent experiences was that I'd done research on a cold case murder and been in an accident involving a collision with a deer.

So what could I tell her now?

"I've been teaching and taking care of my dogs. I bought a new car. Like everyone else, I've been following the Cranbrook case in the paper."

"Poor Jillian," she said. "I've known her since she was a little girl and her dad brought her to the library for her first card. She used to read westerns and books about horses, but now she likes historical novels, practically any story set in England.

"The police talked to me," she went on. "That nice Lieutenant Dalby. I wish I could have given him more help."

Nice? Mac? I supposed he would be with Miss Eidt. She would never challenge his authority or attempt to solve a mystery on her own.

"I read about Jillian's emerald bracelet in the *Banner*. I saw it on her wrist many times, summer and winter."

Miss Eidt didn't know, of course, that I was the one who had found it. I saw no reason to enlighten her.

"I'm not going to believe Jillian is dead until— well, until I read it in the paper. That man they have in custody, that Clancy... I know him. He came in here once and fell asleep. He was drunk. I woke him up and told him to leave the library at once. He gave me an argument. It got pretty nasty."

I shuddered to think of Miss Eidt confronting a possible killer, whether he was drunk or sober. She would have done so with grace and dignity, but how dangerous that encounter might have been for her.

What if he held a grudge against her? That was assuming he remembered an incident that took place when he was drunk. I supposed that didn't matter, as long as he was in custody.

"Guess who came to my rescue that day?" Miss Eidt said.

"Crane?"

"No, dear. It was Brent Fowler. He escorted that Clancy outside, not very gently, I'm happy to say. I don't know what Brent said to him, but he hasn't shown his face around here since."

"Brent is a good man to have on your side," I said.

Now he needed help himself. He was traveling down a dark path and couldn't seem to step away from it. I couldn't think of any way to save him from whatever lay in wait for him at the path's end.

Thirty-seven

"I finally remembered," Brent said. "It happened the way you said it would, Jennet, when I was doing something besides thinking about it."

Brent had waited until he knew Crane would be home to make his appearance. He wanted to talk to both of us, to tell his story once. He was so engrossed in relating his adventures that he hadn't even asked me about the chicken I was roasting for dinner.

I leaned forward on the sofa, eager to catch every single word.

"I was at the barn with my new horse, Incandescent, when it all came back to me," he said. "It was like being hit by lightning."

I was finding it difficult to rein in my impatience. "What do you remember?"

"Lifting a glass of water to my mouth. Before I could take a sip, I was whisked out of that kitchen and into another place. Outside. It was raining. A cold rain. I didn't see any sign of snow on the ground."

He'd not only traveled back in time, but the season had changed.

Brent paused to give Misty a round of petting. He seemed to be reliving that moment, and from his expression I could tell he had been traumatized. I knew how he felt.

"It was dark," he said. "Maybe not exactly dark. Just dusky. There wasn't any light in the sky, and there I was getting drenched in just my shirt sleeves. But why would I have put on my jacket to go into the kitchen?"

"No one would."

Crane took a notebook out of his pocket and began to jot down Brent's remembrances. "Were you on Huron Court?"

I glanced over his shoulder. He had written *glass of water... rain.*

"I don't think so. Since I bought the place, I've been up and down that road a thousand times. Nothing looked familiar. Everything had a weird glow."

I remembered that glow.

Crane turned a page in his notebook. "Some power thrust you into the road. It was pouring out. What did you do?"

"I knew what had happened. I just didn't think it would be like that. I started walking, looking for a house or a barn, any kind of shelter. I heard coyotes howling," he added. "They never sounded more menacing."

I shivered. Those coyotes got around. They had invaded every corner of Foxglove Corners, in the present and the past and possibly in the future as well. They even invited themselves into my dreams.

Brent turned to me. "It was kind of like what you described, Jennet, except I was nowhere near Sagramore Lake, and the road didn't curve. I never had that sensation of being turned around and walking in the opposite direction without realizing what was happening."

"You couldn't have been on Huron Court," I said. "That road has lots of curves."

"Huron Court continues on past Old Resurrection Cemetery," Crane said. "There's no sign, though."

In all the time I'd driven on Huron Court, I never gone farther than the cemetery. "I didn't know that."

"It goes on for three miles or so, then turns into Hickory Lane."

Brent ruffled the fur on Sky's head. Both Sky and Misty had sensed Brent's agitation and were quick to offer a canine's unique comfort to one of their favorite humans.

"I sure wished I had one of my dogs with me," he said, switching his caresses to Misty.

"You were gone five days," I reminded him. "You couldn't have been walking all that time."

"I wasn't. I found a deserted cabin. It must have been somebody's weekend place. The door was locked, but I broke a window."

He cast a sheepish glance at Crane. "What else could I do? I found cans of stew and chili in the cupboard, along with a can opener. There was an open package of Lorna Doones— stale— powdered milk, and a few tins of sardines. I decided I wasn't that hungry. There was no electricity, though. I ate a few meals cold, right from the can."

"You're lucky you didn't poison yourself," I said.

"It was that or starve. I have to find that place again. I need to leave money for what I ate and to repair the window. I had my wallet in my pocket but no cash, only credit cards."

"Wait," I said. "You're overlooking something. This deserted cabin existed in the past. It may be long gone."

"Not necessarily. There are plenty of log cabins in Foxglove Corners."

"It might have a different owner today," I said. "You can't just knock on the door and hand someone a fifty dollar bill and a wild story."

"You're guilty of breaking and entering and theft," Crane said. "But no one's going to hold you accountable."

I supposed he thought he was lightening the mood.

"They'd have a hard time finding me."

"In your place, I'd have done the same," Crane assured him. "But I don't know that I'd eat cold stew from a can."

"The cabin could still be there," Brent said. "Anyway I'm going to look for it and for that road, too."

"What happened after you ate?" Crane asked.

"I draped my clothes over chairs to dry and spent the night on an old cot without a blanket. Here's something interesting. The owner left a stack of newspapers in the cabin. I checked out the date. They were all *Banners* from September, 1986."

At last we had a year, but was that the same year I'd traveled to? When Violet and Ginger were living in the pink Victorian?

"I looked for newspapers when Violet left me alone in the living room," I said, "but she didn't have any. This is good. We have a general idea of the time we were taken back to."

Taken back to. That phrase downplayed the reality of the situation. We had been thrown, flung, catapulted... *Take* implied an escort.

"Go on, Fowler," Crane said.

"In the morning I started walking again. I figured where there was one cabin, there might be another or better still a house with people in it. Anything. Then I heard an engine behind me, and a guy in a blue truck stopped."

Brent was losing me. Not intentionally, of course. I had the feeling he was as lost as I was.

"You're leaving something out," I said. "If the truck driver took you to your house on Wolf Lake Road, he wasn't part of the past. At what point did you cross back over into our time?"

"I'm not sure. It might have been when I walked into a squall. It came up out of nowhere. I couldn't see a foot in front of me, but it cleared up after about five minutes."

Rain on one day, snow on the next. That wasn't unheard of in Michigan. Judging from the date on the papers, Brent must have landed in late September or October.

"That must have been when you returned to your own time," I said. "When you passed through the squall."

"I guess so. How did it happen with you again?" he asked. "I don't remember."

I'd tried not to think about my experience, but I had been unable to banish the memory entirely. It was never too far away to be recalled.

"There was no squall or disturbance in the weather. I was with Misty, and I remember sitting down on the ground, feeling that I couldn't take another step. When I came to or woke up— or whatever— I was in the hospital, and they were telling me that I'd been there all along. I knew the truth, but it took a while for people to believe me."

I reached for Crane's hand, remembering how happy I'd been when I knew he believed I was telling the truth.

"That's as different from what happened to me as night and day," Brent said. "All the way to Wolf Lake, I kept thinking that my house would belong to someone else, that I was still in the past. But when I saw it was exactly as I left it, I knew I was really home again. I kept feeling that I was supposed to be at your house but didn't remember our dinner plans, not at first. You know the rest."

I sat back, reviewing what Brent had told us. Something didn't hold together. Brent had been gone for five days. According to his story, he'd walked in a cold rain for an unspecified length of time, spent the night in an untenanted cabin, and left the next morning, at which point he somehow stepped into the present in time to cross the path of the truck driver who had given him a lift.

It was a tale with the ring of truth, but it didn't add up to five days.

I pointed that out to him. "It appears that there are a few holes in your story."

"That's all I remember."

"Jennet's right," Crane said. "Did you spend more than one night at the cabin?"

He frowned. The effort to recall the omitted days upset him.

"I thought it had all come back, but I see what you're saying. I opened two cans. Two cans. A night and a day. Beef stew for dinner, chili for breakfast."

"Ugh."

"You'd be happy to eat anything, except maybe sardines, if you were starving."

I doubted that, but then I'd never been that hungry.

"This is disappointing," Brent said. "What do I do now?"

"Wait till the other memories return," I said. "That's all you can do. Spend more time at the barn with your new horse. Maybe she's the trigger."

"He," Brent said. "The next time it happens, I'm going to have cash in my wallet."

"The next time?"

"Sure. I want to go back. You can't call what happened to me an adventure in time. I was ripped off."

I sighed. There was no way to save Brent from his obsession without his cooperation. Fortunately he couldn't travel back in time simply because he wanted to. The time slip had its own rules.

Thirty-eight

The next morning I baked four dozen Christmas cookies and sprinkled them with red and green sugar. They were still warm when company arrived— Molly and Jennifer bundled up against the snow and wind.

After I'd hung up their parkas and the collies calmed down enough to allow conversation, Jennifer said, "We have news."

"But it isn't good news," Molly added. "We don't know what to do next. We figured you would."

That sounded ominous. I wished the girls didn't have so much faith in me.

I assembled ingredients for cocoa making and set an assortment of cookies on a Santa Claus plate. That I could do.

"What happened?

"Mrs. West, that's Trista's breeder, went to Beatrice's house with Trista's papers and pictures," Jennifer said. "Trista wasn't there. Beatrice said she didn't own a black collie."

"That's true. She doesn't."

"Mrs. West told her one of the neighbors had seen a black collie in her yard," Jennifer said. "It barked all day. She was about to call the police. Then Beatrice said there was a dog, but it didn't belong to her, that she was babysitting it for a friend."

"And the friend lives up north," Jennifer went on.

"Then, supposedly, Trista isn't in Foxglove Corners any longer?" I asked.

"She's somewhere up north."

"That covers a lot of territory."

"Beatrice told Mrs. West that the dog won't be around anymore."

"We don't believe it," Molly said. "Neither does Mrs. West."

I made the cocoa and filled three mugs to the top. At the last minute I remembered I had a package of miniature marshmallows. Where was it? Searching in the cupboard gave me much needed time to think. At this point, I didn't believe anything Beatrice said. I supposed she was capable of muzzling a dog and hiding it in the basement.

But why? What reason could she have for going to such lengths to keep a dog that didn't belong to her?

"Mrs. West is going to report her to the police," Molly said. "She thinks Beatrice stole Trista."

"Will the neighbor back her up?" I asked.

"I guess so, but she doesn't want Beatrice to know she complained. They still have to live in the same neighborhood."

"She can be an anonymous informer then."

Anyone could have been driven to distraction by non-stop barking. Poor Trista.

"Will the police be able to do anything?" Molly wanted to know.

"It depends."

I hoped they'd take Mrs. West's claim seriously, even though they had serious crimes on their roster. But what if Trista had been spirited away to another town?

"I don't understand why this Busy Bea doesn't buy a collie of her own," I said. "Or better yet adopt one from a shelter. Sue Appleton has a pretty tri all ready for her forever home."

But Beatrice wanted Trista. So did Trista's owner, who had offered a reward equal to the price of a show prospect for her return. This shouldn't be an issue. Trista's owner had the legitimate claim.

"Mrs. West was so nice," Jennifer said. "She gave us the reward money because we found Trista, even though we didn't really. She says we put her on Trista's trail."

"That was nice of her," I said.

"We still want to help bring Trista home," Jennifer said. "Tell us. What can we do?"

Brent had asked me the same question about remembering his lost days. Why did people think I had the answers? At times, I was the most confused person in the room.

If this were my mystery to solve, I would be at a standstill. I was glad the girls had taken it on as their first project.

"It's really up to Mrs. West from now on," I said. "It sounds like she's determined to get Trista back. This is a dog she bred, after all. I don't think she's going to let the matter go."

I helped myself to a cookie. They *were* good. Small wonder they were rapidly disappearing.

"What are you girls going to do with the reward money?" I asked.

Molly answered for both of them. "Split it and save it for college."

Jennifer reached for a star, leaving a trail of sugar on the table. "Trista should be in her own home for Christmas," she said.

~ * ~

Christmas was coming, but except for rare interludes, the Christmas Spirit continued to elude me, even with dozens of cookies stored in nostalgic tins, a wreath on the front door, and a balsam fir in the yard. In a few days, Julia would arrive from

England. I had the guest room ready for her with a white poinsettia and a box of holiday-decorated chocolates on the nightstand.

Wherever she went, Julia brought sunshine with her. We could use a little sunshine in Foxglove Corners.

I sat at the window, watching the snow fall and jotting down ideas for holiday activities Julia and I could enjoy together. A snow carnival at Spearmint Lake, a Christmas sale at the Green House of Antiques with vintage refreshments— whatever *they* were. Dinners out. Brent had mentioned another visit to the Hunt Club Inn during Julia's visit, and Julia liked the food and the atmosphere at the Adriatica.

After the first of the year, she would return to England. I wanted each day to be perfect with no unanticipated disturbance or trauma. No coyotes howling in the night; all mysteries frozen for the next few weeks. Trista's recovery in the hands of Mrs. West. What had I left out?

Veronica the Viper. For her, a transfer to the North Pole for the new year would be acceptable.

Really, Jennet, I told myself. *This is hardly what's meant by peace on earth good will to men.*

I didn't care. Besides, Veronica wasn't a man.

~ * ~

Annica was the embodiment of the holiday spirit in a swishy green dress. Her red-gold hair had a new shine, and her favorite silver bell earrings tinkled when she moved. She was in constant motion, flitting from table to table with a coffee pot and a happy smile. Something was afoot.

Rejoice and be merry... Visit Clovers and have a cup of Christmas cheer.

Well, hot chocolate topped with real whipped cream. This was my second cup today.

Annica slid into the booth, holding a cup of chocolate for herself. "Marcy can handle the crowd. We've been so busy I could drop."

I took my first sip of hot chocolate. "Everything tastes better at Clovers."

"Isn't this the most gorgeous day?" Annica said.

I glanced out the window at the trees across Crispian Road all draped in white. The wind had fashioned a fantastic snow sculpture at the woods' edge. It looked like a winged dinosaur.

"It's pretty but cold," I said.

"I got an A on my research paper on Emily Bronte, it's almost Christmas, and best of all, Brent is back. Now it'll really be a merry Christmas."

But for how long? I didn't say that. Annica must be aware of Brent's desire to return to the past. I hoped she was no longer thinking about accompanying him. Which, in all likelihood, wasn't going to happen.

I couldn't begin to understand the rules that governed the time slip, but I was reasonably certain that two people wouldn't be whisked out of time together, unless perhaps they were holding hands.

"The lady deputy was in for lunch today," Annica said. "You just missed her. She asked about Crane again. She wanted to know if he'd been in lately."

The last vestiges of my chocolate-inspired good mood evaporated. "What did you tell her?"

"Not lately. She asked about you, too."

"For heaven's sake. The woman doesn't even know me. I only saw her that one time she gave me a ticket. What did she want to know?"

"How you were. I said I hadn't seen you lately. That word 'lately' comes in handy when you're dealing with a super snoop."

"She's probably hoping I'll slip on the ice and break my neck."

"It isn't getting icy out, is it?"

"That was just an example. I wish she'd bring her questions to me."

Not that I wanted to talk to her. But maybe I had to.

I entertained a brief notion of speeding through Foxglove Corners in the hopes of attracting her attention. Not the best idea. I didn't want to end up in a ditch.

It almost felt as if I had a stalker, someone slinking around asking my friend about me. More to the point, asking questions about my husband.

What was her next step? I was sure there would be one, and I didn't need the added aggravation.

"I'm going to have to talk to Crane about her," I said. "I'll do it tonight."

Thirty-nine

No matter how I broached the subject of Veronica, I would sound like a jealous wife. But Crane should know about her uncalled-for interest in him— and in me. I, of course, assumed that Crane didn't return that interest. I loved my husband, and I trusted him.

After dinner, when he had finished reading the paper, I said, "Annica told me something disturbing today."

Having his full attention, I told him the whole story. "And she did this on a previous occasion. What do you think?"

He frowned. "I don't know. Offhand, I'd say Veronica is trying to make friends and fit in. She's new in town, and Christmas is coming…"

I hope you're not thinking of inviting her to our home for Christmas.

I had the good sense not to say that out loud. Could I possibly be more uncharitable in this season of good will?

"Aren't there any single men in the department?" I asked.

"We have two bachelors," he said. "Cole and Jim."

Well, then, Veronica. Redirect your focus.

"I can understand why she'd be interested in you," I said. "But why is she curious about me? Does she think I forgot that ticket she gave me? Which, by the way, I didn't deserve."

I shouldn't have mentioned that. Too late. But he didn't react to it.

"Veronica isn't interested in me—not in that way," he said.

Some men were so naïve. Even Crane. Didn't he realize how attractive he was to the opposite sex? The silver strands in his fair hair, the fine lines that bracketed his frosty gray eyes, and his rugged, handsome features added up to a unique and superior man. I couldn't blame Veronica for her infatuation, but she had no right to cast her eyes in my husband's direction.

I could never lose him. All of the color would drain out of my life if Crane wandered away from me.

That won't happen, I told myself. *Crane loves you and he's happy with our life together. How much more proof do you need?*

"I'm uncomfortable with her asking Annica about me," I said. "I don't like her making comments about me. It's creepy."

"If you got to know her…"

I didn't let him finish his sentence. "That wouldn't be a good idea. Maybe I'll meet her someday if the Sheriff's Department has a social event like a picnic."

Or a Christmas party?

That hadn't happened yet and probably wouldn't.

"I can have a word with her, if you like," he said.

"No. Unless she keeps doing it. Even then. I can handle my own problems. I just wanted you to know what's going on."

"Don't get so worked up, honey," he said. "Veronica's not a problem. She's harmless. She's just being friendly."

Candy interrupted our conversation with a spate of ungodly barking. It set all the collies off, even Raven outside in her house. In her rush to the bay window, she knocked a magazine off the edge of the coffee table.

Crane picked it up and ordered her to calm down. "Are we expecting company?"

"I don't think so. It can't be Brent. He'd have come in time for dinner."

I glanced out the window, laying a steadying hand on Candy's shoulder. "It's just deer. Three of them. They keep getting bolder. The poor things are hungry."

I didn't want to discourage them. Against a background of snow, they created a lovely, living Christmas card— for a heartbeat. Then they were gone, leaving seven agitated collies in their wake. One would think they'd be used to wandering wildlife.

It appeared that our discussion about Veronica was at an end. What had I achieved? My goal, I supposed. Crane was aware of Veronica's interest in us, and he knew how I felt about it. In a way, I wished I could summon up a modicum of sympathy for a woman trying to find her place in a new community. Especially during the Christmas season.

But I couldn't. No matter what Crane thought, I didn't believe for a moment that Veronica was harmless. At least I would be on guard from now on, and Annica would keep me apprised of any further developments.

As I always said, forewarned is forearmed.

~ * ~

Murder Suspect Confesses

So proclaimed the *Banner* headline the next morning.

At last. But this must mean that Jillian Cranbrook was dead. Poor Jillian. I'd suspected it all along.

Then I read the sub heading, *Cold Case Solved.* This couldn't be about Jillian. Quickly I read the article.

Clancy had admitted murdering a young girl several years ago. He claimed he never meant to do it, that he had blocked out the incident until the police wouldn't stop questioning him. That brought it all back. But how could he be held accountable for an act he'd long since forgotten?

Yes, he referred to murder as an incident. This was his story:

He was out in the country, minding his own business, when he came across a pretty young girl walking with her dog, a large collie.

Ginger!

He tried to be friendly, saying 'good morning' and telling her what a nice dog she had, but the girl told him to leave her alone. The dog growled at him. It wasn't nice. It was vicious.

Ginger vicious? Only because she sensed that this stranger was up to no good. She was right.

The girl turned around and started walking away. Incensed that she'd spurned his friendly overtures, Clancy pursued her, grabbed her, tried to make her talk to him, and somehow found himself choking her.

Clancy had confessed to the murder of Violet Randall, not Jillian Cranbrook.

Which didn't mean he hadn't killed Jillian as well.

To further confuse the issue, Clancy admitted taking his victim's green bracelet and watch because they were so pretty.

Green. Emerald, not sapphire. He was confusing Jillian with Violet. I couldn't be the only one who thought Clancy had murdered both young women. Two country roads. One in the summer, one in the winter. One girl walking, one in a car that had malfunctioned.

He would have been younger then and presumably stronger, although according to witnesses, already a vagrant and a drunk with a quick temper.

The article contained other facts. Clancy didn't remember what happened to the dog. He didn't think he'd killed it and didn't recall hiding his victim's body in the woods either. He thought he'd left it in the road and taken off. Nobody else was around to see what he'd done, so he certainly wasn't going to tell anybody what happened. It was the girl's fault for being unfriendly. It was always the woman's fault.

The police might have questioned him all those years ago, but it was fuzzy, like a bad dream.

He remembered the jewelry, though. He liked things that sparkled. He collected them.

It appeared that Clancy was indeed unbalanced. Because of that he might not stand trial. Unless the alleged lapses in his memory and the confusion about precious stones were an elaborate act.

Was he crafty enough to create this scenario?

Clancy was in the hands of the law. The police would sort it all out. I wouldn't have to worry about him bothering Miss Eidt in her library again. He wouldn't have a chance to end the life of another innocent girl.

"You can rest in peace, Violet," I said softly. "Your killer has been found."

But was this the end of Violet's story? For some reason I felt that it was only the end of a chapter.

~ * ~

Violet's aunt Viola was ecstatic.

"It's over. I've been praying all these years for Violet's killer to be found, but I never thought it would happen, not after all this time."

She was one of many people who called to talk to me about the newly revealed murderer. I had discussed the revelation with Lucy, Camille, Leonora, and Annica, in that order. I wondered if Crane had more information. I'd have to wait till he came home to find out.

"He didn't say anything about Violet's sapphire bracelet," Viola said.

"I assume he stole that too. Took it off her wrist and probably lost it somewhere along the way or pawned it."

"If Violet hadn't taken that walk and if Clancy hadn't have been in the vicinity, my niece would still be alive. I can't understand why they let him go in the first place."

"Well, they didn't have any evidence."

Crane said they'd most likely questioned anyone who, like Clancy, didn't have a job or a home and had been seen loitering in various parts of Foxglove Corners.

"My niece wasn't unfriendly, but she didn't like to be approached by strangers," Viola said. "I'm that way myself."

"I don't believe he forgot about it," I said. "How could anyone possibly murder someone and not remember it?"

"My poor Violet never had a chance. I've been crying all morning, but I'm happy that her killer is finally going to pay for what he did."

Maybe. I hoped so. I hoped that Clancy wouldn't be locked up, then released at some future time to go back to his rootless, murderous ways.

"I guess I'll always wonder why Ginger didn't defend her," I said.

"Yes, and how she got away without being killed herself."

"I can't see Clancy strangling a strong dog," I said. "Apparently he didn't have a weapon— like a gun or a knife."

"There's so much more I want to know."

"We'll never have all the answers, even if Clancy stands trial. He'll claim he doesn't remember."

A hard note stole into Viola's voice. "I can't forgive him. I know I should, but I can't."

"You're certainly entitled to your own feelings," I said. "They're going to prove that Clancy killed Jillian Cranbrook. Everything points to him as her killer."

I stopped and backtracked. "Scratch that. We don't know for certain that Jillian is dead. It just looks that way."

It wasn't over. Not at all.

Forty

As the collie pack rushed to the front door, I watched from the bay window. Brent lifted boxes of all sizes and shapes out of the Belvedere and set them down on the snow. Until this moment, I'd forgotten my promise to wrap presents for him to deliver on Christmas Eve.

"You have your work cut out for you, honey," Crane said as he threw on his jacket and went out to help him.

The collies were wild with anticipation, thinking, no doubt, that each box held tasty treats for them. Brent never forgot the animals, but these gifts were for the children of Foxglove Corners who would be lucky to have food on the table this Christmas, let alone presents.

In they came. Dolls, stuffed animals, books, games, puzzles, toy drones... He appeared to have shopped in every toy shop in the county— or in Santa's workshop. Along with toys he brought huge packages of wrapping paper, ribbons, tags, and seals.

Oh, my goodness. I'd have to call Leonora or Annica as soon as possible and pray one of them had several extra hours to help me.

Oh, well, it would be a relief to turn my attention to a normal task with a deadline.

Brent set a collie-sized reindeer in my arms. "I know you like deer."

Its red collar jingled obligingly, reminding me of Annica's silver bell earrings. Misty tilted her head, and Candy nudged it with her nose.

"These aren't for dogs," Brent said. "You guys will get yours later."

I shook the reindeer lightly for the pleasure of hearing its jingle bells ring.

"That's the last of it," he added. "Thanks for the help, Sheriff. What's for dinner, Jennet?"

"Something different. Camille gave me her recipe for stuffed cabbages."

"Sounds good. Guess I'll stay, if you made enough."

"Is a dozen enough?"

"Should be."

I'd have made two dozen if I'd known he was coming.

"I only have Christmas cookies for dessert, though," I said. "I'm all baked out."

"That's okay. I had two pieces of pie for lunch."

It seemed he'd been hungry ever since his return from the past.

"Would you and Crane please take these boxes upstairs to the study?" I asked. "Otherwise we won't have room to walk."

When they came back after several trips, Brent said, "I'll bet our Violet is happy now with that lowlife Clancy under lock and key."

"She should be able to rest in peace. Only..."

Perhaps I shouldn't say anything. It was too late, though. I had their attention.

"Only what?" Brent asked.

"I ran into Edwina Endicott at the library a few days ago. She claims she saw a girl and her collie walking on Huron Court in the snow. Who could they be but Violet and Ginger?"

"Didn't Miss Eidt tell you the Endicott woman was delusional?" Crane wanted to know.

"Not exactly. I don't remember her exact words."

"That was before Clancy confessed to the murder," Crane said. "Interesting timing."

I was about to ask him to explain what he meant when Brent said, "I thought Violet only walked in September or October."

"I'm only repeating what Edwina said."

Who said a ghost couldn't change her mind?

Brent sat in the rocker with Misty and Sky at his feet, and Crane poked at the fire. I added another place setting to the table and wished I could drive down Huron Court every now and then to see if the ghostly pair would materialize in the snow.

Impossible, and not only because of Crane's edict. I had never overcome my fear of slipping out of time and finding myself back in the past. Of getting lost in the mists of Huron Court. Of Crane driving by in his cruiser, looking for me, not seeing me because I existed on another plane.

That fear was burned deep in my mind and soul and heart.

A spoon flew out of my hand and landed on the hardwood floor with a clang. Gemmy lunged for it, saw that it was inedible, and backed away.

"Is everything okay, honey?" From the living room, Crane fixed me with a look I couldn't interpret. "Do you need help?"

"It's fine," I said. "I'm fine."

I reminded myself that Edwina Endicott was obsessed with otherworldly matters. If there wasn't a ghost to be seen, she was capable of manufacturing one. Therefore, I should take her story with the proverbial grain of salt.

That didn't alter the fact that Huron Court and the pink Victorian were dangerous for me and others. I was thinking of Brent.

As for Edwina's alleged sighting, with Clancy removed from vulnerable society, Violet had no reason to walk.

At least none that I knew of.

~ * ~

"How did your stuffed cabbages turn out?" Camille asked the next morning as we sat in her country kitchen sampling a coffee cake under the watchful eyes of Holly and Twister.

"Perfect. They're all gone. The entire dozen."

"It's a lot of work, but they're worth it," she said.

Camille was baking Christmas cookies too. Hers were more elaborate. She actually stuffed tiny envelopes of dough with delicious fillings. No simple stars and trees for her.

"So far the trapper has caught five coyotes," Camille said. "If they all move on, maybe we'll see more deer."

Only five? This was proving to be an expensive enterprise. "I think the coyotes have found their home in Foxglove Corners."

"Oh, I hope not. I saw one on Jonquil Lane yesterday. He was standing in the snow and staring at me. It's like he knew we hired the trapper."

"Don't be silly," I said. "He couldn't know."

Could he?

Of course not.

I broke off a piece of coffee cake, craving comfort food.

If the coyotes had howled last night, I didn't hear them. I'd had a rare restful night's sleep without noise or dreams.

Wait a minute!

There was a dream... Only a tiny piece of it remained in my memory.

A curving road. Snow pelting my face as if each flake contained a fragment of ice. A howling in the woods that didn't sound as if it came from the throat of a coyote.

Maybe the coyotes of Foxglove Corners had been howling last night after all.

The teakettle whistled, and Camille rose to pour boiling water over the leaves. I held my hand over the top of the teacup, letting the steam warm it. If only Lucy were here. She wasn't an interpreter of dreams, but she could read our tea leaves and perhaps pinpoint the source of the sudden unease that gripped me.

"What's the matter, Jennet?" Camille asked.

"I just remembered a bit of a dream I had last night."

"Not a pleasant one, I'm guessing."

"I don't remember enough of it to say."

Holly laid her paw on my lap.

"Good dog," I murmured and slipped her a piece of crust.

"Are you still worried about Brent?" she asked.

"In a way. You know Brent. He's always on the lookout for the new project, the beckoning adventure. He has a notion that he wants to go back to the past. Heaven knows why."

Camille smiled. "Because it's there. The opportunity, I mean."

"Probably. He fancies himself a modern day explorer. I wish he'd remember that not every explorer returns from the unknown."

Still he hadn't mentioned the time slips lately, nor the pink Victorian. Only Violet and her killer's surprising confession. Last night at dinner, he had been the Brent of old, a picture of bonhomie, telling stories about horses, laughing, complimenting my cookies. He had devoted a lot of time and energy amassing all those toys for his Christmas Eve delivery. He planned to bring the old-fashioned Fowler sleigh out of mothballs and make his traditional ride through Foxglove Corners.

I reminded myself again that Brent didn't have a choice in the matter, whether he remained in this world or stepped into another one. No one did. He could fall back into the past at any time or never experience a time slip again.

"There's no point in worrying about Brent, I suppose," I said. "There's something else that concerns me."

"The coyotes?"

"Yes, but there's another problem," I said. "There's a snake in my Eden."

And I told her about Veronica.

Forty-one

The gift we deliver and the gift we receive ...

I had brought the CD player into the study so the Kings Singers could provide Annica and me with music while we wrapped the presents.

Annica held up a book with a beautifully illustrated cover. "*Black Beauty*. I *loved* that story. For a long time after I read it, I wanted to have a black horse of my own. Isn't it a bit old-fashioned for a twenty-first century kid, though?"

"You just said you enjoyed it," I said.

"I was born in the last century," she reminded me. "It was my mom's book."

"*Black Beauty* is a children's classic. It'll never go out of style.

Brent had bought dozens of books, at least two for every game or toy. He had his priorities straight.

I felt as if I were drowning in a tidal wave of green and red. An hour of steady wrapping had transformed our neat study into a rustling paper mess. The collies thought they were helping by stealing empty rolls of gift wrap. I suspected I'd find bits of chewed cardboard all through the house.

To think we'd been so organized when we started. Presents on one side of the room; wrapping supplies on the other. We worked well together, though, inspired by the lovely, traditional carols. The upside was the return of the Christmas Spirit. I could almost see her smiling down on me, happy to see I was finally in the proper mood for the season.

"And here's *The Black Stallion*," Annica said. "A good gift for whoever loves horses."

"Here's one for a future chef." I reached for a box that contained a toy stove. It wouldn't be easy to wrap as it was an awkward shape. Red paper, I decided. White ribbon. A candy cane tag.

"Did you finish your Christmas shopping?" Annica asked.

"I haven't started."

"You must know you're running out of time."

"I guess so. Maybe I'll think of a great gift and buy one for everybody."

"Good luck with that," she said. "I have a few more presents to get. When we're finished, let's go to the Maplewood Mall. We can shop and have lunch at a new restaurant called the North Pole."

That was where Leonora had wanted to go on the last day of school. I felt a jab of guilt, wondering if she'd ended up going alone. I had the best friends in the world. Look at Annica giving up her free time to help me, although I imagined that helping Brent as well was a strong motivator.

"Let's do it," I said. "In another hour, we should have all the presents wrapped, and we'll be hungry."

"After the holidays, the North Pole will reopen as Blue Island, a fish place."

"Then we'd better go there today."

"Will Brent come by to pick up the presents?" Annica asked.

"I hope so," I said, envisioning Annica and me plowing through the snow to load my car. I didn't want that to happen.

"When?"

"Soon, I guess."

"He'll probably invite Lucy to go with him on the sleigh," she said.

"Probably. He did last year."

"I want to find a nice present for him," she said. "It has to be special but not too expensive."

"Remember, it's the thought that counts," I said. "He'll like what you give him because it's from you. Brent could have anything he wants."

"Not anything. He wanted to have the Gingerbread House ready for guests on Christmas Eve."

I'd almost forgotten the name Brent had chosen for his inn.

"Surely he abandoned that idea."

"It's in Limbo. I feel…" She taped a perfect green bow to the game she'd just wrapped. "I feel like we're on the edge of a cliff just ready to topple over the next time the wind blows."

Good grief! I almost dropped the scissors.

"We who?" I asked.

"Brent, you, me, all of us."

For a moment it seemed as if Lucy were in the room with us.

~ *~

You couldn't escape from holiday music at the Maplewood Mall. But why would you want to? It surrounded us, sending subliminal messages to shoppers.

Buy, buy, buy. Christmas sales are the best of the year. Buy now before the bargains are gone.

I found a lacy white blouse for Julia, who never had enough dressy blouses in her closet, a holly-and-ivy teapot for Lucy and two decorated with snow scenes for Camille and Miss Eidt, sleigh earrings for Leonora and for Crane a book I thought he'd enjoy,

What I Saw at Shiloh by Ambrose Bierce and a CD of Civil War songs.

"You did well," Annica said. "I wish I could have found something for Brent."

"He'd like the pair of wood horses we saw at the Art Fair. They're a bit pricey, but…"

She shifted her shopping bag to her other arm. "Maybe I'll go back for them on the way out. Brent is worth it, and Mary Jeanne promised us a Christmas bonus."

We were standing in front of a map of the mall, trying to locate the North Pole. The Little Drummer Boy was playing his drums for the Christ Child. The mall's indoor fountain was changing color. Blue… Yellow… Pink… A smell of popcorn filled the air. Suddenly I wanted popcorn more than lunch.

Annica grabbed my arm. "Look, Jennet. Isn't that Brent?"

No other man could stand out in a crowd as Brent did. His dark red hair, the color of a certain kind of maple leaf in autumn, was distinctive enough. Then there was his forest green suede jacket, along with the way he stood, as if he were the lord of the manor surveying his domain. And there was the requisite female companion at his side.

Veronica!

"It's that deputy woman all dressed up," Annica said. "What's she doing with Brent?"

They stood in a long line in front of the North Pole, in animated conversation, appearing to enjoy each other's company.

Veronica was all in white that contrasted sharply with her shining black hair. Even the coat draped over her arm was white. I hated to admit it, but she looked like a goddess. I remembered an old movie I'd seen recently on the Classics Channel, *One Touch of Venus*. She looked like Ava Gardner.

"They happened to run into each other?" I said.

"If you run into a friend, you say hello and go on your way. You don't have lunch together. Where could she have met him anyway?"

"Anywhere," I said. "Maybe they got acquainted at Clovers one day when you weren't working. I remember he saw her with Crane at the Lakeside Diner. Maybe Crane introduced them."

"Speaking of Clovers, if we're through here, why don't we go there for lunch?" Annica said. "I don't want to see them."

Neither did I. I'd be happy to see Brent anytime in any place. Veronica? Never. Veronica and Brent together... Well, I'd try to forget I saw that.

Crane didn't have to concern himself with Veronica trying to fit in her new hometown. She'd managed to meet Foxglove Corners' most prized bachelor.

Maybe she'd given him a ticket.

~ * ~

On the way out of the mall, we stopped at the Art Fair so Annica could buy the wooden horses for Brent. Seeing the man you cared for in the company of another woman would have daunted a lesser spirit. Annica had a generous nature.

"I guess he can see whoever he wants," she said. "We're not going together, and it's a free world."

I nodded. "You know Brent has a lot of girlfriends."

"I just wanted to be the most important one."

"Maybe you are. He chose you to help him furnish the pink Victorian."

"Yeah, I'm a good interior decorator."

She fell silent as we found my car in the crowded parking lot— no easy task— but perked up when we reached Clovers.

Clovers had the Christmas color and ambience without the music. I followed the jingle of Annica's silver bell earrings to the booth with my favorite view of the Crispian Road woods. When Marcy had taken our orders, Annica said, "He gave me emerald earrings last Christmas. I don't wear them often. I'm afraid I'll lose them. I wonder if he'll buy *her* a present."

"I suppose it depends on how well he knows her."

"He never mentioned her, not once."

That didn't surprise me. "Men are good at not talking about Veronica. It's like she's a well-kept secret."

"She's beautiful," Annica said.

I couldn't disagree. Veronica was a beauty in a goddess-movie star way.

"So are you," I said.

"Not like her."

"Well, no. Neither am I. Few women are."

Marcy swooped down on us bearing two large menus. "How does it feel to be a customer, Annica?" she asked.

"Great! I know what I want. A bowl of chicken noodle soup and one to take out."

Comfort food.

"For me, too," I said.

I figured I could stop worrying about Brent getting swept away to the past now. At least for a while.

Forty-two

The night was winter perfection, the kind to inspire a Christmas greeting card. A luminous moon shone above the high silvery branches of a poplar tree, and myriads of stars sprinkled diamond dust on the fresh snow.

Across Jonquil Lane, a solitary lamp burned in the window on the yellow Victorian's first floor. Camille and Gilbert were out for the evening, and the Linton house was dark. Once again I felt as if I were alone at world's end.

It was a night when peace in the world, and in my own life, seemed an attainable goal. Not a sound disturbed the silence, not even the infernal howling of the coyotes. It seemed that all dreams were possible. Christmas was coming. We were all safe during this blessed time. In the words of Shakespeare, *No spirit dare stir abroad...No fairy takes, nor witch hath power to charm, So hallow'd and so gracious is the time.*

So banish disappointment and fear and all things malignant and hungry. This night was going to usher in a new day and a happy era for all.

My work for the day was done. Brent's Christmas presents were stacked in the living room waiting for him to pick them up, Crane's dinner was in the oven, ready for his late arrival home, and I had hung the last ornament on the tree. Finally I'd gone outside to bring Raven's dish into the house.

Something about the night, some unknown and unknowable element, prompted me to stand still for an instant and listen.

Really, Jennet. There's nothing to hear. Nothing there.

Raven wasn't in her house, which wasn't unusual for her. Often she set out on an adventure in the woods before settling down for the night. I'd stopped worrying about her. Unlike the collies who lived inside, she wouldn't be confined, and she always came home.

Anyway, she'd been here to lick her dinner dish clean.

A twig snapped. It seemed louder than it should be, but not loud enough to make my heart skip a beat, not even unusual when we lived in such close proximity to the wild. Nonetheless my heart launched itself into an uncomfortable, erratic rhythm.

All right. It was larger than a twig. A fallen branch then, lying on top of the snow. Some creature was abroad.

I scanned the area, saw nothing but snow and deer tracks.

That's it. A deer had ventured close to the house and, sensing my presence, had melted into the darkness.

Then why hadn't all the dogs barked?

I grabbed Raven's dish and, stepping deep in unshoveled snow, I hurried toward the beckoning kitchen light.

From inside the house came an ungodly howl. Trapped within the walls, it was still a bone-chilling sound.

Candy. She was the prime howler in the pack.

Another closer sound stopped me in mid-step. Breathing. Where there's breathing, expect to find a living creature.

Dear God, not the vagrant killer. Clancy was still in police custody. Wasn't he?

My hand on the doorknob, safety in sight, I searched the darkness, looking for the source of the disturbance.

Nothing.

Breathing. A rustling.

Well, maybe something.

Beyond Raven's doghouse, a form took shape. Unmoving, it fixed me with an ungodly glowing stare.

The creature was enormous, larger than a collie. It was muscular. Black. Standing on four feet. Neither coyote nor wolf. In my territory, but unafraid. Not the Dogman but a coywolf. I'd seen it before, had almost convinced myself it was a creature of my imagination.

Imaginary creatures don't breathe. They don't trod on sticks. They don't challenge you with a cold stare.

Was this the animal Camille had seen?

Without thought, I flung Raven's dish at the shape and...

It wasn't there.

All right, that's impossible. No wild creature runs away that quickly.

For a moment I considered finding the flashlight and looking for large canine paw prints in the snow.

Do it in the morning.

I'd find another dinner dish for Raven, stay in the house, and wait for Crane. And trust that the beast was miles away.

The night hadn't been so peaceful after all.

~ * ~

The next morning I put the last of the breakfast dishes away in the cupboard and refilled the dogs' water pail. It was early, and I had a whole day ahead of me to do whatever pleased me.

Before he left, Crane had investigated the area behind Raven's doghouse, supervised by a curious Raven. Any animal prints had been obliterated by a late night snowfall. Knowing the coywolf had been so near the house unnerved me. Was he looking for food?

Where had he gone? For that matter, where did any of them go during the day?

I could think of several places. The woods adjacent to the yellow Victorian, the unfinished construction, someone else's woods. The bold ones ventured out to the lane, no longer afraid of humans, if they ever had been.

I only knew I didn't want to see the creature again.

A ripple of falling water drew my attention to my phone on the kitchen table where I'd left it. I saw that my caller was Annica.

"Hey, Jennet," she said. "Something's happened. It isn't good. Is it okay if I come over?"

"Sure. I'm staying home all day. What's wrong?"

"I don't want to talk about it on the phone. I'll be there in about twenty minutes. See you then."

It was early in the day for company, but friends were always welcome in our home, and I was always ready for them. I had coffee, tea, and hot chocolate. I took banana nut muffins out of the freezer to thaw and sailed through the living room, gathering stuffed toys and bones. A pity I couldn't relocate Brent's hundred plus presents.

The collies always knew when change was imminent. Misty pulled her toy goat out of the basket and followed me as I brought two blue-checked napkins out of the credenza drawer.

The drive took Annica fifteen minutes and left her breathless. She wasn't wearing earrings, a true indication of her state of mind.

One look at her face told me this wasn't going to be a casual mid-morning get together. I took her coat, told her to leave her boots on, and asked again, "What's wrong?"

"Brent's gone again," she said. "I can't find him. I called Lucy, and she knew. She said he's in trouble again and she doesn't know how to help him."

I pulled out a chair for her and frowned at Misty, who thought she spied a new playmate. "Sit. Start from the beginning. The last time we saw Brent he was with Veronica at the North Pole."

She started to laugh, a nervous laugh that might well move on to hysteria.

"That sounds so funny when you say it like that. The North Pole!"

"Tea or coffee?" I asked.

"Oh, tea, I guess. Yes, tea. I need to calm down. Well, Brent called me after that. He asked me to meet him at the house and bring the lamp..."

"I'm not following you. What lamp?"

"The one I found at the Green House of Antiques. The saleslady called it a *Gone with the Wind* lamp. It was beautiful with pink and yellow roses on the globes."

"It sounds expensive."

"Yes, but Brent gave me one of his credit cards so that if I saw something perfect for the house I could buy it right away," she said. "So I did."

It sounded as if Annica and Brent were closer than I'd thought. How many men would trust a girlfriend with a credit card? Annica must be more secure in her relationship than she'd realized.

"Did you meet him at the house?"

"I waited a whole hour, just sitting in my car in front of the house. He never showed up. It was like before when he stood me up for dinner."

"And you assume he's missing? He didn't just forget?"

"It was his idea, Jennet. How could he forget? Anyway, he had given me a key for emergencies, but I didn't use it until I knew for sure he wasn't going to be there."

The teakettle broke into her narrative with its shrill whistle. I poured water over the leaves and thought about what Lucy had said. Lucy knew. Brent was in trouble. Lucy couldn't help him.

Could anyone?

"So you went inside..." I prompted.

"He'd gone to Clovers. There was a bag of sandwiches on the coffee table, and his jacket was lying on the sofa..."

Just like before.

"I searched the house. All right, Jennet, prepare yourself because this is really, really scary. In the room we decorated for Violet, I found a sheet of paper torn from that notebook Brent always carries with him. It was something new in the house. No, I mean old. It was white, turning yellow, and the ink was fading.

Torn from Brent's notebook.

"And?"

I held my breath.

"It was two sentences in Brent's handwriting. It said, *I came through. I need help.*"

Forty-three

"Brent came through," I said. "He must be referring to a time slip."

"What else?"

Like a danger signal, a picture of Brent standing in line at the North Pole with Veronica flashed on and off in my mind. Apparently he'd had lunch with Veronica, then afterward called Annica to meet him at Violet's house from which he stepped into the past.

He lived his life at a dizzying pace and never seemed to tire. This latest trip was bound to slow him down, though.

I should have known this day would come. Once Brent started traveling down that dark path, this was the inevitable outcome.

But something didn't add up.

"Brent would have had to be inside the house to slip into the past and write the note, wouldn't he?" I asked. "Where was the Belvedere?"

"It wasn't there. That's why I waited outside the house."

"He had to have his car. He couldn't have walked to the pink Victorian from wherever he was."

"You're right. Why didn't I think of that?"

I drank more tea and thought about transportation. Vintage automobiles were rare in Foxglove Corners. A yellow Plymouth Belvedere with soaring white fins would be easy to see unless it was deep in the woods.

What if Brent had had an accident like mine? A deer materializing on Huron Court. A deadly swerving into the woods. Then he would start walking, in search of help, as I had, unless he was injured. He must have been all right, though. One way or another, he had arrived at the house with take-out sandwiches and at some later time had written the note.

Some later time? That should be some *years* earlier. Or later? My head was swimming.

"I have to call Crane," I said. "He can be on the lookout for the Belvedere right away."

"Do you think it's possible for a car to slip back in time?" Annica asked.

"I don't know."

The possibility demanded more tea, more contemplation. I lifted the top of the teapot. We had plenty of tea, enough to see us through the next ten minutes anyway. Then I'd make more. Mint tea, this time. I for one felt in need of something to sooth the clenching of my stomach muscles.

I considered all the time travel tales I'd read over the years. Handy time machines often stood by to transport a traveler to another year. Often an unnatural storm or a powerful bolt of lightning swept a character away. Or fog. *The White Fog*, one of the old Gothics Miss Eidt had given me for Christmas, had a heroine who went back in time when she walked through a fog.

Remember the mists that hugged Huron Court.

Then there were characters who went to sleep in one time and woke in another. I'd never known a character to arrive at a past or future time in a vehicle.

"Like in *Back to the Future?*" Annica added. "Remember the DeLorean?"

Okay. I'd forgotten those movies. But I couldn't see Brent driving back in time in a fifties' vehicle.

On the other hand, why not? It would suit his flamboyant personality.

"I'm having trouble with the note," I said.

Without a doubt, the handwriting on the note was Brent's. I'd seen samples of it countless times. The page looked as if it had been torn from his black notebook, the one he'd left behind on his last time trip. As to the condition of the paper, its yellow tinge testified to its age. I looked at it again, more closely, and noticed a faint smudge of ink at the bottom.

It suggested agitation. A plea for help, written hurriedly, left in a place where Annica would be liable to notice it.

I'd set the note in the middle of the table, far from the teapot and our cups lest it come in contact with even a drop of water. I didn't want to see it ruined in any way. It was a relic, a link to the past. Perhaps a clue.

"That note puzzles me, too," Annica said. "Where was it all the other times we were in Violet's room? You were there yourself once."

"I wish I could explain the intricacies of time, but I'm not a rocket scientist."

Annica's voice took on a desperate note, one I seldom heard. "We have to help him, Jennet. He's counting on us. What can we do?"

"*Nothing,*" Lucy had said.

"Nothing. I can't think of anything except maybe... No, not that."

"What?"

I didn't want to say it, not even think about it, but I did. "To spend time in Violet's house and see if the time slip will activate itself again."

No, my inner voice insisted. *No, no, no!*

Annica was silent. I hoped she wasn't still thinking about trying to follow Brent into the past. I had to discourage her. Quickly. One friend lost in time was one too many.

"There are no guarantees that would happen," I said. "I certainly can't take the chance."

"Yeah, your husband won't let you. But I'm not married. I answer to only one person. Myself."

"It isn't that," I said. "I love Crane and my life in the here and now. I'd never do anything to put it at risk."

Besides, I was afraid of being stranded in the past. As Brent might well be.

A determined paw landed on my lap. Candy was eying the muffin I'd absently crumbled into a napkin. She added the pathetic little whimper of a starving collie.

Well, she might as well enjoy it. My first and only bite had been unsatisfactory. It tasted flat. Maybe I'd left out an essential ingredient.

I held the muffin in front of her mouth and watched it disappear, which was the signal for the other collies to approach the table and beg.

"They're not very good, are they?" I said.

"Not as good as Clovers."

I scooped the remainder up, broke them into small pieces, and spread them on a newspaper. The collies fell upon them, and I knew there wouldn't even be a crumb left to sweep.

"I feel like I'm living in a science-fiction movie," I said, joining Annica at the table again. "I can deal with a mystery and even a murder, but not this. When did my life become so complicated?"

The answer was simple. When I'd walked the dogs down a country road and met a girl playing ball with her collie in front of an elegant pink Victorian house.

Little did I know... In spite of the seriousness of the situation, I smiled. My life wasn't a science-fiction tale; it was a Gothic novel.

"Let's go back to the beginning," I said. "Take Brent's note. Did you ever see it in the house before today?"

"No, and Brent's cleaning service went over that room with a fine tooth comb. Brent and I arranged the furniture ourselves. It wasn't there."

"Because Brent hadn't gone back to the past to write it," I said.

To have aged along with the house, the note *must* have been there somewhere. On that other plane? In the alternate universe?

Brent had scribbled the two desperate sentences. He had relied on Annica to find it. What, exactly, had he hoped she would do?

A growing tension throbbed in the back of my head, a prelude to a headache on the way. I felt as if I were back in Sister Mary Barbara's eleventh grade physics class, attempting to grasp a concept that forever eluded me.

"I can't do it," I said.

"Can't do what?"

"Can't help Brent. I couldn't do anything for him the last time. Nobody could. He had to come back on his own. And if, by chance, you were able to join him in the past, how could that help? There would be two of you in trouble."

Tears glittered in Annica's eyes. Her hand moved toward her ear. If she'd been wearing her silver bell earrings, they would have added a fairy-light tinkle to the silence that followed the collies' loud crunching. She must have forgotten she'd left them at home.

I lifted my cup to my lips and found it was empty. Annica hadn't touched her tea, but she'd eaten the muffin without complaint. I refilled our cups and came to a decision.

I had to visit Dark Gables and talk to Lucy. Not that she would have a neat solution to Brent's dilemma, but this new development would cause me to implode if I didn't share it with her.

~ * ~

Annica left soon after, voicing her intention of going to the university library to research time travel. "Not fiction," she said. "I'll look for scientific articles and books. Maybe I'll find the answer there."

I let the dogs out, stayed with them, and gave them fresh water and the homemade dog biscuits Camille had baked for them. Then I left a message on Crane's voice mail and took one last look at the Christmas tree. It was lovely, and I hadn't had a chance to enjoy it or even plug it in.

Problems never crop up at convenient times, but I could afford a few hours away from the house. Crane was going to meet Julia at the airport in the morning, and I'd already planned a nice welcome meal for her tomorrow as well as dinner for us tonight.

I still had to wrap the presents I'd bought at the mall yesterday, but I could do that this evening.

"Hold on, Brent," I said, willing him to hear me from whatever dark place he'd gone. "We're going to do everything in our power to help you."

And hope it'll be enough.

Forty-four

Lucy presided over her white teapot on the wicker coffee table. Her long black hair fell in glossy waves past her shoulders, and her black dress made her look especially somber. A plate of store-bought oatmeal cookies lay on a magazine, being ignored by us but not by the collie, Sky. We'd been together like this countless times, Lucy, Sky, and me.

Today was different. It was almost like a wake.

"I know about Brent," Lucy said. "I was half asleep early this morning, and I heard his voice. He said two words: *Help me*. At the same time, I had a strong feeling that he was no longer part of our world. By then I was awake and afraid, so afraid, for him."

With her words, the temperature in the sun room seemed to plummet. My turtleneck sweater and long sleeves could never be warm enough to keep this unnatural iciness at bay.

"You're don't mean he's dead, do you?" I asked.

"I can't say, but I don't think so. He's just gone. Tell me about the note Annica found."

"The note. All right. It was a plea for help written in Brent's hand on a page torn from his notebook. It looked like it had been in the house, in Violet's room, for decades. It hadn't, of course."

Lucy nodded. "After Brent returned to the past, he wrote it, and it became something new in the environment."

"Do you understand how that's even possible?" I asked.

"No, Jennet. I'm just going to accept that it is."

We were having tea, Lucy's new favorite, Garden Mint. No matter that I felt as if I'd drunk a gallon of tea with Annica only hours ago.

"Yesterday Brent left a message on my phone to remind me about our plans for Christmas Eve," Lucy said.

When I looked puzzled, she added, "To accompany him on his sleigh ride."

"Oh, yes, to deliver the presents."

Were they doomed to stay in my living room unwrapped and undelivered while the children of Foxglove Corners waited in vain to hear the sound of Brent's sleigh bells? I hoped not, but I could see them taking up space in my living room, which wouldn't do with Julia's visit. I'd have to ask Crane to move them back to the study.

"Brent wasn't expecting this..." Lucy paused, hardly ever at a loss for words until this moment. "What would you call it? Complication?"

"For want of a better word."

I imagined Brent had been thinking of the lunch he'd shared with Veronica at the North Pole or of Annica and the new *Gone with the Wind* lamp. Of how the lamp would look in the pink Victorian or of the new horse in his barn. Anything but leaving all this behind without a moment's warning.

"He wanted to travel to the past again," I said. "But when it was convenient for him. He should have learned the way it works from his last time slip."

Lucy swirled a silver spoon through her tea, stirring up the leaves. "I don't believe he expected to find anything threatening in the past. He told me if he saw Violet, he'd warn her not to go walking with Ginger on that day."

The day Clancy had tried to force her to return his friendly overture with a smile of her own and words of encouragement. The day he'd killed her.

"Didn't he realize he'd be changing the past?" I asked.

"He figured the end would justify the means."

The need to avoid altering the future was a constant in the time travel fiction I'd read. I thought of *A Sound of Thunder* by Ray Bradbury. One minor, seemingly insignificant, change in the distant past led to a future in which dinosaurs roamed the city streets and preyed on humans. The phenomenon even had a name: the Butterfly Effect.

"I don't think Violet would change her plans because of a stranger's wild story," I said.

My sometimes pesky-sometimes wise inner voice was clamoring to be heard. Violet had had a premonition. She knew her life was going to be cut short. Wouldn't she seize any opportunity to change her fate if all it involved was staying home on a particular day?

If she had only done that, she wouldn't have been walking on Huron Court when Clancy came stumbling down the road, perhaps reeling from downing too many drinks at the local bar.

I was overlooking something, though. Brent had sent two desperate pleas to the future for help. In all likelihood, he wouldn't be in a position to tamper with events on Violet's behalf. He would be busy ensuring his own survival.

"It's an interesting idea, the possibility of changing the future," Lucy said. "Suppose Violet didn't die by Clancy's hand but perished in some other way, perhaps on the same day, because it was meant to be?"

I could see another side of Lucy, the horror story writer glimpsing a new idea, her present concerns on hold.

Then she said, "I can't imagine the world without Brent in it. I have no idea how to help him, I haven't a clue, but there has to be a way. And I'm going to find it. *We're* going to find it. You, me, and Annica. Now, drink your tea, Jennet. For a start, we'll see what the tea leaves say."

~ * ~

"I see a road," Lucy said. "There's a fork in it. And here's a figure." She pointed to a long light leaf. "It's you at a crossroad. You don't know which way to turn."

"That was how it all began, except I *did* know the way to turn. I took the road less traveled by."

"It looks to me like you're going to do it again."

"Oh, no," I said. "I'm not. I can't."

"Don't panic. This is what I see. Maybe if I look at it in another way, tilt the cup a bit…"

I waited through a long pause, while Lucy searched for an alternate, more palatable interpretation of the arrangements of the leaves.

"No" she said. "This is a road, here's a fork in the road, and the light leaf is you because this is your cup."

I sat back and let my mind travel back to Huron Court, one of the few places in Foxglove Corners I avoided.

"The last time I set foot on Huron Court, I was following my collie, Misty," I said. "You remember, she'd run away."

What else could lure me back to that treacherous, accursed stretch of roadway?

Brent? I loved Brent as a good friend but couldn't help him this time if by doing so I endangered myself.

He would never expect that of me.

Help me. Lucy had heard his voice.

I need help, he'd written in the note, presumably to Annica, that he hoped would make it intact to the future.

Which meant he'd appealed to Lucy and to Annica but not to me.

That was neither here nor there.

Don't be a coward, I told myself. *We all have to do our part.*

At present, Annica was researching time travel. She would add to her knowledge but that wouldn't bring Brent back to us. Lucy would do something. But what? And I? At this point, I didn't know.

Lucy set my cup on the coffee table. "I'm sorry, Jennet. That's all I see. You know you don't have to believe it."

"It's that house," I said.

"Yes, it's evil. I've known that ever since I first set eyes on it. But all Brent could see was a challenge with a new haunted inn as the prize. He understood the risks."

"How is any of this going to help him?" I wanted to know.

"It isn't, but I'm going to try to think of something."

~ * ~

That evening, Crane said, "We can't report him missing this time. We know where he is."

"Sort of. I've been thinking. He's in Foxglove Corners at a time when it was probably quieter and more peaceful than it is now. What kind of danger could he be in?"

"All I can think of is that he wants to come back and doesn't know how."

I had to marvel at my one time practical, down to earth husband. Since we'd met, he'd dealt with ghosts and ghostly premonitions, and now time travel. He accepted every strange thing that happened.

"I haven't found the Belvedere," he added. "For all we know, it's in the past with Fowler."

"That suggests he was outside the house when he went back to the past. How was he able to leave the note in Violet's bedroom?'

"I see what you're getting at. If Fowler ended up in the same time you did, Violet and her family would be living in the house. He couldn't just walk in and leave a note on a table."

"I can't think about this anymore," I said. "It's making my head ache. Will you keep on looking for Brent's car?"

"Sure will, and I have Mac searching too. He's curious, but I didn't give him any details."

"Julia is going to walk into quite a mystery," I said. "I'll have to tell her what's going on."

And what an interesting conversation that would be.

"Let's hope her flight arrives before the storm," he said.

I'd been so focused on the past that I hadn't bothered to listen to the weather report.

"What storm?"

"The one that's coming in time to disrupt holiday travel. I heard they're expecting a foot of snow."

Forty-five

The snow began at ten o'clock the next morning, right on schedule. It fell steadily and slanted westward. Crane planned to meet Julia's plane at four while I stayed home to take care of the dogs and prepare a welcome dinner.

I played with the collies until we all grew tired of fighting the weather. The dogs came in to take naps, and I wrapped the presents I'd bought at the mall when Brent was still safely anchored to the present. Before the time slip. I'd bought him a set of champagne flutes from Crane and me, hoping the pair of fox cubs painted on the glass might inspire him to rethink his position in the Foxglove Corners Hunt.

Would he be home in time to open his gift on Christmas Day? Was it even winter where he was? At this point I could only hope so.

I taped a silver bow to the box and set it under the tree. Now for Julia's blouse.

I hoped her presence would be a good omen. Friends were wonderful, but I wanted my sister. How many times had I said that over the years? *I want my sister.*

She was on her way.

The teapots for Lucy, Camille, and Miss Eidt were easy to wrap, as were Crane's book and CD. Leonora's sleigh earrings took a little longer, since a small box is always more of a challenge than a large one. Crane had taken the children's presents up to the study. Brent would never make it back in time to load the sleigh, pick up Lucy, and set out on his traditional ride through Foxglove Corners.

I couldn't bear to think of their disappointment— and his.

He might not make it back, period.

But I had promised myself to entertain only positive thoughts. The dogs' bones, balls, and new stuffies were wrapped and stacked on a high shelf in the front closet. Candy and Misty were worse than little kids at ferreting out my hiding places.

As if she knew I was thinking about her, Misty dropped her toy goat at my feet. I was wrong about all the dogs napping. I tossed it for her and found myself engaged in a game of fetch.

Later that afternoon, I called Lucy. "Did you hear anything more?"

"I haven't heard Brent's voice, if that's what you mean, but the strangest feelings are coming through. I know they originate with him."

"Strange in what way?"

"I'm sensing fear, despair, and certainty that all is lost. I'm afraid Brent may not be coming home this time. I had a dream last night about coyotes," she added. "They had banded together and were advancing on the house. They looked like people. Like a mob."

"Jot that down in your idea book," I said.

"I could practically feel their hot breath in my face. My hand hurt. I turned the light on to see if something had bitten me."

"And had it?"

"No. I was sleeping on it, but that dream means something. Something bad."

Why did I think I could summon positive thoughts by talking to Lucy with her gloom-and-doom take on the situation? Despair and fear were not qualities I associated with Brent, even though he was out of his element in whatever alien place he'd landed. Brent should be able to acquit himself admirably in the present or in the past.

"It won't be a merry Christmas without him," Lucy said.

"We still have time for him to come home. Julia will be with us. Come over and join us on Christmas Day."

"I'd love to unless I get snowed in."

I glanced out the window. There had been no break in the snowfall. Jonquil Lane was all but buried, even without about six more inches predicted. Now I could worry about Julia's flight being delayed.

It was going to be a long day.

After a quick cup of tea and a slapped-together sandwich, I called Annica.

"What did you find out at the library?" I asked.

"Nothing I could understand, but I looked up a friend of mine, a physics major. I asked him if he thought time travel was possible."

"What did he say?"

"Only in the movies. Then he laughed. Naturally I didn't give him any details. He asked me if I'd go out with him sometime. I said I was going through a bad break-up. Maybe after that."

"What's our next step?" I asked.

"I'm going back to Violet's house. I'll look in every room. Maybe I'll find another message from Brent. Maybe I'll travel back to the past myself." She paused. It sounded as if she were eating something crunchy. "I don't suppose you'd come with me?"

"No," I said. "And don't go anywhere while it's still snowing. The roads are too dangerous."

I wasn't worried about Crane, who had driven in far worse weather, but Annica was too distracted to be behind the wheel.

"Keep in touch," I said, "and come over on Christmas Day. We're not doing anything special. I'm just cooking a small turkey."

"If I'm still here."

I didn't like the sound of that.

"Don't forget, you have a dog to take care of. You don't want to leave Angel without her owner."

She ignored that grim possibility. "Danger is all around us. Mary Jeanne closed Clovers early. We were closing on Christmas Eve anyway."

So Annica was free to prowl through the pink Victorian, assuming the country roads were passable. Then what? I shuddered at the thought of Annica visiting an isolated house on a snowy night, even if it didn't have a dubious reputation. Anything could happen to her.

~ * ~

They arrived with a wave of snow and Christmas good cheer, Julia all in red and Crane still in his uniform, carrying her suitcase. Like Annica, Julia jingled when she moved. With her it was the gold bracelet loaded with English and Scottish charms.

"Back," Crane told the collies, and miracle of miracles, they fell back.

"It's wonderful to be home," she said. "Home in Michigan, that is."

I hugged her. "I thought you liked it in England a little too well. I thought maybe you'd met a handsome Englishman. A lord or something."

In truth I'd thought she might want to stay there permanently.

"I'll always come home," she said. "My plane made it in just under the wire. They're cancelling flights right and left."

"Well, you're here and safe."

"The roads are bad," Crane said. "I'll take your suitcase up to your room. Then I'd better shovel the walk."

He gave me a special look which I interpreted as 'It's your story to tell.'

"Sit by the fire," I said. "I'll put the water on for tea, and we can talk. You've walked into a mystery."

Her eyes lit up. "I was hoping you'd say that."

The collies had settled down, lying or sitting as close to Julia as they could. Most of them remembered her from her last visit.

Her gaze fell on Star who wagged her tail slowly. "You have a new dog."

"That's Star. She's a rescue."

Star crept closer to Julia, who extended her hand for Star to sniff.

"Tell me about the mystery," she said.

"Let me preface it by saying you're not going to believe it."

"Try me."

I had to start at the beginning, at my first glimpse of Violet with her collie, Ginger. The story grew progressively stranger, but she listened intently, never interrupting me.

"Now Brent is missing," I said. "We think he's gone back in time."

Julia stared at me. "You're serious, Jennet?"

"Perfectly. We don't know for sure, but it seems logical."

"I'm willing to believe in ghosts," she said. "At least I'll keep an open mind. But time travel? My willing suspension of disbelief stops there."

"Then let me present you with proof. I'll be right back."

I didn't have to hunt for the handkerchief my mother had given me that had accompanied me on my journey to the past and remained behind to age along with the pink Victorian. It was neatly folded in a special wooden box, looking fragile, as if might turn to powder in my hand.

Our mother had given Julia a dozen similar hankies of her own, all embroidered with delicate flowers.

Her eyes misted as she touched the soft material, and I told her the story of how it had been found in the house. "I always thought Foxglove Corners was beautiful, Jennet, but now I'm wondering what kind of place you moved to."

"It's a charming little town that happens to exist on the fringes of the other world," I said.

I liked that description. I'd have to remember it.

Forty-six

It was the most unusual Christmas Eve I'd ever experienced. Julia and I sat in the living room in front of a roaring fire with only the tree lights for additional illumination. As Julia said, we were living the American Dream. The dogs were half asleep, waking when deer invaded their territory or one of us mentioned food.

We'd been having a happy time, reminiscing about past Christmases and our age-old debate. Should we open presents on Christmas Eve or Christmas Day? I'd lost that argument long ago. We waited until Christmas Day to exchange gifts.

Missing from the evening was the usual anticipation of Christmas morning. Well, not missing, only lost in occasional sad realizations. Brent wouldn't be here tomorrow to exclaim over the champagne flutes with the fox cub illustrations. He wasn't here to deliver presents to the children who had come to expect them.

I wondered if it was snowing on the Huron Court of yesteryear.

Something else was borderline worrisome. Annica wasn't answering her phone. I'd called her twice and left two messages. It wasn't like her to ignore my calls.

Julia was saying, "I've loved every minute of my time in England, but I'm almost ready to come back to the states. Another six months, I think."

"You've been gone so long," I murmured.

"I wouldn't have missed it for the world."

Crane and Candy burst through the front door. Candy's coat had a thick new layer of white, and Crane hadn't fared much better. He'd been shoveling the walkway once again, and Candy had been supervising. The other collies had elected to stay warm and dry by the fireside.

"It's tapering off," he said. "Then it's supposed to snow again on Christmas night."

"We can stop dreaming of a white Christmas," Julia said. "It's here."

"Did we get twelve inches?" I asked.

"More like four or five."

"You look like a snowman," I said. "Come keep Julia company while I'll make us all hot chocolate."

A sliver of apprehension broke off from the large block that had lodged in my mind unnoticed in the pleasant overload of muted Christmas music and nostalgic conversation.

Something bad was going to happen. It was happening now, far from our cozy, safe hearth.

Was Lucy suddenly aware of a similar feeling across the miles in Dark Haven? A feeling that came out of nowhere and gave no warning of its arrival. All right. Call it by its name. A foreboding.

No fairy takes, I thought, nor *witch hath power to charm…*

The Evil hovered that over Foxglove Corners had never read *Hamlet* and didn't respect this holy night.

The clock struck ten.

"You look so comfortable sitting there," Julia said. "I'll make the chocolate."

She rose. Star and Misty padded after her.

"There's another tin of Christmas cookies in the cupboard," I called. A simple enough statement, it caught the attention of my entire collie family.

Ten o'clock was too late to call anyone, especially on the night before a holiday, but I didn't think Annica would mind, considering the circumstances.

I tapped in her number and listened to her voice mail, instructing me to leave a message. I'd already left two.

She wouldn't have gone to bed so early. She couldn't have decided to go out in this weather, in spite of my warning. Not on this night before Christmas.

I thought again. She would if she believed she could help Brent. I would do the same for Crane.

"What's wrong, honey?" Crane asked.

I told him what I suspected.

"You're really worried about her?"

"I am."

"Tell you what. I'll drive out to Huron Court and see if she's at the house."

"Not in this snow."

"It isn't far. Just around the corner. Almost."

"But..."

"On an ordinary night, I'd be out patrolling the roads."

"Do you think I'm overreacting?"

He dropped a kiss on my head. "I think your friend is over-the-top reckless. I'm glad you have more sense."

~ * ~

Julia set a tray with three mugs of hot chocolate and a plate of cookies on the coffee table. They were too close to collie noses and mouths. I did some hasty relocating.

"Where did Crane go?" she asked.

"He's taking a little spin in the snow down to Huron Court."

"Isn't that the strange road that leads to the past?"

"That's sort of what happens. I like to think of it as the Groundhog Day road. You're driving in a straight line— well, around curves— when all of a sudden, without realizing it, you're heading in the opposite direction."

"I never heard of such a phenomenon. How can you *not* know you changed directions?"

"I can't explain it any better. I just know I experienced it, except I was walking."

"Why is Crane driving to Huron Court?

I told her about Annica, whose fondness for Brent had brought her impulsive nature to the forefront. "She has a wild idea about following him to the past."

"That's crazy," Julia said.

"That's Annica."

"We'll soon know what happens, if anything. While we wait, would you like to play a game? Or should we watch television? There's bound to be a Christmas movie or concert on one of the channels."

"If you would."

"It'll make time go by faster."

She was right. No sooner had I turned on the Classics Channel to *A Christmas Carol*—to Susannah York as Mrs. Cratchit railing against her husband's employer, Scrooge—than the clock struck eleven. Or so it seemed. I hadn't been watching the movie after the first few minutes.

Out in the night, the coyotes began to howl.

Julia jumped. "What on earth?"

"Coyotes," I said. "They're taking over the world."

I couldn't concentrate on the movie. After all, I must have read Dickens' story hundreds of time and seen all the film versions of it, including the musical. At this point, I could have stepped into any one of the roles and recited the lines from memory. At last, mercifully, the movie ended, and I turned off the television.

Julia yawned. "Jet lag is catching up with me. Do you mind if I go to bed."

"Not at all. I'll wait up for Crane."

"I remember you used to wait up for Santa."

"And I never saw him. I was the official waiter. I promised to call you when he came down the chimney. Crane should be back by now," I added.

But he wasn't.

Julia went upstairs and, seeing that the cookie plate was empty, I decided to leave it on the table. I'd take the dogs outside for the night and get ready by bed. Surely Crane would return soon. Any minute he'd come stamping through the door, snow flying in all directions.

With news. Good news. That was the only kind I'd accept.

It's difficult to stay positive when you're worried about the people in your life. First Brent disappears. Then Annica. I felt as if I were in the grip of a weird chain reaction...

Go ahead. Finish the thought.

Then Crane takes far too long to drive over to Sagramore Lake and from there to Huron Court.

Brent, Annica, Crane.

Who would be the next to go?

~ * ~

Some say that ever 'gainst that season comes Wherein our Saviour's birth is celebrated, This bird of dawning singeth all night long...

It was a half hour till midnight, a half hour till Christmas Day, and I didn't hear any bird of dawning. Only coyotes howling in the woods beyond the unfinished construction. Only Misty barking at an oddly shaped snowdrift. Only Gemmy play-growling at her.

Now that the snow had stopped and I'd stepped outside, I could appreciate the beauty of the night. Gilbert had outlined the front of the yellow Victorian with colored lights. The house itself was dark, but the cars were in the driveway, all but buried in the snow.

It was truly a marshmallow world, even though we hadn't received the predicted twelve inches. Yet.

I searched for headlights on the lane. All I could see was the thick all-encompassing darkness of Foxglove Corners and the snow.

And where in this white sparkling world were my friends and my husband?

The dogs were getting rambunctious, all seven of them, as Raven had come out of her house to join them in their roughhousing. Which wasn't why I had brought them outside.

I figured they'd taken care of any business they had.

"Inside," I said. "Now. Or you'll sleep outside tonight."

I opened the side door. They rushed into the house, even Raven who apparently didn't want to go to bed in her doghouse and get snowed in.

For a long, troubling moment I had a familiar feeling akin to my earlier foreboding. Even though Julia slept in the guest room, and Crane was surely on his way home, I felt that I was alone in Foxglove Corners.

Forty-seven

I woke before daybreak, vaguely conscious of a heaviness, a sense of wrongness that lay over my heart. He hadn't come. I'd waited for him with cookies and milk until I gave up and went to bed.

Waiting for... Santa Claus?

Of course not. Waiting for Crane.

His side of the bed was empty. Memories of last night flooded back. Annica's unexplained absence... Crane had driven the short distance to Huron Court to look for her. He planned to return right away, and he would have unless one of a dozen possible mishaps had prevented it.

I pulled my cell phone out of the charger, hoping to see a missed message. No one had called.

I reached over to touch his pillow. It was cold.

At seven o'clock, it was already shaping up to be a Christmas different from any I'd ever known.

I grabbed my slippers and robe and stepped out into the hall. The door to the guest room was open. Misty and Halley had deserted their post. The drone of a television drifted up the stairs, along with the unmistakable fragrance of pancakes and maple syrup.

Julia, in a long pink robe, was busy at the stove, deftly dodging collie paws. The dogs were taking advantage of her. *They know I never let them wander so close to the frying pan when I was making pancakes.* Candy's nose was too near the fire, and Misty was trying to sit up.

"Merry Christmas," Julia said.

"Merry Christmas."

I must sound like a speaking toy, voicing a mechanical greeting.

"Did Crane go out again?" she asked.

I looked through the kitchen window, hoping to see his Jeep. Snow drifted high over his customary parking place squelched that notion.

"He never came home last night."

"Does this happen often?"

"No."

Think positively, I told myself. Perhaps he came home and went out again on some urgent sheriff's business.

No, in that case he would have left me a message.

"He's in trouble," I said.

If only I hadn't told him about Annica, he'd be here with us in the kitchen, telling Julia he had to have bacon with pancakes and he liked his orange juice freshly squeezed.

My throat filled with an enormous lump. I tried to swallow it. After three attempts, I succeeded.

I always worried about Crane when he was on duty and always knew when something was wrong. The feeling of wrongness was stronger than my desire to be positive this Christmas morning.

"I gave each dog a dish of kibble but didn't let them out. I was afraid they'd run away or one of those howling demons would attack them," Julia said.

"The coyotes wouldn't approach a pack of collies. Did you remember to feed Raven and give her fresh water?"

Even though your world is falling apart, don't neglect your dogs.

"Uh, no. I forgot her."

"I'll take care of her." I filled Raven's food dish to the top.

"I turned on the television for the news this morning," Julia said as I became aware of a Christmas carol playing softly in the living room.

Il est ne.

He is born.

"Is anything new?" I asked.

"That evening snow is coming earlier than they thought, and there's been some excitement in town. A prisoner escaped. He's a murder suspect."

"Oh, no! Not Clancy."

"That's the name. Kevin Clancy."

"He's the vagrant who confessed to killing Violet Randall," I said.

"I remember you mentioning him. Also he's a suspect in another young woman's disappearance."

"How did they let that happen?"

"They called it a kind of Christmas-related mix-up."

Being careful not to name names or assign blame. Mac must have been on vacation. He'd never let a prisoner slither out of his grasp.

"Apparently he kept saying over and over again that he had to get out. He had something to do."

"He and just about every other prisoner," I said.

For a moment hope glimmered to life. That must be what had detained Crane. Clancy was dangerous and, for all I knew, armed. The county would want to go after him with all their manpower.

But in that case, Crane would have let me know.

I didn't feel like eating, but knew I'd need energy for whatever the day brought. I suspected it wasn't going to be good, and I had to be strong for Crane. He was counting on me.

"I'm going to clear the snow off the car and drive out to Huron Court," I said.

To do what I'd sworn I would never do. To step inside the pink Victorian, if it became necessary.

Julia gasped. The serving fork hit the floor. "Isn't that the road that…"

"Swallowed up Brent and Annica. Yes."

She turned away from the stove, spatula in hand. "But what if something like that happens to you?"

"I have to take that chance."

"Crane wouldn't like it."

"That's true, but he isn't here."

She tried again. "Aren't you afraid?"

Afraid was too mild a word to express my feelings. Ever since my last time slip, I'd feared being pulled into the past again, dreaded the thought of losing everything that mattered to me.

I hadn't thought it would happen this way.

"I'm afraid, but I'm going to do it anyway," I said.

"Then I'm going with you, but not until you eat. I already had two pancakes."

The thought of having Julia at my side made me feel marginally better about the day's undertaking. Julia and I had faced many an obstacle together in our time. I couldn't ask for a better companion in adversity, and the worst adversity is the unknown one.

Still, I said, "It would be better if you stayed here in case Crane comes home. He won't know where I've gone, and he may be hungry."

"You can leave him a note, and I'll put his pancakes in the oven so they stay warm. Any more objections?"

I forced a smile. "I can't think of any."

I sat down, and she set three pancakes on my plate. Candy eyed them hungrily.

Hungry... Breakfast... Pancakes...

I made myself hold fast to a variety of different scenarios. Even one in which Crane was at this moment eating breakfast at some open-all-night diner with Veronica.

Even that would be preferable to what I was imagining.

Julia poured a cup of coffee and sat down to keep me company. "Well, I'm not staying here alone. It's Christmas morning."

So it was. So easy to forget.

At the last minute, I made a decision. "I'm taking Misty with us," I said.

~ * ~

No one else was driving on Jonquil Lane. It was Christmas morning, after all. People would be going to church or opening presents at home. Our new snow removal service had cleared and salted the roads, determined to meet the challenge of still another snowfall.

I turned on Sagramore Lake Road and drove to the lake, silver and shining in the morning light, with isles of snow floating under a cloudless sky. And from there I proceeded to Huron Court.

It hadn't snowed as much on Huron Court. No one had plowed the road, of course, but tire tracks indicated it had seen light traffic, which was unusual.

Annica would have come this way, and Crane.

"Look!" Julia said.

Beyond the fork in the road, a yellow Volkswagen had apparently skidded into a snowbank and gotten stuck. The car was empty. Had the driver abandoned it?

"Where could he have gone?" I said. "There are no houses this way."

Only the pink Victorian, which was locked, unoccupied at present, or so I assumed, and forbidding.

I pulled over to the snowy verge and came to a stop behind the Volkswagen, letting the engine idle. I wished I knew what time the car had been trapped in the snowdrift. Could Crane have discovered the driver's plight? If so, he would have stopped to help.

"Maybe the driver called for a tow truck," Julia said.

"And waited in his car," I added. "It's too cold to walk and no place to go. Just the cemetery."

He could have returned to the fork in the road and taken his chance there'd be signs of civilization in the other direction.

"How likely is it that a tow service would even be open on Christmas morning?" Julia asked.

"Likely, I think, considering last night's storm. I'll bet this isn't the only abandoned car in town."

"Let's move on," Julia said. "These woods make me nervous."

"They were different the first time I walked on Huron Court," I said. "It was autumn. There was the sweetest smell in the air."

The sweet fields of autumn.

I shivered in the sudden coldness that insinuated itself into the air, the coldness of fear and dread. It seemed as if I could smell that indescribable autumn scent inside the car with the heater on its highest setting and all the windows closed.

Forty-eight

I steered back to the road and drove slowly on. There was always a chance that some clueless motorist had made a fool's decision to go for help on foot. I'd watch for him.

Misty sat in the back seat, mesmerized by the changing scenery. In truth, though, it didn't change, consisting solely of woods, snow, and curves that took us to more of the same.

Julia had been unusually quiet.

"Are you still nervous?" I asked.

"Well, yes. I keep waiting for this time tangle to turn us around. So far I'm unaware of any change."

"There hasn't been one," I said, then added, "Unless we suddenly see Lake Sagramore again beyond the next curve."

"Don't say that. Huron Court looks like any other country road in Foxglove Corners. I'm only nervous because of your stories."

To me, of course, they were more than stories. I wondered if Julia really believed me. She said she did.

"I thought we'd run into the driver of that Volkswagen by now," I said. "Not literally, of course."

"During one of the last big storms, some people left their cars on the freeway and never came back for them. That caused a major problem for the road crews."

She was silent for a few minutes, fussing over Misty, who had begun to whine. "You don't suppose... No, that's borrowing trouble."

"What?"

"I was thinking about that girl who disappeared on Thanksgiving. If Annica was driving on Huron Court last night and had car trouble... She's a young woman alone."

"Clancy is in custody," I said quickly. Then as quickly I remembered.

"No, he isn't. Do they know when he escaped?"

"Sometime yesterday afternoon."

"He could have left the state by now," I said. "It doesn't make sense that he'd stay in Foxglove Corners."

But did anything he said or did make sense?

Annica's goal had been clear. She was heading to the pink Victorian, hoping, I assumed, to follow Brent into the past. And how ludicrous that sounded!

Could Clancy possibly have intercepted her? He had a knack for discovering vulnerable young women.

Guilty of one murder by his own admission, a major suspect in a disappearance, what was one more victim? I had faith in Annica's ability to defend herself, but if she'd had car trouble in a snowstorm, she would have been at a disadvantage. Her car was an older model Honda Accord. Maybe she'd never reached the house.

In that case, Crane wouldn't have caught up with her.

Then where was Crane?

I reminded myself that Julia and I were driving down Huron Court on Christmas morning for one reason— to find him.

I didn't like the direction my runaway thoughts were taking but didn't know how to turn them off, and I had another concern. I glanced at the dashboard clock. We'd been on the road long enough to have reached the pink Victorian. Where was it?

Around the next curve?

"Oh, no!" Julia gasped, and Misty gave a little whimper.

"I don't believe this," I said.

A tree had crashed to the ground, blocking every inch of the road. It must have happened yesterday during the storm, as the trunk and branches were already well covered with snow. Here was an undeniable natural occurrence, an act of God, when I was expecting to be catapulted back in time at any moment.

With the tree in the way and no hope of moving it, even with Julia's help, I wouldn't have a chance to see what was around the next curve.

Not so fast. Remember, positive thinking.

"What do we do now?" Julia asked. "Climb over it?"

I surveyed the mountain of downed tree. It had been enormous and appeared even larger with most of the trunk and branches lying across the narrow road.

"There's an easier way," I said. "We go around it."

"And get out of the car?"

"Sure. How else? We can't drive over it."

How far would we have to walk in the woods? Not far. We would pass the tree on the left, going around the uppermost branches.

"But..."

I anticipated her objections. They were my own.

Once we crossed the barrier— assuming that was possible— we would be placing ourselves at the same kind of disadvantage I'm imagined for Annica. In the wilderness with no easy exit. In our favor, there were two of us and Misty.

Still considering, I said, "The house can't be much farther."

"Inside the car, I felt safe. Sort of. Is there another option?"

"Just one. Turn the car around and go home."

Sing to the merry Christmas!

...and leave Crane to his fate.

I wasn't going to do that. To encourage myself, I conjured a happy scene. Crane would be at home waiting for us. He'd have a reasonable explanation for his long absence and his failure to keep me informed of his whereabouts.

I'd have to tell him that I'd looked for him on Huron Court. He'd be furious. I'd deal with it.

"Will the car be okay if we leave it here?" Julia asked.

"I'll move it out of the way and lock it, but the only one likely to drive by is Brent, and that would be good. He knows my car."

I'd left Misty's leash on. She was dashing from one window to the other, whining, eager to be outside.

As I led her out of the car and caught up to Julia who was waiting for us on the verge, I said a quick and silent prayer.

For Crane, for Annica, and for Brent. For the success of our mission, which I suddenly saw as foolhardy. When we reached the pink Victorian, we had no guarantee we'd find our lost ones.

~ * ~

We entered the woods and saw immediately that someone had been there before us. He'd left a trail of deep boot prints in the snow that had blown and drifted around the fallen branches. The close-growing trees had preserved the path.

Crane?

No. Crane's prints would be larger.

"Someone had the same idea," Julia said. "It must be our missing motorist."

I grabbed for a branch as my foot slid on a slippery patch. Walking in the woods had its own dangers, but the trailing vines notorious for snaring and tripping hikers were buried deep in snow.

We walked alongside the existing prints. They also attracted Misty's attention. She sniffed at the trail, committing the scent to canine memory.

The prints ended when the walker returned to Huron Court. In the road he must have continued in the path carved out by the tire tracks.

I could only hope they'd been made by Crane's Jeep.

Misty came to a halt and, put on her brakes as dogs often do when they don't want to walk any farther. When they sense danger.

Julia took off her gloves and massaged her hands. "A few minutes outside, and my fingers are freezing. What's wrong with her?" she asked.

"We're approaching the notorious pink Victorian."

"I don't see anything."

"It's beyond that curve."

Always beyond the curve. The house. The memories. The bad time. The danger.

"Misty doesn't like the house," I said.

What I wanted to say was, "Misty is aware of otherworldly activity in the area. She's watching for a ghost dog named Ginger and the spirit of a girl murdered long ago."

I didn't think that would be beneficial to Julia's frame of mind.

In my sharpest no-nonsense-now tone, I said, "Heel, Misty."

She moved, albeit reluctantly and with a whine of protest, and we rounded the curve. There was the pink Victorian, silent and sinister. Waiting for us.

Forty-nine

Since I'd last seen Violet's house, it had acquired new stairs and a fresh coat of shell pink paint. The lacy gingerbread trim, repaired and repainted, sparkled in the morning light, and the windows had a newly-washed shine. All of the gutters and shingles were properly attached.

It's a lovely illusion, I told myself. *But the house is still evil.*

At the road's edge, Misty put on her brakes again. I held fast to the leash, telling her that everything was all right.

There were no cars in front of the house. I reined in my disappointment. I hadn't really expected to see Annica's Honda or Crane's Jeep. Still, I'd been hopeful. Were we on a fool's errand?

And where had the stranded motorist gone?

You're not looking for him, I reminded myself.

I couldn't help thinking about the driver of the abandoned Volkswagen. If he had set out in search of help, why would he have bypassed the first house he came to on Huron Court? Viewing it from the road, he couldn't have known that it was unoccupied.

If he had stopped at the house, he'd have left prints in the snow unless a stray wind had obliterated his tracks.

There was no wind to speak of last night.

No footprints.

No snow…

Something wasn't right.

Realization burst through my musings. Where was all the snow? Four or five inches had fallen on and around Jonquil Lane. Here not even a light dusting lay on the ground. Here at the house where seasons moved in the wrong direction. Here in this accursed house.

It was possible for one part of town to receive more snow than another, but that hadn't happened here.

To make sure I wasn't hallucinating, I looked back on the road we'd just left. It was covered with snow as were the woods that lined Huron Court, all shining in a faint light. It was as if a gigantic, acres-wide umbrella had sheltered the pink Victorian and its grounds while snow fell all around it.

Impossible— anyplace but on Huron Court.

Apparently Julia hadn't noticed anything amiss. Should I call her attention to the phenomenon? Not yet. She didn't need to worry about it yet.

"The house is magnificent," Julia said. "I can see why Brent fell in love with it."

"He spent money lavishly on period furniture and vintage oil paintings. You should see the inside."

But I stood unmoving, as if encased in ice. I felt myself moving emotionally away from the house. Fear returned, along with a surge of cold that had nothing to do with the low temperature.

"What are we waiting for?" Julia asked.

"Brent keeps the house locked."

But Annica had a key.

"I thought that's why we were here," Julia said. "To investigate the house."

"We're looking for Crane. I don't see any sign that he came this way."

Unless he parked the Jeep in the road.

The thought of Crane set my momentary reluctance flying.

"Maybe Annica left the door unlocked," I said. "Let's try it."

I was doing this for Crane, not that he would condone it. As for the fear that held me in a death grip, I'd been afraid before and hadn't let it stop me. There was a slight chance I might find some indication that he had been inside. That I might find a clue.

"As long as we're here..." I turned the knob and pushed. The door opened onto the living room, and I saw that Brent's pictures hadn't done the room justice. He'd wanted the furnishings to reflect Violet's time, but his vision was unique. The room was beautiful and filled with color and old time charm, but perhaps not homey.

It could never be homey.

A certain sweetness lay on the stale air. A scent of violets.

"Oh, how gorgeous," Julia said. "But why would Brent make it so easy for a thief to enter?"

He wouldn't.

"Brent was scrupulous about locking the house because it's so isolated."

I recalled the incident involving the mirror that had fallen from the wall twice—and hung itself back up. At a time when Brent was unwilling to accept a supernatural explanation when a natural one would do, he had insisted that somebody had broken in. After that mysterious occurrence, he wasn't about to give anyone else an opportunity to roam freely through the house.

"Annica must have left the door unlocked," I said. Which meant she'd been there. We were on the right track. Perhaps Crane had followed her.

I led a reluctant Misty in the house, or, rather, dragged her, and closed the door.

She remembered being in the living room with me, and her memories couldn't have been happy.

Still, I didn't think that would explain her sudden agitation. Nor did she appear to be reacting to supernatural vibrations. Whining loudly, she struggled to break free of her leash, while I struggled to hold on to her.

Somewhere above a muffled sound broke the silence. Suddenly it became clear to me. Suddenly and too late. Julia and I weren't alone in the house.

"Someone's here," I whispered.

"Where? In the house?"

I nodded.

"How can you tell?"

I pointed to Misty, whose howling was loud enough to wake the proverbial dead. "She knows. And didn't you hear that? Just now?"

"We'd better get out of here while the getting's good," Julia said.

I heard them then, footsteps on the stairs. They were loud stamping noises, the intruder making no attempt to approach in secrecy.

Misty growled a warning. She didn't want to leave. Yanking on the leash, I dashed to the door with Julia in my wake.

We weren't fast enough.

The man stood at the foot of the staircase glaring at us. He had the wizened face of an old man, seventy or more, and there was something odd about his eyes. They didn't seem to focus properly. His faded khaki jacket was too large for him and missing some of its buttons.

I'd never seen him before.

"You're here," he muttered. "You're everywhere. Both of you, and the dog, too." He whipped a gun out of his pocket. "Why didn't you stay dead?" His gravelly voice had a hint of an Irish accent.

I knew him then. Clancy. Killer, escaped prisoner, lunatic. He'd obviously stolen the stranded Volkswagen and probably the clothes and the gun as well.

Misty bared her teeth. If he hadn't had a weapon, I would have dropped the leash and let her make mincemeat of him. As it was, I felt an overwhelming need to protect her.

Hadn't the man noticed that no snow had fallen on the house and the surrounding land?

Did it matter?

"You're making a mistake," Julia said. "You don't know us, and we're not dead. Believe me. We'd know if we were."

The violet fragrance intensified, grew so strong that I thought I'd suffocate if I couldn't escape it.

"Not yet, but I can fix that," he said. "I'm getting out of here. You're staying. I found a way to end this once and for all."

He pointed the gun at Misty. "I hate dogs."

Julia and I exchanged glances. We had no need of speech.

What now?

We're out of options.

"Violet," I whispered. "Help me."

A new smell overrode the fragrance of violets. Smoke!

He shoved the gun in Julia's back. She screamed and tried to push me out of the way, and Misty lunged for him, choking when she couldn't break free of her restraint.

"Move it," he shouted.

Die now or later, I thought.

Later.

Fifty

The smell of smoke was stronger on the second floor. I heard a sinister crackling on the eastern side of the house.

The house was burning. The madman had set it on fire. Once a fire is started, it doesn't take long for it to spread and consume everything and everyone in its path.

The world filled with the hiss and crackle of a building fire and the mindless muttering of the vagrant killer. "Fire is better. No bodies lying around to come back to life."

"In here." He yanked open a door and shoved us inside, one by one. He aimed a kick at Misty's flank.

"No, Misty!" I tugged desperately on her leash as she tried to lunge at Clancy, teeth bared, fury in her eyes.

"Devil dog." He slammed the door.

I grabbed the knob, tried to turn it. It was already warm. How soon before it would be too hot to touch?

"Locked."

"We have to get out of here," Julia cried. "We'll burn to death."

Of all the ways to leave the earth, dying by fire was the one I most dreaded. Visions of horror danced crazily through my mind. Joan of Arc tied to the stake. Animals fleeing a raging forest fire. A chicken sizzling on a grill.

"It'd be better if he shot us," Julia cried.

"We'll get out." I didn't wholly believe it. I just wanted to, unable to accept the alternative.

I tried to remember what to do. Keep your face covered. Stay close to the floor. Break down the door? With our bare hands? The room was empty. No hope of finding a tool.

I glanced at the window. Our way out of the conflagration. The only way.

I wrapped my scarf around the lower part of my face and motioned to Julia to do the same with hers.

Was the smell of smoke growing stronger, the crackling of the flames louder? Was it getting harder to breathe?

Yes, yes, yes.

Time was running down, racing to Stop.

The lunatic's laughter seemed to override the fire's roar. It came from a distance. He must be leaving the house.

Our chances of escape were evaporating with the dying air.

Julia pulled her scarf away from her face. "I can't breathe." She took a great gulp of poisoned air and coughed.

"Keep your face covered," I shouted. "Don't waste breath talking."

"I have to. Jennet, I love you."

"Love you, too, Julia."

Thank heavens Brent had installed new windows. This one opened easily. I lifted the screen and looked down. The fire had moved quickly, already reached the west side of the house. Flames licked the exterior wall, devoured lengths of gingerbread trim. All I could smell was nauseous, deadly smoke. Not even the faintest whiff of violet fragrance.

Through the haze, I saw the ground below, hard and hostile terrain, without the drifted snow that should be there to cushion a fall.

Heaven helps those who help themselves.

I said, "We have to jump."

"I can't."

"It's the only way. You can, if you have to."

"We're two stories up. I'll break something or crack my head open."

"Better than roasting."

And better to do it quickly.

"I'll go first."

I pushed the loop of Misty's leash higher on my arm and tried to lift my frenzied struggling collie.

That wouldn't work.

Julia grabbed my arm. "She's too heavy for you. Let her go. Let her jump on her own."

No.

I sat on the sill and tried again to lift her, using the last ounce of strength I possessed.

No time to think she was too heavy, no point telling myself the fall would probably kill us both. Only time for a short prayer.

I had her. My arms tightened around her wriggling body. I swung my legs over, eased myself off the sill, and let myself fall, holding fast to Misty as if she were my last link with life.

~ * ~

The impact knocked the breath out of me, but I remained conscious, or thought I did. When I opened my eyes, my arms were empty. I'd lost Misty in the fall. I didn't remember when she'd left.

All at once, feeling returned. I became aware of a heat so intense I feared I would melt. The pain began seconds later. Every part of my body, especially my left side and my head, felt as it were on fire. Where was…?"

Julia!

I didn't see her.

Hadn't she followed me out of the window? If not...

I'd have to go back for her. Back into the inferno.

If I could move. If the fire hadn't engulfed the entrance.

Somewhere near I heard a faint whimper. The cry of a baby who has been hurt by a loving hand.

The crying continued. It seemed like the only sound in the world.

There should be sirens, firemen manning hoses, people on Huron Court come to gape at the spectacle. There was nothing. Nobody.

I forced myself to get up slowly, riding with the pain. I could do this.

You can if you have to.

That was what I'd said to Julia.

My eyes were watering. I wiped them on the sleeve of my jacket and looked up, expecting to see the skeleton of the pink Victorian, its pieces torn away, hanging loose, burnt to a crisp.

And there it was. Whole and elegant, pink and glowing, a virtual palace set down in a landscaped setting with trees that had died long ago.

The intense heat had gone. There wasn't so much of a hint of smoke in the air. I breathed in the mellow warmth of a sweet-scented autumn day.

I had gone somewhere, only not to my planned destination. And...

The cry turned into a howl of despair. Misty crept up to me through autumn-dry grass, her ears flattened, her eyes haunted. She looked like a dog who has been beaten by a beloved owner and cast away to fend for herself.

...I wasn't alone.

She who has a dog is never alone.

~ * ~

Here we go 'round again...

An aura of peace hung over the pink Victorian with puffy white clouds low in the sky. It was simply a beautiful country house, a well-tended relic of an earlier century.

Where Julia might be?

No, she wouldn't be there, not until some years later when many of the trees would be gone. I couldn't bear to think of her in the small locked room with the fire coming closer every minute.

She would have jumped. I was certain of that. Jumped to safety but landed in a different time. I held fast to that idea.

I love you, Julia.

The thought provided a modicum of comfort. If I believed Julia was still trapped in the burning house, I couldn't bear to walk away from it, and I had to leave. I'd left things undone in the future. I had no idea where Crane was.

I wouldn't be able to resume my search until I found my way back to my own time.

With a last look at the shimmering pink Victorian, I reached for Misty's leash— miraculously still attached to her collar, dragging behind her— and led her out to Huron Court.

What I wanted to do was stay where I was and run my hand through Misty's soft fur and wait for the cessation of the pain. But that was a luxury I couldn't afford.

At some point, I'd become separated from my purse. I thought with longing of the small pill box with the aspirin, hopelessly out of my reach. I'd have to function without it.

"Come girl," I said. "Good girl. We have to go home."

She came, wagging her tail.

So back to Huron Road, back to another season. The snow was gone, the world colored for fall in green and russet and gold. The sweet fields of autumn. Leaves crunched underfoot as we set out in the direction of Sagramore Lake.

And please, God, let the pink Victorian stay behind us. Iron out that time twist that sends the traveler back in the opposite direction.

We walked on, although every step brought fresh stabs of pain to my body. I did my best to ignore them. Obviously nothing vital had broken in my two-story tumble to the ground. And what a miracle that was!

Restored to her former happy self, Misty trotted along at my side, stopping occasionally to sniff some marvelous find that was invisible to me. She was limping a little, but then so was I. If only we'd walk into snow. Then I'd know we were home.

Misty uttered a low growl. I froze, all senses heightened. Could Clancy have followed us to this earlier time when he left the house?

No, I would have known if someone were stalking us. Misty would have done more than growl. We were alone on Huron Court, and somewhere a bird sang. We had nothing new to worry about. But as we walked, I took my eyes of the road, looking first to the right, then to the left, as if that would prevent an assailant from leaping out at us.

About sixteen yards from the edge of the road, I spied a splash of yellow. It had a definite shape, and there was something familiar about it. Leading Misty over dried brush, over a crackling of fallen leaves, I came to a vehicle with a streamlined body and long white fins.

It was Brent's Plymouth Belvedere.

Fifty-one

Was it Brent's car?

It was yellow, it had long white fins, it was a Plymouth Belvedere manufactured in the late nineteen fifties... But it was hardly the showcase model Brent had driven. Unsightly rust had eaten its way through the paint. The body was thickly coated in the mud of past years. It looked as though it had been driven into the woods straight into a tree where it came to a stop and stayed for decades unnoticed by the infrequent passerby.

There was one way to know for certain. Brent always hung Saint Christopher medals in his cars. I pulled open the driver's side door, surprised to find it unlocked, and there it was, the medal with its silver tarnished and the ribbon from which it was suspended in tatters.

How long had the car sat in the woods, abandoned by its owner, slowly but surely deteriorating?

And where was Brent?

The last time I'd seen his meticulously restored car, it had been in mint condition. Bright lemon yellow, sparkling white fins, sleek, a prehistoric bird too rare and fine to last. Not a speck of dirt on the body.

I rested my hand on its gritty fender. Misty sniffed at it, whined. Did Brent's scent still remain on the Belvedere? Maybe so, or, to her, this might be just another curiosity. In any event, the car couldn't tell me what had happened to Brent.

"Let's go, Misty."

The discovery of the Belvedere only added to the general confusion. Suppose Crane's Jeep had suffered a similar fate? What if it was hidden so deep in the woods I would never see it? What if I never found him?

Don't think of that. Remember, be positive.

The sun was hot. It was too early in the season to wear a jacket with a heavy lining. I took it off and draped it over my arm. In this world where the seasons were out of sync, I might need it by the time I rounded the next curve.

Keep walking, I told myself. *Look for the lake. Look for snow.*

Thank God Huron Court hadn't sent me back the way I'd come. Yet.

Thinking of the lake made me aware of how thirsty I was—with a half dozen bottles of water in my car and the car lost in time. I couldn't last much longer without something to drink. Neither could Misty. And that made me think of food. It had been hours—in any time, future or past—since Julia and I had sat down to a pancake breakfast.

I couldn't know those pancakes would have to last me to the end of my life. And thank heavens Julia had fed Misty.

My thoughts were erratic, careening into one another, my mind reluctant to deal with the most crucial issue of all. I needed to go home.

How did I find my way back the last time?

Think.

"Do you remember, Misty?"

She looked at me and wagged her tail.

You're the alpha dog, she might have said. *You lead, and I'll follow. I don't have to remember.*

I spied a fallen tree trunk that would serve as a makeshift bench and sat, wishing I had a wall to lean against.

The last time I had been sitting on the ground. Then, as now, I was exhausted. I'd had a headache. Now there was no part of my body that didn't hurt.

What can you expect when you throw yourself out of a window two stories above the ground?

That last time, I thought I had reached the end of the road. I knew I had reached the end of my endurance. I'd closed my eyes, thinking it was fitting a collie should be with me at the end.

When I had opened them, Crane had been with me.

Later he told me I'd been in the hospital, in a coma. That my time slip, my time with Violet, was a figment of my imagination.

Of course, I didn't believe him.

Of course, he didn't believe me. Until Brent found the handkerchief I'd taken with me and left in the past.

Proof positive. It had turned Crane into a believer.

Maybe the magic would work again.

Close your eyes. Think of home. A green Victorian farmhouse with a stained glass window between twin gables on a lane where jonquils and daffodils bloom in the spring...

Nothing happened.

But for the first time I remembered my collies waiting for me to return. I *had* to find the way back. In the meantime, Camille would realize that neither Crane nor I were home. She'd take care of them. It was Christmas Day. I could almost see her crossing the lane, a Christmas coffeecake in her hand. She would see the note I'd left for Crane on the kitchen table.

I let the pleasant image drift away. If I didn't start walking again, I would stay forever on this fallen log in the autumn of another time, rather like Brent's prized vintage car, rusting away in the woods of Huron Court.

~ * ~

A drop of moisture landed on my face, then another. Snow!

Suddenly the air filled with snow falling, blowing in a high wind that had come out of nowhere. Out of a sky that had been, moments earlier, deep blue with cloud wisps moving lazily over autumn-colored treetops.

Misty yelped her excitement. Within the confines of her six-foot leash, she danced and circled around me, entangling both of us in leather. Snow! Fun time!

I freed myself, slipped into my jacket, and pulled the hood over my head. The wind tried to snatch it back. It shrieked, almost sweeping me off my feet. It was stronger than any wind had a right to be unless it was part of a hurricane or a tornado. Like the tornado that had brought me to Foxglove Corners.

I could feel it lifting me off the ground, pushing me to one side.

Find a sturdy tree. Wait it out.

An old willow grew close to the edge of the woods. I grabbed hold of a low-growing branch and held on to Misty's leash.

It was no tornado that forced the snow into high drifts. It was an unnatural wind, an anomaly born of the time twist. How else could the season have changed from sun-warmed autumn to furious winter between one footstep and the next? With one teardrop-flake of snow?

I pressed my face against the rough bark of the willow's trunk and waited.

Time passed. Time twisted. The wind blew and finally blew itself out. The snow still fell. Lightly, gently. It fell on existing snow, and the ground began to rise.

I remembered that snow was supposed to begin again later in the day.

Was I home then? In my own time? If so…

Julia!

Instinctively I turned around and retraced my steps. I had to go back to the pink Victorian, or what remained of it, and see if Julia was still there— in our time, when the lunatic Clancy had set fire to the house.

It was important that I know my sister's fate before continuing my long journey home.

~ * ~

I gazed on a scene of utter devastation, the burnt-out wreck of a once proud, always mysterious Victorian mansion. It was nothing but scorched walls and melted building materials. Glass and tiles and shingles and items so misshapen I couldn't identify them. Charred bits and pieces that might have been vintage oil paintings or lamps or chairs.

Snow fell on the ruins, giving them a pristine white appearance. The area was no longer protected by time's invisible umbrella. An acrid smell lingered in the air. And perhaps a whisper of violet scent?

There was no sign of Julia.

Farther down Huron Court, I saw two figures, a young girl in blue pants and a white top, nothing more substantial, and a sable and white collie. They were walking at a leisurely pace toward the cemetery. They didn't look back.

So Violet had come and gone, never letting herself be seen until now, not lifting a hand to help, and my sister was dead, my beautiful golden sister who carried sunshine with her wherever she went.

Misty whimpered and scratched at the ground. I let my tears fall.

"I love you, Julia."

I couldn't say 'loved.'

I could do nothing more at this place of death. Once again I walked away from the pink Victorian with Misty in tow.

It seemed as if I'd been walking for weeks, but assuming time had straightened itself out, it was still the same day. Maybe early afternoon. Still Christmas. The most unusual Christmas I or anyone had ever experienced.

I was going home. I felt sure of it. What I was afraid to think about was what I'd find— or wouldn't find— when I arrived.

Fifty-two

I hadn't thought about my car until I saw the vehicle at the side of the road, its form almost obliterated by snow.

I brushed the snow off the window and peered inside. I'd left my purse on the seat. What a foolhardy thing to do, and thank heavens I'd done it. And there was Misty's toy goat in the back.

There would be aspirin in my purse and bottles of water in the backseat. Shelter and transportation. I didn't have to walk another step. I really had come home.

But without Julia.

Don't think about Julia now. There'll be time to mourn later. A lifetime of tears. For now, concentrate on getting yourself and Misty home.

I gave Misty a gentle pat, but she needed no encouragement. She leaped into the back seat and promptly curled up into a snow-covered ball.

I pulled my keys out of my pocket and started the engine. Every move I made felt strange. It was as if I hadn't sat in a car before, had never driven one. As if the seat were too close to the steering wheel.

The feeling passed. Familiarity returned. I turned on the windshield wipers, got the scraper out of the back, and cleared the windows. In the time it took me to brush off the snow, the car had warmed up nicely. I broke into one of the water bottles, took a drink and gave one to Misty, after which I lost no time in making a U-turn on the narrow road and heading toward Sagramore Lake.

I didn't even take the time to swallow two aspirin.

It was still snowing, reducing visibility drastically, and I had to drive at a snail's pace lest I slide into the woods. But finally I was moving in the right direction.

At the fork in the road, I spied a solitary walker so bundled up in a hooded green coat that I couldn't tell if it was a male or female.

As I drew near, the walker turned, scrambled into the brush, and after what seemed like a long moment, waved to me.

I recognized her then. Annica, her face bright with sudden joy. She stumbled toward the car. Her hood fell back, freeing a tumble of red-gold hair.

Misty scratched at the window as I brought the car to a careful stop and flung the door open.

"It's you!" Annica cried. "Jennet! Oh, thank you, God. Thank you. Thank you. I thought I was hallucinating. I had stopped hoping."

She was inside, sitting beside me, shedding snow, and shaking. Her face was free of makeup and tear-stained. The jingle of her silver bell earrings added an incongruous note to her feverish speech.

I reached for another bottle of water and untwisted the cap.

"Drink," I said. "Don't try to talk."

But she couldn't stop talking. She babbled on about wind and seeing strange things in the snow. Between gulps of water, she said, "I came out here in my car, but I don't know where it is."

"You were looking for Brent," I said.

And Crane was looking for you.

"I never found him. I checked at the house, but he wasn't there. I was on the way home when my car just stopped, out in the middle of nowhere. I tried to call my mom on the cell, but I couldn't get a signal. It feels so wonderful to be warm again," she added and drained the water bottle.

I gave her another one.

Not getting a signal was strange. But why expect electronics to work in a world where time had gone mad?

She said, "I left the car where it stopped in the road. What else could I do? I thought I'd walk over to Sagramore Lake Road. But I couldn't reach the lake. I kept walking in circles, just like you said. So I decided to go back to the house and try the landline, but when I got there... It wasn't there."

"It burned to the ground this morning," I said. "That crazy Clancy set fire to it."

Now was the time to tell her about how he had locked Julia and me in the room and left us there to burn to death, about my jump and landing in another time, but I couldn't bring myself to say a word. I'd have to talk about Julia.

"No," she said. "If it just happened, there'd be something left, like all kinds of burnt debris. The house simply wasn't there. Where it had been was a field filled with flowers."

"You must have been in the wrong place."

"No. I walked all the way down to the cemetery. Over and over and over again. I didn't see any houses, and everything looked different. It wasn't quite so woodsy. And where the pink Victorian should be, all I saw were flowers."

"Flowers in winter?"

"It wasn't winter by then," she said. "The season changed in the blink of an eye."

She began to cry, great gulping sounds. Misty laid her paw on Annica's shoulder and licked her face.

"Then it started snowing, and I saw your car. I can't tell you where I was," she said when her sobs had subsided. "I don't know."

I thought I did. After leaving her car, Annica had experienced a time slip, but she had ended up in the future when flowers bloomed where a house once stood. I thought it best to distract her until she regained her equilibrium.

"Well, *I* know where we are," I said. "Look, it's the lake. I'll take you home with me. We can sort everything else out later."

~ * ~

Home. Where a green Victorian farmhouse with a stained glass window between twin gables wasn't a dream. Where high drifts of snow were real, and tree lights shone through the bay window. Where collies barked and collie faces appeared in the window.

Best of all, Crane's Jeep was in the driveway. By the goodness of a benevolent God, my husband had come home.

I pushed open the side door and stepped into a maelstrom of yelping, crying, jumping collies. Beyond them was the oak table with Camille's coffee cake in the center, just as I had imagined it, and Brent in a chair drinking coffee, a person who hadn't been in my fantasy scenario.

Where was Crane?

My eyes fell on the breakfast dishes, rinsed but not washed. On the pitcher of syrup still on the counter.

Oh, Julia. My sister.

The tears were back.

Brent waded through the leaping dogs and folded me in his arms. "Jennet! We thought…"

"I'm here, too." Annica came in with Misty who carried her toy goat gently in her mouth.

"Hey, Fowler, what are you doing? Step aside."

Crane's voice. Crane.

He grabbed me away from Brent. In that moment, sadness disappeared. I leaned against him ...his strong, sturdy, real chest. I hadn't lost him.

"I thought you were gone," he said.

"I was, for a while. Julia... She's dead." I made a valiant effort to speak clearly. "She died in the fire at the house. That crazy Clancy set it."

"No, she didn't," Crane said quickly. "She's in the hospital with a few broken bones. Lucky for her she landed in a snowdrift."

Julia alive?

Still, I couldn't make the tears stop.

It was too much to take in, impossible to untangle without days of thought. I'd landed in the past on an autumn-hardening ground. Julia had stayed in the present, jumping into snow which hadn't prevented her from serious injury— where there hadn't been snow when we'd entered the house. But she was alive, and the lost ones were where they belonged. I had a lifetime to understand exactly what had happened.

It wouldn't be long enough.

~ * ~

I made another pot of coffee and one of tea, and we sat together demolishing Camille's coffeecake with the collies around us, even Raven who had been scratching at the door to be let inside.

Annica had told her story, earning a loving look from Brent, one I'd never seen on his face. She'd risked her life for him. He wouldn't forget it.

Crane said, "I hit the roof when I read your note, Jennet. Didn't I tell you never to go near Huron Court again? Under any circumstances."

"You may have, but I had to find you."

I glanced at the last piece of coffeecake, the one with the largest dollop of red sugar. Did anyone else want it? Could I still be a gracious hostess if I took it for myself?

Maybe I'd go over to the yellow Victorian to thank Camille and see if she had another coffeecake or some muffins.

Crane had obviously gotten over his anger, but as I put all the pieces together, I felt a little angry myself. I'd been overjoyed to find him home. Still...

"So you thought I was gone, and you stayed here in the nice warm house instead of going out to look for me?"

He laid his hand over mine. "I was going to, but I called Lucy. She told me you were all right and on your way home with Annica."

I took a moment to digest that. Lucy knew? How? Well, why bother to wonder? Lucy was another one of the mysteries of Foxglove Corners.

I said, "Tell me where you were. You went out to find Annica. You said you'd be right back, and you were gone all night. Christmas night."

He didn't answer.

I waited a moment, letting him think, gather his words. "What happened to you?"

"Right after I passed that fork in the road I got caught up in your time twist. I thought I'd been driving long enough to reach that damned house. It isn't really that far. But I just kept driving and the road never ended."

"Like the Flying Dutchman," Annica said.

"Believe it or not, I thought of that. By rights, I should have eventually come to the cemetery, but all I found was more road. Then I drove right into a blizzard and this time, I saw the house. It was on fire, and someone was lying in front of it. It turned out to be my own sister-in-law. I took her to Emergency."

"And the rest is history," Annica added.

While I'd been listening to Crane's tale, someone had taken that last piece of coffeecake. Brent, I'll bet. Or... Candy. She was looking pretty pleased with herself.

"What's your story, Brent?" I asked.

He drained his coffee cup. "Tell you tomorrow, Jennet. I missed Christmas Eve, so I'm going to deliver the kids' presents today. They're already loaded in the Jeep. I just have to pick up Lucy, and we're off. We'll celebrate Christmas tomorrow."

"I'll take you home in Jennet's car, Annica," Crane said. "But come back tomorrow. What about your car?"

"It can stay on Huron Court for all I care. I'm never going back there again."

"That's pretty drastic," I said. "Call a towing service."

"And have them get lost in time?"

"Maybe not." I reconsidered. "Let's save that problem for another day."

My mind had already leapt ahead to tomorrow's dinner. Turkey, stuffing... I had to make the cranberry relish and pies."

This was one Christmas I'd never forget.

Fifty-three

During the night, a howling in the woods woke me. I never thought I'd welcome that ungodly keening. Tonight, I didn't mind it. They were the coyotes of home, and Crane lay beside me. We had visited Julia, and we were going back to the hospital tomorrow to bring her home.

Once again all was well in my life. It had been a close call. A little like death. But we'd come through the madness unscathed, all except Julia.

The next day, on the twenty-sixth of December, we celebrated Christmas, all of us, including Lucy and Camille and Gilbert who hadn't been part of the dark adventure. After dinner, Brent, sipping brandy, told us what had happened to him.

Ironically he wasn't thinking about going back to the past until it happened.

"I was driving down Huron Court, going to meet Annica," he said. "She had a lamp she was all excited about. So I was driving along, nothing unusual was happening, when all of a sudden a snow squall came up. Just like the one I walked through the last time. It didn't last long, but when it stopped, all the snow was gone. Even the snow that had just fallen."

"The season changed," I said.

"It looked like spring. The leaves were green again, and I saw grass and wildflowers blooming along the woods. I knew I'd crossed over to the past then. So I drove on around a curve in the road, and there was the pink Victorian glowing in a mellow light. The way I'd never seen it. It was brand new, sparkling with what looked like a fresh coat of paint.

"I thought I'd have a chance to meet Violet and warn her. I wanted to change her future. If she hadn't met up with Clancy that day, she could be alive today. Someone else would lie in that grave in Old Resurrection Cemetery."

Crane refilled Brent's glass. "Drink it up."

"What *did* happen?" I asked.

"No one was living there. I looked through the windows. All the furniture was gone."

Brent had slipped back in time, all right but ended up in the wrong year. After Violet's murder, I'd guess, after her family had boxed up her possessions and stored them in the attic. After they'd moved away.

How strange. Annica and Brent had both traveled in time, Brent to the past and Annica to the future. In my flight from the burning house, I'd been in another season but had no idea whether I'd gone back or forward.

"You told me the family left the house after Violet was killed," Brent said. "I was too late to warn her. Fate was working against me."

"It's for the best," I said. "Changing history is dangerous. Just think what harm you could have done. Your mother and father might never have met. You'd have erased your existence."

He drained the brandy snifter. "I wouldn't have liked that, but I don't see how saving one girl from her killer could affect me."

I didn't either, but who knew the power of the Butterfly Effect?

"What did you do then?" I asked.

"I had the car. I wasn't on foot and vulnerable. I figured I'd drive out to Wolf Lake Road and look for my house."

Crane refilled Brent's glass yet once again. "I'll drive you home tonight," he said.

"After that it gets fuzzy. I drove and drove but was still on Huron Court. I never made a turn, but I kept approaching the pink Victorian. I wanted to drive to the lake."

"You fell into that twist in the road that turns you around when you're not aware of it," I said. "I remember how that felt. It was like being trapped on a demented carnival ride."

"It was so foggy," Brent added. "I had to turn my lights on and by then I only had a quarter tank of gas. I had cash in my wallet this time, but how could I fill the tank if I couldn't get off that damned road?"

This must have been the moment when those feelings came through to Lucy. Fear and despair.

"So the car was useless," Crane said. "Mac and I looked for it. Where is it now?"

"Somewhere in the past, I guess."

"I saw it," I said. "Rusting away in the woods. I knew for sure it was yours when I saw the medal."

"Maybe it's still there," Crane said.

Brent shook his head. "I doubt it."

The room seemed to lose its solidity. It must be the brandy. I wasn't used to it. Well, either that or all the time travel talk.

"How can we ever make sense of this?" I asked.

"Don't even try, dear." That was Camille, the voice of comfort.

"We're just glad you all are back," Gilbert added.

"I'm glad I was only here for the end," Julia said.

I smiled at her. There was so much we could have said, all of it better left unsaid. I had my sister back. We had agreed not to talk about the fire. Not yet.

Brent set his glass down. Empty.

"Before I ran into that twist, I thought I'd see if I could find Clancy in some nearby watering hole. I planned to tell him I knew what he'd done."

"That would have pushed him over the edge."

"Yes. Too bad I never met up with him."

"He's dead," Crane said. "Mac figures he tried to get out the door after he started the fire, but it must have stuck. Or maybe he tripped. Anyway, he was trapped inside."

Perhaps Violet had caused her house to malfunction. I'd seen her walking away from it with Ginger.

Good work, Violet, I thought.

"It should have been dark on Huron Court, but it wasn't," Brent was saying. "There was just a strange yellow light."

"Perpetual twilight," I murmured.

"Then I had an idea. I went back to the house, broke a window, and left a note for Annica. Maybe she'd never find it, but I couldn't think of anything else to do. I wrote: *I came through. I need help.*"

"I found it," Annica said. "What were we supposed to do, though?"

"I wanted you to know where I was. Jennet, I know it's late, but do you have anything to eat? Even a sandwich?"

"I'll make you something if you promise not to talk till I get back," I said.

He promised, but when I came back with a tray of sandwiches, I realized that his story was winding down. After writing the note, he had started driving again until he'd experienced the same instant blizzard that had whipped Crane back to his own time. And he'd seen what was left of the pink Victorian.

"Charred ruins and ashes," he said. "That beautiful old house."

"I'm sorry you lost it, Brent, and all the beautiful furnishings you and Annica got together."

"I'm not."

"That house was evil." Lucy spoke for the first time since Brent had begun talking. "It needed to be destroyed. Once you started down that dark path, there was no going back." She turned to me. "I've been thinking, Jennet. That big coyote you saw. I think it was a foreboding of all the terrible things that followed."

"I think it was a coywolf," Brent said, "and I'll bet it's still prowling around."

"To each his own," Lucy said primly.

"I still own the land," Brent added. "I was wondering what to do with it. I don't think I want to build another house on the site."

"Why don't you plant it with wildflower seeds in the spring?" Annica asked. "I'm pretty sure that's what you did."

"Good idea," he said. "Hey, Jennet, do you think I could have another piece of pie? I have to have something to counteract that brandy."

I smiled. Brent was back and still hungry in spite of the big turkey dinner we'd just had.

Perpetual hunger must be one of the after effects of time travel.

"Sure thing," I said.

He followed me into the kitchen to supervise the cutting of the pie, I assumed. At least that's why Candy and Misty were there.

Since we were alone, I said, "Just before you took off to times unknown, I saw you at the North Pole with the new deputy sheriff. I didn't think she was your type."

"Veronica? She isn't. It's simple. I knew you were concerned about her interest in the sheriff and thought I'd let her know there were other fish in the sea."

"Did she take the bait?"

He smirked. "They all do, but the lady's too bossy for my taste."

I could hardly wait to repeat this to Annica. She'd be happy to hear it, and I knew Brent expected me to pass the message on.

~ * ~

Later that afternoon, Jennifer and Molly came over for a Christmas visit. They brought a tin of homemade chocolate fudge, home-baked biscuits for the collies, and good news which they related over cocoa and Christmas cookies.

"Trista is back with her real owner," Molly announced. "She was in her new home for Christmas."

"How did that come about?" I asked.

"Beatrice gave up. She admitted she'd taken in a lost black collie but honestly didn't think it was Trista."

"She was saving face," Jennifer added. "So she handed her over to Mrs. West and said she was happy to get rid of her."

"Yeah," Molly said. "She said Trista barked too much. Stupid woman. That's what collies do."

Jennifer said, "This mystery solving business is easier than we thought it would be. We can't wait till the next one."

Such charming enthusiasm. As if they were sugar plums, the memories dance in my head. A pink Victorian house and an old murder. Coyotes howling in the woods and the strangest road in the world. Ghosts and a grave and a killer who almost got away with murder.

"As for myself, I'm more than willing to wait," I said, and toasted my resolve with a mug of Christmas cocoa.

Meet

Dorothy Bodoin

Dorothy Bodoin lives in Royal Oak, Michigan, about a half hour's drive from the town that serves as the setting for her Foxglove Corners cozy mystery series. A graduate of Oakland University with Bachelor's and Master's degrees in English, Dorothy taught secondary English for several years before leaving education to write full time and stay at home with her collies. *Down a Dark Path* is #22 in the Foxglove Corners series. She is also the author of one Gothic romance and six novels of romantic suspense.

95702617R00184

Made in the USA
Lexington, KY
11 August 2018